Murder Creek

Jeff Kerr

Book Cover by Cheynne Edmonston

Three may keep a secret, if two of them are dead.
—Benjamin Franklin, *Poor Richard's Almanack*

Chapter One

Dieter Bergheim clicked off the TV in disgust. War, a mass shooting, a jackass politician who couldn't keep his zipper shut—there was nothing but bad news these days. The Barbie doll news anchor with shellacked hair and impossibly white teeth had closed with a report of yet another failing bank begging for a government bailout. *Typical,* thought Dieter. *Liars and thieves, that's what bankers are. Eager to take your money and give it to their fat cat friends while sticking it to the little guy.* Dieter had seen through that charade decades ago. That's why he kept his money in much safer places than banks.

Someone rapped on the door. A smiling young woman poked her head in. "Hi, Mr. Bergheim. I'm just here to remind you that lunch will be served in ten minutes."

"Damn it, I know when lunch is," Dieter said with a scowl. "I haven't lost my mind yet. And I told you last time not to come into my room unless I said you could."

"Sorry. I just thought since you're new you'd—"

"I'm not senile! Do you really think I can't remember when lunchtime is? Now get the hell out of here and leave me alone."

She quickly shut the door. Dieter swore for the umpteenth time since moving into the assisted living facility. He paced his small apartment, taking small steps, and tried to ignore the tremor in his left hand. Damn his Parkinson's disease and damn the doctors who couldn't make it go away.

Already Dieter's new home felt like a prison. Communal dining. Rules for all this and all that. People popping in whenever they damn well pleased. Why the hell had he agreed to move into this place? Who had given his older brother the right to dictate how he should lead his life? Especially since that son of a bitch was still living free and easy on the ranch they inherited from their parents. The ranch that until last week had been his home. Where Dieter had been just fine, thank you very much.

Dieter stumbled on the towel left on the floor after his morning shower. Kicking it out of the way, he dropped into a leatherette easy chair and looked around the room with disgust. A wall-mounted TV loomed before him. Behind him, what passed for a kitchen, all sixty square feet of it. To his left, a sofa and tiny desk. To his right, the door that led to the bedroom. A bedroom that held only a dresser and the bed he would die in someday. If he was lucky enough not to spend his final hours in a hospital with tubes sticking out of every orifice in his body.

Loud knocking roused him from his self-pity. "Goddamn it, I know when lunch is!" he shouted.

The door opened. A man stepped into the room and closed the door behind him. "What are they serving today?" he asked with a mirthless grin. "Pudding?"

Dieter's eyes bulged. "You!"

"Yes, me. How long has it been, Dieter? Eight, ten years?"

"A hundred would be too soon. Get the hell out of here."

The man sauntered over to Dieter and towered over him. "You're hurting my feelings. I'd have thought you'd be happy to see your old business partner."

"I'd be happier to have a porcupine wipe my ass."

The man pulled a chair out from the desk and sat. "I always liked your sense of humor. You're a funny guy."

"And you're a piece of shit."

"How can you say that?" the man said. "Am I the one who cheated his partner out of a small fortune?"

"I didn't cheat you out of anything. You got cold feet and sold out. I gave you a fair price."

"It was only a fair price if you hadn't known you just landed the contract that would put you on easy street. That contract turned a struggling company into a booming corporation."

"Is it my fault you were too busy screwing the secretaries to pay attention to the business? You were lucky I gave you anything."

"Dieter, you owe me."

Fighting the rigidity caused by his failing nervous system, Dieter struggled to stand up. "I don't owe you a dime."

The man leaped to his feet and, with a light shove, knocked Dieter back into the easy chair. "Sit down," he said sharply. He waited for Dieter to make a move. When he didn't, he sat back down.

"How did you find me?" Dieter said.

The man scoffed. "How many Dieter Bergheims do you think there are in Central Texas? Despite what you may think, I'm not an idiot."

"Whatever. Just leave."

"I came here to give you a chance to do the right thing. I deserve a piece of the windfall you knew was coming when I left."

"Well, you wasted a trip."

"I can see that." The man paused, thinking. "The thing is, you think you've got the upper hand. I can go take my share anytime I want."

Dieter snorted. "Yeah, right."

Someone knocked at the door. "Come in!" Dieter shouted, this time glad for the interruption.

The same young woman he had yelled at earlier nudged the door open and stepped tentatively into the room. "I'm sorry, Mr. Bergheim, I didn't know you had a visitor."

"He was just leaving."

"They told me to remind you again about lunch. It started fifteen minutes ago."

Dieter's visitor stood up and ambled to the door. "Enjoy your pudding, Dieter."

Chapter Two

Adam Cash yanked the bedspread taut and stepped back to admire his work. The twin bed was new, purchased three days ago in San Antonio. Cash and his girlfriend Edie James had taken her son Luke to SeaWorld for the boy's fifth birthday. On the way back to Pinyon they detoured to Costco for Cash to buy the bed. He had just finished assembling the frame, dropped the mattress in place, and fitted it with sheets and a pillow. He gave the pillow a final straightening twist and told himself the job would have passed inspection during his army days.

On his way out of the room, Cash spotted a battered guitar case in the closet. He had been telling himself for months he should get his old instrument out and see if he could still play. At one time he had been good enough to join a country band organized by his friend Steve Jenkins. The Prickly Pears performed at several school dances and rodeos. They even played a gig as the warmup act at Kendala Halle for Cody Joe Krause, a local singer who had once appeared on the Grand Ole Opry. Although Steve was the band's front man, Cash occasionally sang lead without embarrassing himself. At least, that's what Edie had told him at the time.

The band broke up when Cash joined the army. Edie broke up with him as well, saying she had no intention of waiting for him unless he was ready to make theirs a committed relationship. To Cash, that meant they wouldn't see other people. To Edie, it meant marriage. Cash hadn't felt ready for that, so she moved on. Now, ten years and Edie's divorce from that scumbag Randy Webster later, they were back together. Cash had no intention of screwing it up this time.

Cash removed the guitar from its case and took it into the den. After tuning the instrument, he began strumming and sang the first line of the old Kenny Rogers hit "The Gambler." Unable to remember the rest of the verse, he launched into the chorus but stopped when a shadow flashed across the front window. He put the guitar down and went outside. A blue Ford Focus rolled to a stop in the driveway. He smiled and waved at the driver.

Cash's brother Reid stepped out. With a baby face and four inches shorter than his older brother, Reid looked younger than his twenty years. He opened the car's hatchback and pulled out a pristine black guitar case.

Cash whistled and led him inside. "I see you took the plunge on the Martin."

"Yep." He followed Cash into the house. "It cost me three thousand bucks. I'll be living on ramen noodles for a year."

"What did Mom and Dad say?"

"What do they always say?" He adopted a whiny voice. "'You should get a real job.'" Switching to his regular voice, he said, "I tell them being a musician *is* a real job."

"Let me guess," said Cash. "Dad said, 'I mean one that pays.'"

"You got it." Reid spotted Cash's guitar on the sofa. "Are you playing again?"

"Not really."

"Liar. Let me hear you."

With a shrug, Cash sat on the sofa and pulled the guitar onto his lap. He was embarrassed to play for his brother, as accomplished as he had become. Gritting his teeth, he played and sang what he remembered of "The Gambler." When he finished, he grinned sheepishly and said, "Like I told you, I suck."

"You're just rusty. Why don't you practice some and I'll get you up on-stage tomorrow night?"

Cash laughed. "I don't think so." He headed toward the kitchen. "You want a beer?"

"I'm still underage."

"You want a beer or not?"

"What do you think?"

Cash fetched two beers and returned to the den. He handed one to Reid.

"Is this from the Packsaddle?" Reid asked, referring to Steve's brewpub in Pinyon.

"Yeah. Pillbug Pils."

"Stupid name," said Reid, taking a sip.

"Not as stupid as 'The Whistling Armadillos.'"

Reid frowned. "You can laugh now, but you won't be laughing when we get a gig at the Grand Ole Opry." He set his beer on the coffee table and took out his guitar. "Now, let's jam."

***

The loneliness Emil Bergheim felt in the house now that his brother was gone surprised him. As cantankerous as the son of a bitch could be, Emil missed him. Theirs had always been a stormy relationship, but one in which fraternal loyalty trumped all else. Ever since he could remember Emil had looked out for his little brother. As kids, they played together, hunted deer and wild turkeys together, and fought each other's fights no matter what. But Parkinson's disease and its ravaging effects was one foe Emil felt powerless against. It pained him to see how helpless Dieter had become. After his third serious tumble in as many days, Emil had put his foot down. His brother needed more help than he was able to give. He needed to move to an assisted living facility.

Emil had seen this coming for at least a year. He had already researched facilities in San Antonio and Austin before settling on Avonwick Retirement Community, a sprawling complex adjacent to Mopac Expressway in the Texas capital. Dieter had balked, but Emil's uncompromising attitude held sway. "It's time. I'll help you move in," he told his brother.

"I don't need your damn help."

"You sure as hell do."

Dieter's voice turned pleading. "Don't make me do this."

"Goddamn it, Dieter, you can't take care of yourself and I'm no God damned nurse. You can't cook, you can't do chores—hell, you can't even take a shit by yourself. You damn near broke your arm getting out of bed yesterday. So, quit whining and face the facts."

Dieter's lower lip trembled. "Who's gonna pay for that fancy place?"

"You've got plenty of money."

"I ain't giving it to you."

"No, you're not giving it to me. You'll just be paying your bills like you've done all your life."

In the end, Dieter relented. Emil helped him select the clothes and furniture he would take with him, threw everything in the back of his pickup truck, and drove them both to Austin. After an awkward goodbye, he returned to the ranch alone. And now Dieter was gone.

Emil took his supper dishes to the kitchen sink. He hadn't felt like cooking, so his meal consisted of leftover deer sausage and beans eaten cold from the can. He was rinsing the can when he caught a glimpse of movement through the window.

Emil retrieved a pistol from his nightstand and went outside. He'd spotted the movement near his workshop, a four-hundred-square-foot tin structure a hundred feet from the house. He'd probably just seen a deer, but it paid to be cautious.

"I know you're there," Emil called out as he neared the workshop. "Come on out." When there was no answer, he said, "Don't try anything stupid. I've got a gun."

Muffled conversation reached Emil's ears. Alarmed, he strode toward the shop, only to hear the heavy footsteps of somebody running down the incline toward Caliche Creek. He jogged around the building in time to see a man descend the creek bank, cross the dry creek bed, and scramble up the other side. He couldn't make out any distinguishing features.

"Don't you come back," Emil shouted into the darkness. "Next time I'll shoot!"

The footsteps receded into silence. A car started in the distance, and the vehicle roared away. Emil could hear its tires spitting sand and gravel from the hard surface of the dirt road bordering his property. Then all was silent.

An owl hooted overhead. Emil saw a great horned owl flapping silent wings as it disappeared into the cedars. He had once read that the Comanche saw the giant bird as a harbinger of death. Maybe it was and maybe it wasn't, Emil told himself as he plodded back to the house. What did it matter? Death was just a part of life.

Chapter Three

Cash climbed out of the Noble County sheriff's department squad car he used when on duty, and nodded at the old man waiting outside the modest ranch house. It had been built at least a century ago, but with its immaculate white siding, spotless windows, and crisp blue trim, it looked many decades younger. Cash bounded up the steps of the porch. "Good morning, Mr. Bergheim."

Bergheim crossed his arms. "Morning." His face remained a mask of stone.

"I hear you had some intruders last night."

"Yep."

Cash waited, but Bergheim said nothing more. "Do you want to tell me about them?"

"Why do you think I called?"

Cash told himself to be patient. As long as he had known the crusty old bastard, Emil Bergheim had doled out words as if he was paying for them by the syllable. Before being hired as a Noble County deputy, Cash had built fences with the old guy. Back then his reticence annoyed Cash. Now, Cash found it amusing. Well, two could play at that game. "I'm listening."

The old man unfolded his arms and, without a word, descended the porch steps. He marched past Cash and headed for the workshop. Cash followed.

"They were right here," Emil said when Cash caught up.

"They? Was it more than one person?"

"Had to be at least two. I heard them talking."

"What were they doing?"

"I don't know. About to break into my shop to steal my tools is my guess."

Cash leaned in to examine the metal door. It was held shut by a deadbolt operated by a Schlage electronic keypad. "Wow, Mr. Bergheim," Cash said. "You've gone high tech."

Bergheim grunted.

Cash peered closely at the frame adjacent to the lock. He saw no scratch marks or other signs of tampering. He tried the handle. It resisted his effort to turn it.

"Shouldn't you be wearing gloves?" Bergheim said.

Blushing with embarrassment at his boneheaded mistake, Cash said, "I guess I'm still getting the hang of this job."

"You never forgot them building fences with me."

Cash ignored the remark but donned gloves. He stepped back from the door and noticed a plastic candy wrapper in the dirt. He picked it up. "Do you eat Jolly Ranchers?"

"What's a Jolly Rancher?"

Certainly not you. "Never mind. Let's look inside."

Bergheim keyed in the code and they entered the shop.

Cash flipped on the lights. "Is anything missing?" he said, taking in the neatest workspace he had ever seen. Tools hung from a floor-to-ceiling pegboard next to a spotless ancient oak workbench. Above the bench were two shelves, from which dangled glass jars, each one neatly labeled to indicate its contents. The lids had been glued to the boards so that the jars could be screwed into place. Larger implements hung from another wall: shovels, a pickaxe, several rakes, and a chainsaw. A drill press, a scroll saw, and a lathe formed a line below the room's only window. In the center of the shop was a table saw.

Bergheim made a slow inspection tour of the room, pausing briefly to look closely at each of the power tools. "Looks like everything's here," he said.

They went outside, Bergheim locking the shop door behind them.

"Did you get a good look at them?" Cash asked.

"No, they ran off when I told them I had a gun."

"Did you shoot at them?"

"No."

"Good."

"I will next time."

Cash knew that was true. Emil Bergheim was an old-breed Hill Country rancher. If he perceived a threat, he shot it and sorted it out later.

Cash said, "Which way did they go?"

Bergheim pointed. "Yonder past the creek. I heard them drive off. Their car must have been on the county road."

Cash paced the distance to the creek. He studied the ground for footprints, but a careful search of the parched ground yielded none. The same held for the dry creek bed. He retraced his steps to Bergheim. "All right. Let me know if you see them again."

"You're not going to do anything?"

"I could get Frida out here to dust for fingerprints."

"What for? All she'd find are yours."

"I'll file a report back at the department."

Bergheim spat. "That ought to scare them off."

***

The man called Hooch tossed a roll of copper wire onto the scale at Grant's Scrap Metal. "I got one more," he said. He wiped his brow and reached into his truck bed.

"I've always meant to ask you," Dick Grant, the owner, said. "How come they call you Hooch?"

Hooch tossed the last roll onto the scale. "I used to make my own whiskey. I've been known to drink my share, too."

"Why did you stop?"

"Something got into my last batch. Hell if I know what it was. Sent three people to the hospital. The sheriff started nosing around and I sold the still for scrap. It was you that bought it."

"I'll be damned," said Grant. "I don't remember that."

"I didn't tell you it was a still when you bought it. Just busted it up and brought in the pieces."

Grant chuckled. 'You don't trust me?"

"Not one damn bit." Hooch looked at the scale's digital readout. "Two hundred eight pounds."

Grant brought an ancient calculator out of his pocket. "Let's see," he said, punching the keys. "Two hundred eight pounds at a buck fifty a pound comes to three twelve."

"You told me two dollars a pound on the phone."

"What can I say?" Grant said with a shrug. "The price has dropped."

"Like hell it has. It's two bucks a pound or you can go fuck yourself."

"Sorry. A buck fifty."

"You'll sell it for three times that."

"If you think you can get a better price for your stolen wire somewhere else, then be my guest."

Hooch stomped to his truck, flung open the door, and reached under the seat. He came out with a Walther PK380 pistol and brandished it at Grant. "What's the price now, asshole?" he said.

Grant emitted a nervous laugh. "You're not gonna shoot me over a hundred bucks."

"That's not the right question," said Hooch, stepping up close to the scrapyard owner. His arm whipped up and he clubbed the smaller man's face. "The question is, are you willing to die for a hundred bucks?"

Grant staggered backward, clutching his bleeding nose. "You son of a bitch."

Hooch raised the gun. "Two bucks a pound, right?"

The dazed man nodded. "I'll go get the money."

Chapter Four

Beads of sweat dripped from Cash's armpits, further soaking his shirt. Blurred faces whirled past him as he spun in ever-faster circles. Fixing on Edie's radiant smile, he kept his feet moving in time with the music while dodging the other couples swirling around them. *One-two-three, one-two-three, one-two-three.* But the band, already playing at an impossibly fast pace, somehow kicked up the tempo another notch and Cash stumbled on Edie's foot trying to keep up. She grabbed his arm to save him from falling. Mercifully, the music came to a halt. As the last echoing strain of "Orange Blossom Special" faded away, they fell laughing into each other's arms.

"All right, folks, we're gonna take a short break," bellowed Roger Sanders, lead singer of The Whistling Armadillos. "But don't go anywhere because the beer is cold, the music is hot, and the night is young!"

"Oh my God," Edie said, fighting to catch her breath. "I gotta go sit down."

Cash followed her to their table. As they pulled up chairs, Cash's boss Gabe Santos, one-time army buddy and Noble County sheriff, slid two Shiner Bock longnecks to them. "Looks like you need these."

"Thanks," said Cash, taking a long pull. "That was brutal."

Edie gave him a playful punch. "Dancing with your girlfriend is brutal?"

"I mean, it was very romantic."

"That's more like it."

Cash and Edie shared the table with Santos, his wife Katrina, and fellow deputy Keisha Hodge. Hodge had come without a date. At first Cash and Santos had taken turns dancing with her but in a short while, she had drawn the attention of enough single men that they no longer had to.

They sat in the century-old barn-like building known as Winkler Dance Hall. Beer-stained pine tables arranged on a concrete slab surrounded a wooden dance floor large enough for dozens of two-steppers to circle counter-clockwise. Plywood sheets that could be lifted in cooler weather covered the windows lining either side of the air-conditioned hall. The band performed on an elevated platform at one end. At the other was the entrance and an oak bar where patrons could order drinks, nachos, and jalapeño sausage wraps.

Cash's brother Reid squeezed in between him and Santos and set a bucket of beers on the table. "Here you go, folks. Drink up."

"How'd you buy those?" Edie said. "You're not twenty-one yet."

"I didn't hear that," said Santos.

Reid said, "I have a mature face."

"No, you don't," said Cash. "You look like Doogie Howser." He grinned. "You guys sound great tonight."

"Thanks. There's still time to get you up there."

"Not a chance."

The band's drummer, Eddie Kincaid, pulled up a chair. With his beard, black ponytail, arm tattoos, and silver skulls dangling from pierced ears, Kincaid would have looked more at home in a metal band than one covering Tim McGraw and Reba McEntire songs.

Accompanying him was a young couple, whom he introduced as his friends Slater Cobb and Willa Dearborn.

Kincaid reached into the bucket for a beer. "Don't mind if I do." He took a long drink, wiped his mouth, and looked at Reid. "Is this your cop brother?"

"Adam Cash," he said, sticking out a hand. "Call me Cash."

Kincaid gave him a quick shake, then scanned the others at the table. "And your friends?"

Cash introduced everyone at the table. "How long have you been with the band, Eddie?"

"About six months. Before that, I was slapping skins for a Thomas Rhett wannabe named Tom Paul Jackson."

"I never heard of him."

"He moved to Nashville. Last I heard, he was working at a car wash."

Edie said, "Willa, how long have you guys been together?"

The young woman smiled. "Eight months. But we're not married or anything."

"Not by a long shot," said Cobb with a sarcastic laugh. He wrapped an arm around Willa's shoulders and squeezed. "But who knows, maybe she'll get lucky someday."

An older man who looked at home in his boots and weathered cowboy hat sat down. Gray hair poked out below the hat brim, matching a short beard. He slapped Kincaid's back. "There you are, Eddie. Jeez, can't a guy take a piss around here without getting ditched?"

"I didn't ditch you. I didn't know where you went."

"I'm kidding. So, introduce me to your friends."

Kincaid pressed his lips into a thin smile. "This is my grandfather, everybody."

Cash reached across the table for a handshake. "Adam Cash. Call me Cash."

"Roy Baxter," said the older man with a grin. "Call me whatever you want."

Kincaid drained his beer and stood up. "Come on, Slater. There's someone asking to see you."

Cobb and Willa rose from their chairs. He snatched a beer from the bucket before following Kincaid toward the exit. Willa tossed out a hurried, "Nice to meet you folks," and hustled to catch up to him.

Cash gave his brother a look that showed what he thought of Kincaid. He turned back to Baxter. "I hear your grandson is a helluva drummer."

"Yeah, he's always banging something. Drums, cymbals, cocktail waitresses."

Everyone laughed. Cash said, "Do you live around here?"

"No, I'm in Austin. Been there about six months."

"What do you do?"

"A little of this, a little of that. I guess you could call me retired. I love sports, especially the Astros. I go to a game whenever I can."

Cash's face lit up. The Astros were his favorite baseball team. "Me too! My grandfather lives in Houston. I get down there for a game at least once or twice a year."

"Really? Maybe we could go together sometime."

"I'd love that." He registered Baxter's gray hair. "I'll bet you've got some memories."

"Oh, yeah," Baxter said. "I've been a fan since they were the Colt .45s."

"The Colt .45s? Like the gun?"

"Yeah, not a very PC name these days."

"When did they become the Astros?" Cash asked.

"When they built the Astrodome. Nineteen-sixty-five."

"Did you ever see Jeff Bagwell play?"

"Sure! Bagwell, Biggio. Hell, I go back to Joe Morgan and the Toy Cannon, Jimmy Wynn. Now, there's a nickname for you."

Cash had heard the name but knew little about Wynn, who played decades before he was born. "He was their first big slugger, right?"

"Yessiree. I saw him hit three dingers in a game once. I was just a kid. It was hard to hit home runs in the Astrodome, much less three in a game. The guy had power. He was one of only a handful of guys to hit one into the upper deck in the Dome. They painted a cannon on the seat the ball landed in."

"Cool."

"I ran into him at a restaurant about twenty years ago. I asked him what they did with that seat when the team moved to the new ballpark. He said it was in his living room."

Cash noticed the bored look on Edie's face. "Well, I could talk baseball all night with you," he said, "but maybe I should get Edie back out on the dance floor."

Baxter flashed an impish grin. "If I were you, I'd do whatever it took to please such a pretty lady. Go on, git. We'll talk more later."

Cash led Edie away from the table. Luke Bryan's "Most People Are Good," a classic two-step song, was playing. As he took her hand, he said, "Nice guy."

Edie smiled. "He sure does love the Astros. I think you've found your soulmate."

"You're my soulmate," he said and gave her a quick kiss. "But he might be a close second."

***

Cash considered himself a good, if not great dancer. Country dancing wasn't all that complicated. The two-step got you through most songs. Then there was the waltz, which anyone with the remotest sense of rhythm could manage. Finally, the polka was just a speeded-up waltz to Cash. Beyond those essentials were the Cotton Eye Joe and the schottische. For those dances, rhythm and style counted for less than enthusiasm and blood-alcohol content.

What separated the good from the great dancers were the moves the great ones supplemented the two-step with. And just knowing the moves wasn't enough. You had to flow seamlessly from one to the next, improvising with the music and timing your steps to avoid bumping into the other couples swirling around you. Cash had never mastered that trick. He could twirl his partner easily enough but lacked the confidence to try anything fancier. Edie had been pressing him to attend a dance class with her. So far he had resisted but knew she'd win out eventually.

Edie flashed a captivating smile as Cash twirled her halfway through the Whistling Armadillos' rendition of "Itty Bitty." As she completed the move, she slipped a hand behind his waist and pulled him closer. "Thursdays at seven at the community center. Only six weeks and we'll be the best dancers on the floor."

"You're already the best-*looking* dancer on the floor," he said with a grin. "That's good enough for me."

"Flattery won't get you out of this," she said, playfully slapping his chest.

He gave her a lingering kiss. "What about distraction?"

"Yeah, that might work." Her eyes caught on something past Cash's shoulder. "Hey, is that Bernadette?"

Two years ago, Cash and Bernadette Fenster had crossed paths one night at the Dizzy Dillo on Pinyon's town square. Cash bought her a beer. Several beers later they were both drunk. Cash insisted on walking her home, partly because he was horny and partly because he knew he was too far gone to drive to his own house. They weaved their way to the trailer she shared with her mother. Before she could open the front door, Cash kissed her. She said, "Wanna come in? Momma's visiting my aunt in San Angelo." Catching her drift, he quickly said yes. They made wild, drunken love and fell asleep in each other's arms. Emma was born nine months later. After a rocky start in which Bernadette blamed Cash for "ruining my life," the two new parents made peace with each other. Cash gave her money for childcare expenses; Bernadette agreed to let Cash visit his daughter regularly. The last time he was over, he asked if he could sleep on her couch. She threw him out of the house.

Cash spun around to see Bernadette dancing with a tall, gangly man in a crisp work shirt and spotless cowboy hat. She looked good in tight jeans, a satin blouse with one too many buttons undone, and red boots. Cash said, "I guess her mom is watching Emma."

"Look how they're dancing."

Cash looked again and saw what she meant. They danced like a couple looking for a dark corner so they could rip each other's clothes off. The man pressed himself up against Bernadette, his arms wrapped tightly around her waist and his hands pressed firmly against her buttocks. She leaned her head against his chest and stroked his back with her free hand. They swayed rather than two-stepped with the music. As Cash watched, Bernadette tilted her head back and kissed the guy. Cash saw tongue.

"I better go meet this dude before they elope," Cash said.

"Just be nice."

"I'm always nice."

The song ended. Cash twirled Edie a final time and approached the couple. Bernadette was still locking lips with her partner.

"Hey, Bernadette."

She popped free of the kiss. "Cash." She wiped her mouth with the back of her hand "Hey. Hi, Edie."

"Hi, Bernadette. It's good to see you out having fun."

"Yeah." She forced an uncomfortable smile. "Momma's with Emma, so you don't need to worry."

"I'm not worried," Cash said. "You're a good mother."

The man thrust his hand at Cash. "Clint Morgan." His voice thundered above the background din.

They shook. Bernadette said, "Clint, this is Cash and Edie. Cash is Emma's father."

Morgan cocked his head and grinned. "So this is my competition, eh?"

"No competition," Cash said. He jerked his head toward Edie and grinned. "Unless you're talking about her."

Morgan threw an arm around Bernadette and squeezed. "No, I'm talking about this hot tamale right here."

Bernadette blushed. "It was good seeing you guys." She cut her eyes to Morgan. "Let's get something to drink."

They wandered off. Edie said, "Did he just call her a hot tamale?"

"I know, right? You're the only hot tamale here tonight."

She swatted his rear. "Keep it up and you'll be leaving by your lonesome."

***

Cash couldn't remember the last time he had had so much fun at a dance. He relished every moment on the floor with Edie, especially during the slow songs. The feel of her head resting on his shoulder sent chills down his spine. In between dances, he and Baxter talked baseball. They exchanged phone numbers, promising to attend a game in Houston as soon as possible. Edie endured the baseball talk with only a few eye rolls.

Baxter finished his beer and stood up. "I better get going." He winked at Edie. "Thanks for letting me hog your boyfriend tonight. I hope you weren't too bored."

"Not at all," Edie said. "You guys were made for each other."

Hodge and Santos left an hour later when the Whistling Armadillos ended the evening with "Burnin' the Honky Tonks Down." The few remaining dancers drifted toward the exit as the lights came on. Cash and Edie helped the band load the sound equipment into a van. As they were loading the last piece, Cash's phone rang.

"This is Cash." He listened without comment before heaving a sigh and sticking the phone back into his pocket.

"Who was that?" Edie asked.

"Dispatch," Cash said. "Somebody shot Emil Bergheim."

Chapter Five

Cash waited with his hands on his hips while Santos searched for the switch to the outside floodlight at Emil Bergheim's house. Who would have shot the old man? He had reported intruders the other night. But why had they come back? What were they after?

A wave of sorrow washed over Cash. As abrasive as Bergheim could be, Cash liked the old guy. In keeping with his German heritage, he was a straight shooter, someone who spoke his mind without apology. You might not like his rough talk, but to him, that was your problem. He was only speaking the truth, he would say, and if he didn't let you know about it, it would rise up to bite you in the ass later on. He had thrown Cash a lifeline by giving him a job when he moved back to Noble County. And Bergheim was generous. It wasn't great pay, but it was more than Cash had expected.

"Found it," Santos called from the house, and the area was bathed in artificial light. Santos came outside and headed toward Cash.

"We better hurry," Cash said, looking at the ominous clouds overhead. "It looks like rain."

"Check the workshop. I'll search out here."

Cash grunted and first went to examine the structure's door. Someone had pried it open with a crowbar, smashing the door frame but leaving the lock relatively intact. Wood splinters littered the ground.

The strike plate lay among the rubble, still attached to a jagged piece of the frame. Scratches marred the metal door around the keypad. A deep dent on the door edge marked the spot where the crowbar had been inserted.

Cash flipped a light switch. His heart ached at the sight of the destruction. Tools lay strewn about the floor. The glass jars had been removed and the contents dumped. The larger power tools had been overturned. A gaping hole beside the table saw drew Cash's attention. Next to it was a two-by-two square of concrete that looked like its cover.

Cash peered into the hole. About the size and depth of a large suitcase, it was lined with black plastic. He knelt and peeled away a loose flap to reveal concrete. He rapped his knuckles against the other sides to find the same. This had been no spontaneous dig.

Outside, raindrops pinged arrhythmically on the metal roof. The banging grew in volume and intensity until a steady roar echoed throughout the shop. Santos rushed in, his shirt spattered and water dripping from his hat brim.

"This is going to screw up our search," Cash said.

"We'll see." He eyed the mess in the shop. "Find anything in here?"

Cash gestured at the hole. "Just that. It's empty. Lined with plastic and concrete, though, so he was keeping something in there he didn't want getting wet."

"Money?"

"That would be my guess."

Santos held up a gloved hand. In it was a damp hundred-dollar bill. "I found this outside."

"All right, so Bergheim was hiding a stash of cash. Why?"

"People hide money for one reason. They got it illegally."

"I can't believe that about Emil Bergheim. I used to work for the guy. He's as honest as they come. I remember once when the price of wire went up before we could start a job and he ate the increase. Anybody else would have just bumped up the bid. Know what he said?"

"What?"

Cash rasped out an impression of Bergheim's voice. "I quoted the man a price and by God, I can't go back on my word." He dropped the impression. "He lost money on that job."

"Okay, so he's honest with his business," said Santos. "But you never can tell about someone you don't know well. My dad used to think OJ Simpson was a great guy." He looked at the hole. "It took them a while to find this. They dug several holes outside."

"It must be the same guys he chased off the other night."

"Didn't he say he heard a car drive off?"

"Yeah. He said it was parked on the county road beyond Caliche Creek."

A brief burst of light flashed through the window, followed by a wall-rattling thunderclap. Santos said, "We can't search those woods in this storm."

"I can wait here until it stops."

"It'd still be pitch dark. Come back in the morning. Bring Hodge with you."

"You're not coming?" Cash asked.

"I'll drive over to Junction and see if Bergheim is in any condition to talk."

"He's alive?" That was good news.

"I guess so. They're operating on him."

Cash noticed something shiny sticking out from beneath the concrete square. He slipped on a pair of gloves and tugged a plastic candy wrapper free. He held it up for Santos to see.

Santos said, "Jolly Rancher."

"Yeah," Cash said with a chuckle. "If there's one thing Emil Bergheim isn't, it's jolly."

"Come on, he's a pussycat."

"So is a mountain lion."

***

Cash was up at first light, eager to resume his search. He had set his coffee machine to turn on fifteen minutes before he got up, so as he dressed, he savored the smell of fresh coffee wafting in from the kitchen. He filled a Yeti with the hot liquid, grabbed a banana, and hustled out the door.

At the department, Hodge was waiting for him when he got out of his Ram pickup. She held up a key fob. "I'll drive."

"Do you know the way?"

"No, but you do. And I know how to use a GPS."

As the two of them strode to the squad car, Cash couldn't help but smile. From the day Hodge first reported for duty two months ago, she had assumed as much responsibility as she could get away with. Cash liked her enthusiasm. He also respected her courage. Within two weeks of starting the job, she accompanied Cash to an arrest of Bonnie Hart, aka Jessica Patrice, a woman who had attempted to kidnap Emma and Bernadette. When Maurice Trahan, a con man who murdered his wife in Louisiana and started a new life in Noble County as Dennis Webb, tried to intervene, a shootout broke out. Hodge kept her cool. She chased Patrice down and immobilized her before rushing to Cash's aid. Her fearlessness reminded Cash of the more daring men and women he had served with in Afghanistan.

Cash jumped into the passenger seat while Hodge settled in behind the wheel. When they were underway, she said, "Santos says you used to work for this guy."

"Yeah. When I first moved back to Pinyon after college. I was desperate for a job and the department wasn't hiring. My dad suggested I give him a call. Dad still remembered when he built a dry-stack stone wall around our backyard. It's still standing."

"How long has he lived here?"

"Since before I was born."

"By himself?"

"His wife died maybe twenty years ago. His two kids moved out of state. I went to school with the younger one, a girl named Lily. She couldn't wait to get out of Noble County. His brother lived with him until recently when he had to go to an assisted living facility in Austin. So now he's by himself."

"Why would somebody shoot him?"

"I don't know," Cash said. "But if anybody can survive a shooting, it would be a tough old coot like Emil Bergheim."

They started their search at the house. Cash studied the back door. He saw no signs of forced entry. He showed Hodge where the ambulance crew found Bergheim leaning against the house. Pointing to the workshop, he said, "He got shot over there but crawled back here before calling 911." He gestured at the ground. "Look at the blood."

Hodge knelt to examine a dark splotch in the dirt. She peered beneath the pier-and-beam house. "Hand me some gloves."

Cash produced a pair from his pocket and gave it to her. "You should always carry some of those with you."

"Duly noted," she said without emotion. She slipped on the gloves, reached into the crawl space, and came out with a compact Beretta pistol. "Bergheim's?"

"Must be," said Cash. He slipped out an evidence bag and opened it.

"You got another one of those?" Picking up on his puzzled look, she added, "The magazine goes in a separate bag."

"Right," Cash said, chagrined at his mistake.

Hodge removed the Beretta's magazine, took the bag from Cash, and dropped the magazine in. She pulled the Beretta's slide to eject the round in the chamber. That went into the bag as well. By now Cash had a second bag ready. Hodge slipped the pistol into it.

"You've done this before," Cash said.

"Yep."

The sound of a car engine reached their ears. The unseen car's motor cut off, a door slammed, and footsteps approached from the front of the house.

"That will be Frida," said Cash.

"The crime scene investigator?"

"Crime scene investigator, medical examiner, and my old babysitter. Frida's a one-woman show."

Hodge chuckled. "You gotta love small towns."

Frida Simmons hustled around the corner of the house. "Sorry I'm late," she said. Ten years older than Cash, Frida had indeed once been his babysitter. More recently, she provided surreptitious assistance as he fought to clear his name after being falsely accused of murdering the Noble County sheriff, Griff Turner.

"We just started," Cash said as Frida approached. He held up the evidence bags. "Hodge found this. We think it was Bergheim's."

"Interesting."

Cash handed the bags to her. “Gabe and I searched the shop last night.” He explained about the hole in the floor. “You two go over it again and make sure we didn’t miss anything,” he said. “I’ll search the woods.”

“What’s in the woods?” Hodge asked.

“Bergheim had visitors a few days ago. When he confronted them, they fled past the creek toward the road beyond. The most likely scenario is that the same people came back. They probably would have escaped in the same direction.”

Hodge and Frida disappeared into the shop. Cash walked the shop’s perimeter and saw several shallow holes that had been dug next to the foundation. What had the intruders been looking for? Money? Probably. That would explain the hundred-dollar bill found by Santos.

Cash left the shop and followed a footpath to the creek. Last night’s rain had obliterated any footprints. He walked slowly, searching both sides of the path for anything that might have been dropped. He saw nothing.

Reaching the dry creek, he descended the six-foot embankment and stopped. Unlike the caliche above, much of the creek bed was coated with black clay. Numerous footprints were visible in the moist substance. Cash saw two different sets. One was larger and had been left by boots or hiking shoes. The smaller set looked to have been made by sneakers.

Cash followed the creek for fifty feet in both directions but saw nothing else that caught his eye. He strode across, taking care to step on rocks or gravel to avoid leaving footprints of his own. He climbed up the bank and spotted two round-mouth shovels lying in the grass. The metal shone and the wooden shafts looked fresh. These were new tools.

After making a wide berth around the shovels, Cash entered the cedar. The dead lower branches of several trees had been snapped off. The lighter appearance of the exposed wood indicated that the breaks were recent. In their haste to flee, the intruders must have missed the path.

Watching closely for footprints, Cash started up the path. A sharp bend led through an open area before the woods started up again. He made his way across the opening and pushed aside a large cedar branch blocking the trail. He froze. A man's body sprawled before him, face down, arms extending outward, ski mask pulled over his head. An irregular patch of blood stained the man's shirt, in the middle of which was a small dark hole. Breathing hard, Cash knelt and felt unsuccessfully for a radial pulse. He tugged off the ski mask. "I'll be damned," he said. "What the hell are you doing here?"

***

"His name is Slater Cobb," Cash said, indicating the corpse. "I met him at Winkler's."

"Is he a friend of your brother's?" said Hodge, still breathless from sprinting to the scene at Cash's shout.

"No. The drummer introduced him to me. His girlfriend, too."

"What's her name?"

"I don't remember."

Cash held up a large evidence bag. Inside it was a Sig Sauer P365 handgun. This time he had remembered to put the magazine in another bag. "I found this on him."

By now Frida had joined them. "Think that's what he shot the old man with?"

"Unless we find another gun, that's the working theory,"

Frida performed a quick scan of the body. "I just see the one wound," she said. "Through and through chest wound. It looks like it missed his heart, so he could have been shot back by the tool shed, then made it to here."

Cash squatted to study the man's shoes, dirty Adidas high tops that looked the size of the smaller prints in the creek. "Hodge, retrace your steps and look for blood stains. I want to know where this shootout took place. And get some pictures of those footprints in the creek. I'll go toward the road and see if they left any other surprises."

"Like what?" Hodge asked.

"Footprints, money, another body."

"What makes you think anyone else was here?" said Frida.

"There are two shovels. And two sets of footprints."

Hodge set out on her quest. Cash said, "Frida, you'll want to test Bergheim for gunpowder residue. This guy, too."

"Not my first rodeo, Adam." Unlike most people, Frida addressed Cash by his first name.

Cash left Frida to her work and continued up the trail. He scanned the ground closely for bloodstains but spotted none. He stopped when he reached the county road and scrutinized it for tire marks. The road was little more than a primitive track barely wide enough for two vehicles. The surface was the same caliche mixture of sand and gravel that was found throughout Noble County. Clumps of weeds grew between two sets of tracks. Cash sighed. No discernible tire imprints. His pulse quickened when he noticed a shallow trough gouged into the road a few feet away. Rainwater covered the deepest part. Distinct tire tracks extended from the water on either side. "Bingo," he said and went to fetch Frida.

Chapter Six

Hooch pushed through the flimsy trailer door to find his live-in girlfriend Addie stuffing a wad of chewing tobacco into her mouth. "I wish you'd quit that," he said. "It ain't exactly pleasant to pick tobacco out of my teeth after we kiss."

"Then don't kiss me," she said, snapping the lid back onto the can. "Besides, you smoke like a damn chimney. Kissing you is like kissing an ashtray."

Hooch plopped down in a lumpy lounge chair. "Look, I don't want to start no fight."

"Where were you last night?"

"Like I told you, I went to the Tall Tale to shoot pool."

"That place closes at two. That was eight hours ago."

Hooch was ready with the lie. "I fell asleep in my truck."

She spat into an empty Coke can. "With who?"

"Damn it, woman, with nobody." He reached into a pocket and came out with a wad of bills. "I got some money," he said, tossing it onto the rickety coffee table.

"How much is it?"

"Over two hundred bucks." She didn't need to know about all of it.

Addie snatched the money and began counting. "Well, ain't you Jeff Bozos?"

"Bezos. His name is Jeff Bezos."

"Who gives a shit?" She stuffed the bills into a pocket. "It ain't enough to pay the bills."

Irritation crept into Hooch's voice. There was no satisfying this woman. "I can get plenty more."

"How?"

"Never you mind."

"I'll tell you how, you dumb bastard. By getting a fucking job."

Hooch kicked the coffee table. It flipped toward her, striking her shin. "It ain't my fault I got laid off. My boss had it in for me."

Addie shot to her feet. "Get out."

"Fuck you."

"I mean it. I'll call the cops. I'm sure they'd like to know where you got that two hundred dollars."

Hooch slowly climbed to his feet. "You'll regret this."

She followed him to the door and watched him stride toward his truck. "Like hell I will."

***

Santos leaned his elbows on the table and clasped his hands to signal the others to stop talking. "Let's review what we know," he said.

They sat in the conference room: Cash, Santos, Hodge, and the department's fourth member, Deputy Deke Conrad.

Santos said, "Emil Bergheim caught somebody nosing around his workshop earlier this week. He heard multiple voices, so we assume there were at least two intruders. Cash was called out the next morning but didn't find anything significant. Bergheim must have caught them before they broke into the shop. Last night they came back. Not only did they get into the shop but they shot Bergheim. Right, Cash?"

"That's right," said Cash. "Bergheim was shot near the shop and crawled to the house, where he called for help."

Conrad interrupted. "How do you know he was shot near the shop? Did he tell you?"

"No. He left a blood trail from there to where the ambulance crew found him. We also found bloodstains leading in the other direction toward Caliche Creek. These continued on the other side of the creek, where we saw more on some broken cedar branches. Beyond that was Slater Cobb's body."

Santos said, "Cash found a gun underneath Cobb. A Sig P365. Frida will test Cobb for gunpowder residue to see if he fired it recently. The chamber wasn't full so it could have been the gun Bergheim was shot with." He caught Cash's eye. "Tell them what else you found."

"A bundle of hundreds," Cash said. "Nineteen bills in all. I didn't see it at first but found it near the body."

Conrad gave a low whistle. "That's almost a thousand bucks." He was known for his bravery, not his mental acuity.

"Just under two thousand," Santos said. "Put it with the bill I found last night and it's an even two grand."

Cash said, "How about what we saw in the shop?"

"I was getting to that. The place was ransacked. Broken jars, tools everywhere, overturned table saws, and the like." He explained about the hole. "It's lined with concrete and plastic, so clearly was meant to keep its contents dry."

"So, what you're saying," said Hodge, "is that Bergheim might have been hiding a lot more than two thousand dollars."

Santos said, "Right."

"Where does an old geezer like that get that much money?" Conrad asked. "He didn't make it building fences."

"Do we know for sure it was his?" Cash asked.

"Who else could it have belonged to?"

"We'll have to ask him."

"We can't," said Santos. "At least I couldn't this morning. He was still pretty drugged up from his surgery."

The conference room door opened and Frida bustled in. "Sorry I'm late."

"About time," Santos said before she could find a seat.

"Patience, Sheriff," she said, dropping into a chair. "Okay, here's what I found out. Slater Cobb's gunpowder residue test is negative. So, he didn't shoot Bergheim."

"Interesting," said Hodge. "What about the blood?"

"The stains we found leading from the shop to the house match Bergheim's blood type, O positive. That's the most common type, so we can't assume it's his, although it probably is. I'll send it for DNA testing, but that will take a while."

"And the other stains?" Cash asked.

"They match Slater Cobb. And he's AB positive, which is found in only two percent of the population. It's a safe bet they're from him."

"What about prints on the shovels?"

"Nada. They must have been wearing gloves."

"And the guns?"

"Nothing unexpected. Bergheim's has only his prints; the Sig has Cobb's."

"We need the slug they pulled from Bergheim," said Cash. "See if it matches the Sig."

"That's what I told them when I was at the hospital this morning," Frida said. "I was hoping one of you could drive over later and pick it up."

"I'll go," said Conrad.

Santos dropped his head in thought and ran his fingers through his hair. "Cash, find out what you can about Slater Cobb and his girlfriend."

Cash said, "Keisha, how about I take the girlfriend and you take Cobb?"

"Sure."

Santos continued. "I'll check with Ace and Tractor Supply to see if they remember anyone buying two shovels recently." He paused. "Anything else?"

No one spoke.

Santos shot to his feet, reminding Cash of Sergeant Malkoff, his team leader in Afghanistan. It was a signal for everyone to get off their asses and get to work. The sheriff said, "Keep me posted."

***

Cash left the conference room and made for the exit. On the way, he passed Vicky, the young receptionist who had been crushing on him since his unsuccessful job interview with Griff Turner, the sheriff he had been falsely accused of murdering. He steeled himself for a flirtatious comment, but instead of flashing her usual coy smile, she brushed a tear and turned away. Against his better judgment, he said, "Are you okay, Vicky?"

She wiped her cheeks and looked up at him. Her eyes glistened as she struggled to compose herself. With a final sniffle she said, "I'm fine."

"You don't look fine. What happened?"

"Tyler broke up with me."

Cash silently cursed himself. He had stepped into a Texas-sized cowpie. "I'm sorry," he said, and meant it. Tyler had dampened Vicky's obsession with him. Now that the ex-boyfriend was out of the picture, Vicky might redirect her attention back in his direction.

She fingered the heart-shaped pendant hanging from her necklace. "Guess I don't need this anymore."

Guess not, Cash thought, but didn't say.

She used a tissue to dab her eyes. "That jerk."

Cash saw a chance to slip away, but she wasn't finished. "Cash?"

"Yes?"

"I could use some company at lunch today. Would you take me to Sonic?"

Not in a million years. She was a nice kid, but she was just that, a kid. "Sorry, I've got work to do."

She sniffled. "Maybe another time?"

"You bet."

Before she could say anything else, Cash beat a path to the door. Outside, he blew a long breath and swore. One of these days he would just have to be rude to her. There seemed to be no other way to shut her down. He pushed Vicky from his mind and made a call. "Hey, Reid."

"Hey, big bro. What's up?"

"I need the name of that woman who was with your drummer's friend last night."

"My drummer's friend? Oh, you mean Slater."

"Yeah. Slater Cobb."

"That was Willa Dearborn," Reid said.

"Dearborn. Is she related to the Dearborns that used to live on Kitzler Road?"

"I think so. I know she went to Pinyon High. She was in the class ahead of me, so I don't know her all that well."

"What about Cobb? Is he from around here?"

"Not that I know of," he said, suspicion growing in his voice. "What's with all these questions?"

Cash told him about Cobb's death. "He and at least one other person broke into Emil Bergheim's workshop last night. We think Bergheim shot Cobb but not before getting shot himself."

"Whoa. Slater's dead?"

"Yes."

"What about Mr. Bergheim?"

"He survived but needed surgery. Now I'm trying to figure out who shot him."

"Did you ask him?"

"He can't talk. He's in critical condition."

Reid let out a low whistle. "Wow, they're making you earn your keep down there."

"You could say that. What can you tell me about Cobb?"

"Nothing, really," Reid said. "Just that he's a friend of Eddie's."

"Speaking of Eddie, did he ride back to Austin with you last night?"

"No."

"What about the other band members? Did he go with one of them?"

"No, he was by himself. I know that because I saw him in the parking lot."

"Okay," said Cash. "Can you give me Willa Dearborn's contact information? Eddie's too, if you have it."

"Yeah, I think so."

"Text it to me, okay?"

Moments after Cash ended the call, a text came in from Reid with the phone numbers. He called the girlfriend first.

"Hello?"

Cash said, "Willa Dearborn?"

"Yes."

"This is Adam Cash. We met last night at Winkler's."

"I remember."

"I need to talk to you. It's important."

"Okay, so talk."

He paused. He hadn't thought out what he would say, but he knew he didn't want to tell her about her boyfriend's death over the phone. "It would be better if we talked in person."

She responded with a long silence, finally broken when she said, "You're a county deputy, aren't you?"

"That's right."

"Did something happen to Slater?"

"Where are you? I'll come to you."

"Speedy Chicken. I'm working."

"Be there in ten."

Chapter Seven

Before going to see Willa Dearborn, Cash called Eddie Kincaid. After identifying himself, he said, "You may remember I'm a deputy with the Noble County Sheriff's Office."

"Yeah." Kincaid's voice was guarded.

"I'd like to ask you some questions about an investigation I'm conducting. How well do you know Slater Cobb?"

"Why? Is he in trouble?"

"I'll get to that," Cash said. "How close are you guys?"

"Close enough, I guess. We went to high school together."

"In Pinyon?"

"No, here in Austin. At Bowie."

"Do you guys hang out a lot?"

"I'm not answering any more questions until you tell me what's going on."

Cash paused to consider how much he should reveal. "Slater Cobb is dead. Somebody shot him last night after the dance."

"Shit!" The surprise sounded genuine. "Who did it?"

"We're working on that. Did you see him after you left the dance hall?"

"No, he left before we were done playing. He said Willa was getting tired."

"How long have those two known each other?"

"A few weeks. They're not engaged or anything."

Frustrated that the conversation was going nowhere, Cash decided to show his cards. "Your friend was shot trespassing on a local ranch. Do you know what he would have been doing there so late at night?"

"Hell if I know." Kincaid's irritation was obvious. "Like I told you, he said Willa was tired and left. That's all I know."

"One more question. When—"

The line went dead.

***

Speedy Chicken shared a building with Avi Rao's gas station and store on the south end of town. Cash was pleased to see Avi had reopened after the building was damaged last month by Ralph Spencer's fatal truck explosion. Cash's investigation of what at first seemed like a fluke accident culminated in the exposure of a ruthless con man.

It was late morning and the chicken restaurant had just opened. Cash found the dining room empty. A dozen red laminate tables awaited customers, each one stocked with napkins, ketchup, and salt and pepper shakers. An enticing aroma of fried chicken greeted him as he approached the stocky man behind the counter.

"Hey, Cash. What can I get you?"

"Do we know each other?"

The man smiled. "We've never met, but everybody in town knows who you are. You're a damn hero for busting up that human trafficking ring."

Cash blushed. "I had a lot of help."

"Yeah, but those guys would have gotten away with it if not for you. You even figured out who killed Sheriff Turner." He stuck out his hand. Cash shook it. The man said, "The name's Ellis Doran."

"Good to meet you, Ellis."

"There's a special on today. Buy any combo and get a free ice cream cone. But I'll comp your meal anyway."

"Thanks, but I'm not here to eat. I'm looking for one of your employees, Willa Dearborn. She's expecting me."

"What's this about?"

"I'm not free to discuss that."

"Wait here, I'll go get her," Doran said, looking disappointed.

"If you don't mind, I'd rather talk to her in private."

He gave Cash a quizzical look. "Okay, follow me. You can use the break room."

Cash followed Doran through the kitchen to a room barely big enough for a card table and three folding chairs. A young woman with a drawn face slouched in one of them. Cash recognized Willa Dearborn as she looked up from the phone in her hand.

"Hi, Willa. Thanks for meeting with me."

She nodded but didn't speak.

Cash said, "Is it okay if I sit down?"

"Are you here as a cop?"

"Sheriff's deputy."

"Is there a difference?"

"I guess not. Can I ask you some questions?"

"Okay."

He noticed Doran standing by the door and said, "Would you mind closing the door on your way out?"

Taking the hint, Doran spun around and left, pulling the door shut behind him.

Willa turned suspicious eyes on Cash. He said, "I have bad news, Willa. Slater was killed last night."

Cash expected a more dramatic reaction. She merely stared at her hands and swallowed hard. "He's dead?"

"Yes. I'm sorry."

Finally, the grief broke through. She covered her face with her hands and let out a low moan. Her shoulders shook as she began sobbing. Cash had known she might cry but still didn't know what to do. Should he touch her arm to console her? Get her a box of tissues? How long should he let her cry before speaking again? She made it easy for him by saying, "What happened?"

"He was shot."

"Who shot him?"

"We think it was a man named Emil Bergheim."

"Who the hell is that?"

"A local rancher," Cash said. He waited for another question but none came. "He was shot, too."

"Slater didn't shoot anybody. He'd never do that."

Cash carefully considered his next question, for he knew it could upset her. "This happened on Bergheim's ranch late last night. Do you know why Slater would have been there?"

She drew a deep breath and let it out. "No."

"When did you see him last?"

"We left the dance around eleven. He drove me home and we said good night. I thought he'd be going home, too."

"Willa, I'm going to ask you something that might upset you. Please understand that I'm not accusing Slater of anything. I'm just trying to figure out what happened."

"Okay."

"Why would Slater have gone to Bergheim's place so late at night?"

"I don't know."

"It looks like some money was stolen from his workshop."

She turned a scornful look on him. "He's not a criminal."

"I'm not saying he is. I'm just telling you what I know. It does appear there was somebody else there. Do you know who that was?"

"No."

Her answer was so quick, Cash was alerted. "He didn't tell you he was meeting anyone last night?"

"Like I already said, no. He dropped me off and then went home. At least that's what he said he was doing." Now she sounded angry.

"Who are his friends? Who does he hang out with?"

"I don't know!" she shouted, becoming more agitated. "Why are you asking me these questions?" When Cash didn't answer, she took a deep breath and glanced at a wall clock. "I need to get back to work."

Cash drummed his fingers on the table. Something didn't seem right.

Willa said, "Can I go now?"

He handed her a card. "If you think of anything else, call me."

Chapter Eight

Cash drove back to the station in search of Hodge. He found her at a computer in the conference room. "What did you find out?" he said as he pulled up a chair.

Hodge swiveled her chair toward him. "Cobb has lived in Pinyon for a year. Before that he was in Austin. Why he came, I don't know."

"Job?"

"Maybe. I have his address. It's a rent house on Hackberry. We could get a search warrant."

"Or we could just go knock on the door," said Cash. "Maybe he has a housemate."

Hodge stood up. "Let's go."

***

The house looked like a rental. No live-in owner would let it deteriorate like this. A lone plum tree with multiple dead branches shaded a yard of withered grass. Huge flakes of peeling paint hung from the eaves like bats. Weeds poked through the crushed-shell driveway, threatening a chalk-blue Chevy Blazer.

Cash pointed at the SUV. "Somebody's home." He and Hodge dodged inch-wide cracks in the front walkway on their way to the door. Cash rapped on it and heavy footsteps responded from the other side. Over a blaring TV a man called out, "Who is it?"

"Sheriff's department," said Cash. "Please open the door."

There was a pause. "I'm not dressed."

"We can wait while you put some clothes on."

"Give me a second."

More footsteps. The TV went silent. The door opened a crack. A man's face peered through the narrow opening. His eyes darted between Cash and Hodge. The pungent odor of marijuana smoke drifted onto the porch. "What do you want?"

"I'm Deputy Cash and this is Deputy Hodge. We're here to talk to you about your roommate, Slater Cobb."

"What about him?"

"May we come in?"

"You got a warrant?"

"I could get one based on what I'm smelling right now. But that's not why we're here. I can overlook it if you'll talk to us."

The man hesitated, then stepped back. "Okay."

Cash nudged the door open and stepped inside. Neither Cobb nor his stoner roommate devoted a whole lot of energy to housekeeping. Overflowing ashtrays, empty beer bottles, and dirty dishes covered every horizontal surface in the small den. A jumble of rumpled clothes were piled in the corner. On the floor next to the battered couch was a well-used bong.

The man noticed Cash staring at the bong. He immediately shoved it under the couch. "You said that's not why you're here, right?"

"That's right. May we sit?"

"Sure." He swept a pile of dingy white socks from the couch and took a seat in the adjacent lounge chair. Cash and Hodge eased onto the couch.

"What's your name?" Cash asked.

"Aiden."

"Your last name?"

"Camp."

"Thank you for speaking with us, Aiden," Cash said, trying to put him at ease. "We're here to talk about Slater."

"What did he do this time?"

"This time?"

"Whatever it was, I didn't have anything to do with it."

That was an answer in itself. "Nobody's accusing you of anything. We're just gathering information."

"Just so we're clear. He has his life and I have mine."

"Noted." Cash made a mental note to check for an arrest record on Cobb when they got back to the station. "When was the last time you saw Slater?"

Camp grabbed a beer can from the coffee table and took a gulp. "Yesterday. He said he was going to Winkler's with Willa. That's his girlfriend."

"Do you mind if we look in his room?" Noticing the frightened look on Camp's face, Cash added, "I meant what I said about the weed."

"You're here about Slater, right? Not me."

"Right."

"Okay, you can look in his room, but stay out of mine. His is the one on the right."

"Got it."

At a nod from Cash, Hodge stood up. Cash followed her down the hall. The trashed appearance of the den was matched by what they encountered in Cobb's room. An unmade bed, dresser drawers left open, clothes strewn about: the guy was a slob.

They donned white plastic gloves. "Check the dresser," Cash said. "I'll look in the closet."

A glance in the closet was all Cash needed. Only a winter coat hung from an otherwise empty rack. From the clothes on the floor, he pulled a black polo shirt and tossed it on the bed. He knelt and peeked under the bed.

Hodge finished going through the dresser drawers. "Nothing here."

"Nothing under the bed, either," Cash said, climbing to his feet.

They returned to the den. Cash held the shirt up for Camp and pointed at the Sonic logo over the breast pocket. "Does he work there?"

"We both do. That's where we met."

That explained why they were housemates. "Where were you last night, Aiden?"

"You said you weren't here about me."

"Just answer the question," said Cash.

"I was here watching TV."

"What were you watching?"

"*A Quiet Place: Day One.* Freaked me out, man."

"Was anyone with you?"

"No."

Cash had no real reason to suspect him and asked instead, "Who were Slater's friends? Who did he hang out with?"

"Me mostly. And Willa. They banged like rabbits."

"Nobody else?"

Camp gave it some thought. "There's this one dude that's come around a few times. Says his name is Hooch."

"What did he look like?" Cash asked.

"Normal, I guess."

"Think, Aiden. White? Black? Tall? Short?"

"White. Beyond that, I can't say." He lowered his voice. "I was pretty high when he was here."

Cash waited, but Camp didn't elaborate. "Okay, Aiden, thanks. We'll get out of your hair now."

"Come on, man, you're killing me. What's this all about?"

"Slater Cobb was killed last night. He was robbing a ranch at the time."

Aiden nearly reared out of his chair. "Shit!" He began waving his hands, like a referee calling no play. "As I said, I don't get mixed up in his stuff. I don't know anything about a robbery."

"We'll get out of your hair now."

On their way out, Cash stopped at the door.

"Hey, Aiden."

"Yeah?"

"Is that your car in the driveway?"

"No, it's Slater's."

"You don't have a car?"

"No."

"How do you get around?"

Camp raised his arms and flapped. "I fly, man. I fly."

***

Outside, Cash pondered whether Cobb's space cadet roommate could have been the other intruder. It seemed unlikely. An airhead like that would face an uphill battle to unzip his fly in the dark, much less aim a gun well enough to hit Emil Bergheim. And yet he had no alibi.

This Hooch character loomed as a better candidate. Who was he? That would be a good question for Willa Dearborn.

Hodge headed for the car. Cash stopped her with a raised hand and called Santos. "Hey, Gabe," he said. "Any word from Deke?"

"He just called. They gave him the bullet at the hospital. He's on his way to Frida."

"What about Bergheim?"

"Still in no condition to talk."

Cash shuffled through his mental list. "Any luck at the hardware stores?" he asked.

"No, nobody remembers a thing. They must not have bought the shovels in Pinyon."

"Do you have anything on the tread marks I found?"

"Tires or shoes?"

"Either one."

During the ensuing pause, Cash could hear the sound of rustling paper. "Here we go," said Santos. "Frida says the tires might be Bridgestone Weatherpeaks, but don't hold her to that. No word yet on the shoes."

"Don't hold her to that?"

"The marks weren't all that distinct. Plus, she says it's an inexact science. I was looking through a tire database when you called, and several other models could be a match."

"What other models?"

Santos recited the list.

"So, David Caruso lied to us?"

"Who's David Caruso?"

"You know, *CSI: Miami*. He could identify a killer from a speck of dust."

"I'm more of an *American Idol* guy."

Cash laughed. "I'll give Kelly Clarkson a call." He pocketed his phone and walked over to the Blazer.

"What was that all about?" Hodge said.

Instead of answering, Cash knelt next to one of the SUV's tires, read the writing on the sidewall, and stood up. He started toward the squad car.

Hodge cut him off. "Am I going to have to beat it out of you?"

She looked irritated enough to do it. "Sorry." He nodded at the Blazer. "I thought we might have found the getaway car, but those aren't the right tires."

She didn't look surprised. "What now?"

"Let's get some lunch."

Chapter Nine

Cash and Hodge were halfway through their chicken enchiladas at Flor de Sotol restaurant when their phones dinged in unison.

"It's from Frida," Hodge said. "She wants to see us."

"Why didn't she just call?" Cash said.

"She must want to show us something."

He shoveled a forkful of refried beans into his mouth. "I guess we better eat fast."

***

They found Frida in her office, staring at her laptop screen. Three plaster casts cluttered her desk. Without looking up, she said, "Took you ten minutes to make a two-minute drive. Let me guess. You were at the Firewheel."

"Nope," said Cash. "Flor de Sotol."

She swiveled around in her chair to face them. "Keisha, if you ever need to bribe this guy, enchiladas never fail."

"I've heard chocolate chip cookies are a good bet, too."

"They worked when he was a kid."

Hodge gave Cash a surprised look.

"She was my babysitter," he said.

"If that don't beat all."

Cash redirected his attention to Frida. "Do you have something for us?"

"I do." She rearranged the three casts in a neat row. Pointing at the first one, she said, "This is the tire tread from the road by Bergheim's ranch. Notice how indistinct it is."

"What are the other two?"

"Shoes. I'll get to those."

Cash studied the tire cast. She was right. He could make out a pattern, but it was blurred like an out-of-focus photograph.

"Given the rain that night, I'm surprised we got anything at all," Frida said. "Anyway, look at this." She swung the laptop around so they could see the screen. Cash counted eight different tread patterns. Frida said, "Santos told me you were surprised I couldn't be sure about the Bridgestones. Take a look here." She pointed at the screen. "Look at that cast and match it to one on the screen. I've removed identifying information."

They leaned in closer. Hodge said, "Top row, second from the right."

Cash took more time. Surely there was an accurate way to make a call. Finally, he said, "It's either the first one on top or the middle one on the bottom row."

"And that's why this doesn't help us much," said Frida. She clicked the mouse so that the identifying information appeared on the screen.

"Son of a gun," said Cash. "We were both wrong."

"See what I mean?" Frida said, turning the laptop to face her. "I *think* it's the Bridgestone, but I couldn't swear to it. All I can say for sure is that it's a symmetrical pattern. That's no good, though, because that's the most common pattern out there. That's why tread marks aren't used in the courtroom much anymore. They're notoriously inaccurate. Good defense attorneys eat them for breakfast."

Cash said, "So, we wasted your time."

"I wouldn't say that. We know the vehicle you're after won't have an asymmetric pattern. That rules out a lot of sports cars." She slid the two shoe imprints closer to them. "We have the same problem with the footprints. They're not regarded as definitive unless you can spot something unique about the print you're looking at. The clay at the bottom of the creek gave us better resolution than the road. That said, an exact ID is difficult. I looked for footprints on the concrete floor of the shop but the problem there is that the two of you and Santos were in there as well. Not to mention Emil Bergheim. I couldn't find any clear prints that didn't have others superimposed on top of them."

Cash's face turned red. "We should have worn shoe covers."

"Don't beat yourself up," said Frida. "Griff Turner never wore them even *after* I asked him to."

Hodge said, "So, the footprints are useless as well?"

"I didn't say that," said Frida. "I'm almost positive the tennis shoes were made by EP American Footwear. That's the company that makes Wal-Mart's shoes."

"We already knew that," Cash said. "That's what Cobb was wearing."

"True. But these"—she pointed at the larger prints "—are Timberland Pro True Grit work boots. And look here." She used a pen to indicate one of the treads. "See how that one is smaller than the rest? Part of the tread broke off. Find that boot and you've got the other guy."

Cash scoffed. "So all we have to do is check the boots of every person in Noble County. If the guy is still *in* Noble County. It's Sleeping Beauty all over again."

"Cinderella," said Hodge.

"What?"

"Sleeping Beauty got pricked with a spinning wheel and fell asleep. Cinderella lost her glass slipper and the prince had to try it on every woman in the kingdom to find her."

Cash grunted at his mistake. "I think we've found the missing Grimm sister."

Hodge smiled in answer. "I know my Disney princesses."

"Anything else, Frida?" Cash asked.

"Quite a bit, actually. Deke got back with the bullet they pulled from Bergheim. It's a nine-millimeter slug, which is the type used by the Sig Sauer you found on Cobb. But here's the problem. Cobb didn't fire that gun."

"How do you know?" said Cash.

"There was no gunpowder residue on his hands."

Cash's mind leaped to the obvious conclusion. "The Timberland boot guy shot Mr. Bergheim."

"Yep."

Cash stood up. "Thanks, Frida. You've given us something to go on."

"I've got something else for you. You too, Keisha." She removed a pack of cookies from a desk drawer and held it out. "Chocolate chip."

***

They ran into Conrad on their way to the parking lot. "Hey, Deke," said Cash. "Thanks for fetching that bullet."

"No problem," Conrad said. "Gave me a chance to hand out some speeding tickets."

Cash chuckled inside. Unlike the other members of the department, Conrad loved pulling over speeders on the interstate. Cash said, "I understand Bergheim isn't able to talk yet."

"No. Not today, anyway. They said he might be more alert in the morning."

"In that case, I'll head over there first thing. You want to come along?"

Conrad shook his head. "No, thanks. Santos said I could get out on the interstate again. Three more tickets and I'll break my monthly record."

"Go get 'em, Deputy."

When Conrad left, Hodge offered, "I'll go with you to the hospital."

"Let's divide and conquer," Cash said. "I'll go to Junction while you go to Sonic and talk to Cobb's co-workers."

"Will they be open?"

"Sure. They serve breakfast."

"Okay." She sounded less than excited. "Hey, do you want to shoot hoops later? I've got my shoes in the car."

Hodge had played basketball for the Lady Longhorns of the University of Texas. She had also played one-on-one more recently against Cash. He had yet to beat her. "I can't. This is my afternoon to be with Emma. I'm already late."

She flapped her arms and squawked like a chicken.

"Yeah, yeah," said Cash, waving her off. "You won't be doing that when I kick your ass next time."

Chapter Ten

Easing his truck to a stop in front of a mobile home, Cash experienced the same excitement he always felt when visiting his daughter. He'd never planned having a child after a drunken one-night stand with a woman like Bernadette. Yet he was glad it happened. It reminded him of Philip Seymour Hoffman's CIA agent in one of his favorite movies, *Charlie Wilson's War*. The character tells of a Zen master proving a point with the tale of a boy who receives a horse as a gift. Subsequent events stemming from the gift alternate between the positive and the negative, with the Zen master cautioning villagers each time not to pass judgment on the wisdom of the gift by saying, "We'll see." "We'll see" in Cash's case meant a beautiful daughter that had captured his heart.

Waiting for the door to open after knocking, Cash was relieved to see Bernadette's blue Hyundai Elantra in the driveway. That meant he wouldn't have to make small talk with her mother. His relationship with Mrs. Fenster remained rocky, especially after Jessica Patrice tried to kidnap Emma and Bernadette a few weeks ago.

Cash wondered about the Yamaha motorcycle parked behind the Elantra. As far as he knew, Bernadette didn't ride. Maybe it belonged to Mrs. Fenster.

Once the door opened, Bernadette greeted Cash and led him into the den. Mrs. Fenster occupied her usual place in the rocker, her substantial bottom oozing between the seat and armrests. Emma entertained herself with baby toys in the playpen Cash had brought over at his last visit. He rushed to pick her up.

A man rose from the couch. Cash didn't recognize him at first but then remembered meeting him at the recent dance. It was Clint Morgan, the guy who had been tongue-wrestling with Bernadette much of that night.

Cash shook Morgan's hand. "I didn't expect to see you here."

"If me and Bernie are gonna be together, I figure I better learn how to take care of a baby."

Cash didn't like the sound of that. How serious was this relationship? And how much time was Morgan spending with Emma?

"You want a beer, Cash?" Bernadette said.

"Yeah. Thanks."

Morgan made a move toward the kitchen. "I'll get it, babe. Anybody else want one?"

"I do," said Mrs. Fenster.

"Bernie?"

"Why not?"

Morgan left. Watching Emma snuggle against Cash's chest, Bernadette said, "She sure likes her daddy."

Cash tickled the child's chin, eliciting a joyful laugh. "Of course she does," he said in a baby voice. "And daddy likes her, too."

Morgan returned with the beers. He popped the tab on his and held the can up in a toast. "Here's to Cash. From what I hear, he's the best father in the world."

"I don't know about that."

They passed a pleasant ten minutes in small talk. Cash found Morgan overly gregarious but likable, nonetheless. When Emma woke up, Bernadette fetched her and set her up in her highchair. Cash sat down and began feeding her.

Morgan stood up. "Are you ready, Bernie?"

"Just about," she said, then disappeared down the hall.

"Are you guys going somewhere?" Cash asked, nervous about the prospect of being left alone with Mrs. Fenster.

Morgan said, "We're going over to Junction to shoot pool."

Bernadette returned with a motorcycle helmet. "Okay, I'm ready." Before Cash could react, she and Morgan tossed out hasty goodbyes and left.

Cash gulped. He had planned to stay for a couple of hours, but not with Mrs. Fenster. She caught him looking at her. "I guess it's just you and me," he said.

"I don't like that fella."

No surprise there. She didn't like anybody, as far as Cash could tell. "Why not?"

"I don't trust him. He's slick. Not like you."

Cash had never thought about whether or not he was slick. He bounced Emma again to stall for time. "I'm not slick?"

"You're a straight shooter. You say what you mean. I don't have to worry that you might be up to something. And you've had a good effect on Bernie. She's quit staying out till all hours. Gave up smoking dope. Doesn't drink as much. You and Emma have settled her down."

Cash had noticed the same thing. Bernadette was taking her role as Emma's mother more seriously. Since that night months ago when he caught her naked and high at Roadrunner Pete's Gun Range she had transformed herself. Cash didn't credit himself for that. He credited Emma.

"Anyway," Mrs. Fenster said, "you're a good guy. That don't mean I like what you done to Bernie, getting her pregnant and all."

Cash was touched. Up until now Mrs. Fenster had been nothing but disdainful of his mere presence in the same room. "Thanks," he said. Giddy at their newfound camaraderie, he added, "Can I call you Wanda?"

***

Edie was expecting Cash to bring supper and he didn't disappoint. He showed up at her house with brisket and sausage from Grumpy Frank's Barbecue. He also brought coleslaw, pinto beans, and potato salad, as well as a hefty portion of peach cobbler. He entered the kitchen to find Edie's son, Luke, playing with Legos at the table. "What are you making?" he asked.

The boy didn't look up. "A robot. He's got laser beam eyes and shoots bullets from his fingers."

"Can I see?"

Luke held up his project.

If that was a robot, Cash thought as he looked at the amorphous block, the boy had a terrific imagination. "That's awesome. I used to build things like that when I was your age."

Luke grunted a disinterested response.

Cash said, "Where's your mom?"

"In her bedroom."

Cash set the food on the table and headed down the hall. He found Edie working at her desk. "What are you doing?" he said, pecking her cheek.

"Just filling in some forms."

"Forms for what?"

She hesitated, then turned to face him. "School."

"What are you talking about?"

"You remember, I've always wanted to be a nurse."

Cash did remember. When he and Edie graduated from Pinyon High ten years ago, they had planned on attending Sam Houston State together. Cash would study criminology, and Edie would take prerequisites for nursing school. Then Cash joined the army, prompting a tense discussion about their relationship. Cash said he wasn't ready for a ring. Edie said she wouldn't wait for him without one. Crushed, he left for basic training with a hole in his heart. Edie stayed a year at Sam Houston before returning to Pinyon. She married Randy Howser, a new doctor in town who soon began bedding local ranchers' wives. She divorced him a year after the marriage, but not before getting pregnant with Luke. Single motherhood had prevented a return to school. She'd been working at the Firewheel ever since.

"Yes, I remember," Cash said.

"I'm applying to UT and Texas Tech."

"What, for your prerequisites? You can probably do those online."

"I've been doing that for three years. I finish in a couple of weeks."

Cash gaped, open-mouthed. She'd been taking college courses? How had he not known that? "So, if you're accepted, when would you start?"

"This fall."

His throat tightened. "You're leaving Pinyon?"

"Not permanently. I'll come back after I graduate. Assuming I can find a job around here."

Cash didn't like the sound of that. "When you graduate? How long is the program?"

"Two years."

Cash drew a deep breath. "I thought we were going together."

"We are," she said, her eyes narrowing.

"How can we be going together if you move away?"

Her voice turned cold. "Do you want me to sling hash at the Firewheel for the rest of my life?"

"No. It's just ..." His voice trailed off.

"Just what?"

What indeed? What was he trying to say? He didn't want to stand in the way of her pursuing a career, but he also didn't want her to leave. Not after he had just gotten her back so recently. "I don't want to lose you."

She stood up, crossed the room, and sat in his lap. "You won't." She kissed him long and hard. "Now, what's for supper?"

Chapter Eleven

Cash couldn't understand why Edie wanted to be a nurse. He hated hospitals. The smell, the somber atmosphere, people crying in the waiting room: he always left a hospital feeling depressed.

When Cash was a boy, his paternal grandfather had died in a hospital. Cash had never forgotten the sight of the once strong and joyful man lying in bed with tubes and wires protruding from his body, his face gaunt, his voice weak, his usual smile replaced by a pained expression. Now Cash was on his way to see another man whose strength had always amazed him lying in a hospital bed. He'd wanted Hodge to accompany him, but Santos had sent her to quell a domestic disturbance.

Cash found Bergheim's room. A woman in scrubs was working at a laptop cart by the door. She looked up. "Is it okay if I go in?" he asked.

"Yes. He's tired, but I think he'll be able to talk to you. You're the only visitor he's had so far, so he's probably ready for some company."

Cash tapped on the door and entered the room. Bergheim was asleep. An IV line snaked from one arm to a bag of clear fluid hanging overhead. Wires ran from his chest to a bedside heart monitor. A bag of dark yellow urine sagged from the bed frame.

Cash positioned himself at the foot of the bed. "Mr. Bergheim?" No response. He patted a foot. "Mr. Bergheim, are you awake? It's Adam Cash."

Bergheim stirred and opened his eyes. "Those peckerheads came back," he said with a frown.

"I know. That's why I'm here."

Bergheim sipped from a bedside cup. "It's a helluva thing, getting shot. I don't know what I'm going to do now."

"The doctor said you should make a full recovery."

"But when will I be able to work again? The bullet hit the bone in my thigh. I can't walk."

"It will take time, but you'll get back on your feet."

Bergheim grunted and pulled himself to more of a sitting position. "Some people work so they can live. I live so I can work."

Cash had never looked at it that way. Inactivity would be difficult for a man like Bergheim. "Who shot you?"

"I never saw them good enough to know. There were two of them. I caught them coming out of my shop. They took off running. I hollered at them to stop, and one of them shot me. I shot back. I think I hit him."

"You hit the man who shot you?"

"No, the other one. They were right next to each other. I never was a good pistol shot."

"What were they after in your workshop?"

"Tools, I guess. There's nothing else out there."

That didn't make sense. How would they have carried enough tools to make the robbery worthwhile back to their vehicle? It was a long haul from the shop to the road. "We found a hole under your table saw," Cash said. "It's lined with concrete and plastic. What did you keep in there?"

Bergheim's head jerked up in surprise. "I don't know anything about a hole. Maybe it was Dieter's."

"Your brother?"

"Yeah. He spent a lot of time out there doing God knows what. I asked him once and he told me it was none of my damn business."

"We found some money near the body of the man you shot."

"I killed him?"

"It was self-defense."

Bergheim fell silent.

"About that money," Cash said. "It was a roll of hundred-dollar bills. It added up to two thousand dollars."

The old man cleared his throat. "Is that all you found?"

Cash didn't want to tell him about the gun just yet. "Yes, just the money."

"I mean, you didn't find more than two thousand dollars?"

"No. Should we have?"

"I don't know." Bergheim paused to think. "Dieter has never trusted banks. He used them for his business because he had to. But he hated putting his own money in a bank. Said they were all run by crooks. If he was hiding money out there, it would have been more than two thousand dollars."

"How much more?"

"Hard to say. He wasn't hurting. He made a fortune when he sold his business." He coughed and laid his head back. "This is wearing me out."

Cash took the hint. "I'll leave you be, Mr. Bergheim. I can come back."

"One more thing before you go. Could you see the men on my game cameras?"

"What game cameras?"

***

"He told me there were two," Cash said. He occupied a vinyl guest chair opposite Santos, who sat transfixed behind his desk. Hodge was to his left. "One on a tree near the shop door and another out on the road. He wanted to put up more, but that's all they had at Tractor Supply."

"How the hell did we miss it?" Santos said.

"We didn't. At least not the one by the shop, because it's not there anymore. Those guys must have spotted it and taken it with them."

"Well, hell."

"We had better luck at the road." He held up a memory card. "Let's take a look."

Taking the card from Cash, Santos positioned his laptop so they could see the screen. A moment later, several rows of video files popped up. He clicked on the first one.

Hodge said, "It's just a deer."

Santos tried the next file. "More deer. Let's skip ahead to nighttime."

He clicked on another file. This time a rabbit scurried across the road.

The next file produced results. A dark late-model Buick Encore eased into view and stopped. Two people wearing ski masks got out. One carried a tote bag. Cash thought they were both men but couldn't say for sure. The taller one appeared to say something before they both disappeared into the woods.

Hodge said, "Are they wearing gloves?"

"Too dark to tell," said Cash.

"Can't see the license plate, either. The car is facing the wrong direction."

"Fast-forward to when they come back," said Santos.

Cash moved the pointer until he saw the taller man emerge from the woods, carrying the tote bag. From the way he moved, it appeared to be heavy. He opened the car's rear gate and hoisted the bag inside, after which he tossed in a small object and closed the gate.

"Was that a gun?" Hodge asked.

Cash nodded. "I think so."

The man's head jerked up as if he had heard a noise. He walked out of view. Moments later, he returned, climbed behind the wheel of the Encore, and executed a three-point turn. Santos replayed the sequence, this time pausing halfway through. "Bingo."

Cash locked eyes on the legible Texas license plate. "We've got the bastard."

Seconds after the car disappeared, the engine of an unseen vehicle started up. "What's that?" said Hodge.

Cash said. "There's another car."

"So there were at least three people."

"Had to be."

After the meeting broke up, Cash signaled to Hodge. "What did you find out at Sonic?"

"Nothing. Nobody saw this coming. They all said he was a great guy."

"Aren't they always? All right, let's go."

"Where to?"

"Do you like chicken?"

Chapter Twelve

Ellis Doran slid a tray of chicken and fries across the counter to a waiting customer, turned to the two stern-faced deputies, and said, "We're right in the middle of the lunch rush. Can it wait?"

"No," said Cash.

Doran sighed. "Hang on, I'll go get her."

Cash motioned for Hodge to follow and stepped around the counter. "We'll use that break room again."

"Juanita's eating her lunch in there."

"She'll have to move."

An unhappy Doran led them through the kitchen. On the way, he got Willa Dearborn's attention and motioned for her to follow. She did a double-take at the sight of two uniformed deputies.

They found Juanita enjoying a plate of chicken fingers and mashed potatoes. When Doran asked her to leave, she opened her mouth to protest but stopped when she saw Cash behind him. Taking her food with her, she beat a hasty retreat. Doran followed her out.

"What's going on?" Willa said.

"Have a seat," said Cash.

Once she was sitting down, he went on.

"Who's Hooch?"

"I don't know."

"He hung out with Slater. Does that ring any bells?"

"I heard Slater mention the name, but I never met him."

"What did Slater say about him?"

"I don't know. Just that they went out drinking a couple of times."

Cash waited but her eyes flashed in defiance. "Really, I don't know who he is."

"How well do you know Aiden Camp?"

"Who's that?"

"You're testing my patience, Willa."

She pursed her lips in thought. "Oh, you mean Slater's roommate. Not well. He was always stoned out of his mind when I saw him."

Cash pulled out his phone, tapped the screen, and laid it on the table. "That's your car, isn't it?"

Willa studied the screen. "It could be. It's hard to say since there's no color."

Cash swiped the screen to bring up another photo. "Look at the number on that plate."

She looked at the screen again. Cash thought he detected fear in her eyes. Then the look faded.

"I don't have my license plate memorized."

"It's your car, Willa. We checked."

She sat back in her chair and said nothing, just stared at them.

"What was it doing at Emil Bergheim's ranch the other night?"

"I don't know."

"Lying to us will make it worse for you in the long run."

"I swear I don't know." She looked cool. Had she rehearsed these lines?

Hodge said, "Let's assume that's true, Willa. Can you think of some way it could have gotten there?"

"Was this the night when Slater was shot?"

"It is."

"He probably took it. He had a key."

"You gave him a key?"

"Not to keep. He borrowed the car last week and never gave the key back. I'd been meaning to ask him about it."

Cash said, "Why did he borrow your car?"

"His was getting an oil change at Ike's. He needed to go grocery shopping."

"Were you at work?"

"Yes."

That made sense to Cash. Ike's Auto Shop was across the street from Speedy Chicken. Cobb could have left his car there, walked across the street, and borrowed the car. "How did you get home without a key?"

"I had my other key in my purse that day."

"Why?"

"I don't know. I just did."

Cash drummed his fingers on the table. "Did you know he took your car that night?"

"I already said. No."

"How did it get back to your house? As you know, Slater didn't return from that trip."

A tear rolled down her cheek. "You don't have to remind me."

"You said you never knew he borrowed it. That would mean somebody returned it to your house while you were asleep. Who?"

"I don't know." She slammed a fist against the table. "I don't know. I don't know. *I don't know!"*

Cash held her gaze. Was she putting on an act? "Who are you covering for?"

"Nobody, damn it."

"Don't lie to me."

"I'm not lying!"

Cash wasn't so sure, but he did know she was in no mood to talk. And at the moment, he had no way to force her cooperation. "All right, Willa. We'll stop. For now. But we may think of more questions later on. And I need your car key."

"What? Why?"

"We need to search the car. That's best done back at the station."

"Forget it."

"Don't be an idiot. Searching that car is the fastest way for us to clear you."

She thought about it. "Will I get it back?"

"If we don't find anything, then yes."

She fished her key out of her purse and handed it over. "When?"

Cash stood up and signaled Hodge to do the same. Looking at Willa, he said, "I don't know, but you'll want to call someone for a ride home."

Chapter Thirteen

Cash drained the last drop of his Coke and wiped his mouth. He didn't drink much soda but when he did, he preferred it like this, the old-fashioned way, made with cane sugar and served in an ice-cold glass bottle. Drinking it from a can or plastic bottle just didn't deliver the same satisfaction.

Thoughts swirled through his mind as he waited for Frida to finish searching Willa's car. He recalled Mrs. Fenster's, or Wanda's, assessment of Bernadette's new boyfriend, Clint Morgan. He had seemed polite enough, if overly amorous at the dance. He just hoped that Bernadette wouldn't rush into the relationship. She was an adult and could make her own choices, but to the extent that those choices affected his daughter, Cash felt entitled to render an opinion. He'd keep his eyes and ears open.

Then there was Edie's plan to continue her education. He knew he should encourage her but where would that path lead? Going to nursing school meant moving away from Pinyon. Would their relationship survive a two-year separation?

Finally, he considered the issue he knew he should be dwelling on: Willa Dearborn and her potential involvement in Emil Bergheim's shooting. Could he believe her claim that Cobb had taken her car without her knowledge? And who was the mystery person who returned it?

A ding from his phone brought Cash out of his ruminations. Frida informed him that she had finished her search of the Encore. He jumped up, dropped the Coke bottle into a recycling bin, and hurried out of the conference room.

He found Frida peeling gloves off in the department garage. "What did you find?"

"Nothing exciting. A bunch of fingerprints. It would help to have Willa's for comparison. I already have Slater Cobb's."

"That's it?"

"The floor was muddy on both sides in the front seat, but not in the back, suggesting only two people in the car."

"We could already tell that from the video."

"True."

Cash contained his disappointment. He had hoped for more.

"What now?" Frida asked.

"It's time for a road trip."

***

Because it was late in the afternoon, Cash put off his trip to Austin until tomorrow. The drive would take almost four hours. Even if he left now, he would get there too late to visit Dieter in the retirement home. He decided instead to stop by the office of Bernadette's employer, veterinarian Elizabeth Manor, on his way home.

The lobby was empty. Cash slipped off his hat and smiled at Dory, the receptionist. "Is Bernadette here?"

"Yeah, I'll go find her."

She started to rise, but Cash held out a hand. "Just a second. Let me ask you something. Has a guy named Clint Morgan been coming around lately? Bernadette's been seeing him."

"As a matter of fact, he has."

"What's your take on him?"

Dory shrugged. "I don't know. He's good-looking, polite. I haven't seen any problems. Why do you ask?"

"I just wondered. They've been spending a lot of time together. The last time I went to see Emma, Morgan was there."

Dory's face lit up with understanding. "I get it. I'll keep my eye out."

"Thanks."

Dory led him to the back, where they found Bernadette cleaning an exam room. "Good seeing you, Cash," Dory said before spinning on her heel and returning to her desk.

"Cash," said Bernadette in a voice indicating displeasure. "What are you doing here?"

"I was driving by on my way home and thought I'd stop in to see how you're doing."

"How I'm doing? What does that mean?"

"Nothing. How was your day?"

"How was my day?"

"Are you just going to repeat everything I say?"

She eyed him coolly. "My day was fine."

"How was your date with your boyfriend last night?"

"Are you checking up on me?"

That's exactly what he was doing. "No. Did you guys have a good time?"

Bernadette leaned her broom against the wall and folded her arms. "Yeah. We had a good time. Thanks for asking."

"Good. Tell me about the guy. How long have you known him?"

"Why are you being so nosy?"

"I'm not. I just want to know more about the guy spending time with my daughter."

"Do you mean *our* daughter?"

This was going south in a hurry. "Sorry. Our daughter."

"What do you want to know?"

"Do you like him? Is he nice to you?"

"Of course I like him," Bernadette said. "Why else would I go out with him?"

"Your mother isn't too hot about him."

"My mother doesn't like you, either."

Ouch. He decided to try a different approach. "How long has he been living in Pinyon? I've never heard of him before."

"Do you think you know every person in the county?"

"No, but I've at least heard of most of them."

"He moved here about two years ago. He's got a place on ten acres south of town that his uncle left him."

"What's his uncle's name?"

"What does that matter? He moved away a long time ago. The house sat empty until Clint moved in. Now, if you don't mind, I have to finish cleaning this room."

Cash figured he might as well say what was on his mind. "I hope you don't move too fast with him."

"What does that mean?"

"Just be careful. I'd hate to see you get hurt."

She rolled her eyes at him. "Who are you, my father?"

He stood transfixed, frozen by the sarcasm in her voice. She hadn't spoken to him like that in a long time.

"I'm only saying … if you guys have a relationship, then Emma is part of that. And if Emma is part of it, then so am I."

She gave him a disdainful glare. "What I do with Clint Morgan is none of your business. Now please, leave me alone."

Before Cash could react, she snatched the broom and left, pulling the door closed with a bang on her way out. A moment later, the door cracked open and Dory poked her head in. "Is everything okay in here?"

"Everything's fine," said Cash. He put on his hat. "Just peachy."

Chapter Fourteen

The following morning Cash wanted to send Hodge to collect Willa Dearborn's fingerprints, but Santos had already dispatched her to another domestic dispute. Conrad overheard their conversation and said, "I'll go."

Cash groaned inside. Conrad wasn't known for his tact. "Tell her we just want to be able to ignore her prints on her car. Don't say anything about her being a suspect. A gentle approach would be best."

Conrad shot Cash a scornful look. "Don't worry. I'll sweet talk her."

Right, thought Cash. Conrad possessed the finesse of a hippopotamus.

Santos said, "What do you hope to learn in Austin?"

"Bergheim claims not to know anything about that hole in the shop floor. If that's true, his brother must know what was in it. Plus, I may also have another chat with Eddie Kincaid."

"What about Cobb's roommate? Anything new on him?"

"No, but something occurred to me. He said he was watching a movie the night of the shooting. If he paid for it, we should see a record of the transaction on his streaming platform."

"Good thought. Deke, can you check that out after you talk to Willa?"

Conrad nodded. "Sure."

"Get to it, then. Good luck."

***

Cash followed Interstate 10 east through Junction before turning onto Highway 290. Driving through the town of Dripping Springs confirmed his belief that he had chosen correctly by settling in Noble County instead of Austin. Urban sprawl was hitting the town hard. The once-rural hamlet was turning into another Austin suburb. A massive new housing development greeted him at the city limits. Beyond that he encountered "Land for Sale" signs, newly cleared land, and highway construction. Before long big box stores would pop up, destroying what small businesses remained.

Avonwick Retirement Community was located on the east side of Mopac Expressway across from Camp Mabry, a Texas National Guard base. Cash introduced himself at the reception desk and asked if he could speak to Dieter Bergheim.

The smiling man behind the desk said, "Of course. Just let me get you a visitor's badge." He printed a sticker and handed it to Cash. "This goes on your shirt. You should know Mr. Bergheim can be pretty feisty. And he doesn't always have a firm grip on reality, if you know what I mean."

Cash thanked the man and took the elevator to the third floor. As he stepped out, he was surprised at the fresh, clean appearance that greeted him. He had always imagined retirement facilities as dark, depressing places smelling of urine. Instead, he encountered a brightly lit hallway and walls decorated like an upscale hotel. A pleasant flowery scent wafted into his nostrils.

He found Dieter's door and knocked. "Goddamn it, what is it this time?" came a shout from within.

Dieter Bergheim was already living up to his reputation. "It's Adam Cash with the Noble County Sheriff's Department," Cash said. "I used to build fences with your brother."

After what seemed an eternity, the door opened. There stood a frail, wiry man who could have passed for Emil Bergheim's twin. "Are you here to arrest me?" Dieter said.

"No, sir."

"I'm joking, you jackass." He turned and made his way to a lounge chair.

Cash took note of the old man's shuffling gait and hand tremor. Parkinson's disease. He had a great-uncle affected by the disorder. He followed Dieter inside and shut the door.

"Sit down," Dieter said in a voice that reminded Cash of his army days with Sergeant Malkoff. He sat in the desk chair.

Dieter's speech was slow and halting. "Why are you here? Is this about my brother?"

"I'm afraid so." He explained about the shooting. "I visited him yesterday. He's doing great. The doctors expect him to make a full recovery."

"It'll take more than a bullet to kill that old bastard."

Cash agreed. "There's something else I wanted to talk to you about. We know there were two intruders. Your brother shot and killed one of them—it was self-defense—but the other one got away. They trashed the workshop—"

"What do you mean, trashed?"

"Ransacked. Tools everywhere, the table saw turned over." Cash thought he saw Dieter blanch. "We found a hole beneath the saw. There was nothing in it."

Dieter swore. "There was *something* in it."

"Was it money?"

"How did you know?"

"We found a bundle of hundred dollar bills with the dead man. Two thousand dollars' worth."

Dieter stared past Cash and worked his jaw. "That's my money."

"That's what your brother said. He told us he didn't know it was there."

Dieter grunted but said nothing.

"How much was it?" Cash asked.

"A million four."

Cash blinked hard. "One point four million dollars?"

"Maybe more. I can't remember."

He was stupefied at the idea of that much cash being hidden away in a workshop. "The dead man's name was Slater Cobb. Did you know him?"

"No."

"We don't yet know the identity of the other man, but we're working on it."

"Hell, I know who the other man was."

"You do? Who?"

"Rick Smith."

"Who's Rick Smith?"

"He used to be my business partner."

"Can you describe him?"

"Yeah, he's a real piece of shit."

Cash fought his impatience at the unhelpful response, as well as the glacial pace of Dieter's speech. "Could you be more specific? Tell me what he looks like."

"Normal height. Long black hair. Beard. About as handsome as a dog's ass."

"How old is he?"

"Fifty, sixty. Could be in his seventies by now."

That didn't narrow it down much. "Where does he live?"

"Hell if I know. We don't exchange Christmas cards."

"How about when he was your business partner?"

"Back then he was in Buda," Dieter said, referring to a small town south of Austin. "After I bought him out, he said he was going back to where he was originally from."

Cash waited for Dieter to elaborate. "And where was that?" he prompted.

"California. Don't ask me what part because I don't know."

Great. There were probably more Rick Smiths in California than there were people in Noble County. Cash stood up. "Thank you. You've been a big help."

"Are you going to get my money back? Because if you don't, I'll be out on my ass. Emil sure can't afford this place."

"Mr. Bergheim, why didn't you have that money in a bank? Why keep so much at home?"

Dieter looked at Cash as if he was stupid. "I wanted it to be safe."

***

Cash assessed the rundown apartment complex and shook his head. If this was all Eddie Kincaid could afford, his career as a drummer hadn't yet taken off. The thought that Reid lived in a similar dump saddened him. He had faith in his brother but secretly shared their parents' concerns about his future.

The door to the apartment looked the same as all the others, with peeling paint and warped strips of veneer threatening to jump ship at any time. When the door opened, he was surprised to see Roy Baxter. A pleased look spread on his face.

"Cash!"

"Roy?"

"Nice uniform."

"I didn't expect to find you here."

"I was just leaving. Are you here for Eddie?"

"Yes. Is he home?"

"Sure, hang on."

Moments later, he reappeared with Eddie Kincaid in tow. Baxter said, "I gotta get going, Eddie. I'll see you later. Cash, we're still going to an Astros game, right?"

"You bet."

After Baxter left, Cash said, "May I come in?"

Kincaid hesitated before pulling the door open. Cash followed him into a den furnished with junk that would embarrass a college student. "Can we sit?"

"If we have to." He dropped into a threadbare La-Z-Boy.

Cash sat on the couch and immediately wished he hadn't. An unidentifiable, noxious odor jolted his senses. Recovering, he said, "We didn't get a chance to finish our phone conversation."

Kincaid grunted but said nothing.

"Your grandfather is a fun guy."

"Yeah, he's a real laugh riot. What do you want?"

"I'm still investigating your friend Slater's death."

"I told you I don't know anything about that."

"I'm not saying you do. However, I have some follow-up questions. First, who did Slater hang out with? Other than you, of course."

Kincaid considered the question. "I don't know. We were friends in high school, but I haven't seen him much since. That night at the dance hall was the first time in at least a year."

"You may remember me saying he was shot while trespassing on a ranch near town. The rancher shot him in self-defense."

"Slater wouldn't kill anybody."

Didn't they always say that? "He was with another man. Evidence suggests that's who pulled the trigger."

Cash noticed Kincaid's boots as he crossed his legs. Trying not to be obvious, Cash studied the exposed sole but saw no broken tread. Kincaid said, "Like I told you, I don't know anything about that."

"What kind of boots are those?"

Kincaid pointed at a tag stitched onto the boot that read "Ariat."

"Ariat makes comfortable boots," Cash said. "What size are they?"

"Why do you care?"

"I need me a pair. I'm going to Cavender's after this." Cash always bought his boots at Cavender's.

Kincaid stood up. "Maybe you should go there now."

Cash didn't budge. "This is a murder investigation, Eddie. Don't you want to help find your friend's killer?"

Kincaid's eyes looked sharp enough to drill a hole in Cash's forehead. "Look," he said, "I may be in your brother's band, but that doesn't mean you can come in here and harass me in my own home. I'm telling you to leave."

Cash started to say something, but Kincaid cut him off. "Please go. Now."

On his way to the door, Cash said, "I hope you're not hiding anything, Eddie. That wouldn't go well for you."

"No offense, Deputy, but I hope I never see you again."

Chapter Fifteen

Ellis Doran frowned at the deputy across the counter and said, "Adam Cash has been here twice already."

Conrad stuck his thumbs in his belt. "Are you going to get her or not?"

Doran sighed. It was a bad look for the restaurant to have sheriff's deputies constantly showing up to talk to his employees. How much trouble was Willa Dearborn worth? "Follow me."

He led Conrad through the kitchen, picking up Willa on the way. As he closed the break room door, he said, "Please make it fast. This leaves me short-handed."

"Duly noted," said Conrad. He pulled index cards and an ink pad from his shirt pocket.

"What's that?" Willa said.

"We need your fingerprints."

"Why?"

"Because they must be all over your car. We need to know what they look like so we can ignore them"

"I don't feel comfortable doing that."

"It doesn't matter how you feel about it. You have to do it."

"What if I say no?"

Conrad cocked his head and gave her a stern look. "Then I'd have to get out my handcuffs."

Willa didn't know if he was serious. Could he arrest her for refusing to let him fingerprint her? She didn't want to find out. Besides, what he said made sense. They would find her prints on the car. She placed her hands on the table. "Okay."

***

Willa fumed as she returned to her workstation. Those damn deputies wouldn't leave her alone. The first one had at least been polite, but the guy today was a total asshole.

She fretted for the next hour. Her thoughts so distracted her that she screwed up two orders and accidentally knocked a basket of raw chicken onto the floor. Although she immediately scooped up the pieces, that jerk Doran told her to throw them away. "Five-second rule, right?" she joked but instead of smiling, he pointed at the trash can and said, "After you throw those away, I want to see you in my office."

He was already seated behind his desk when she got there. "What's going on?" he said, frowning.

"What do you mean?"

"You know damn well what I mean. The sheriff's office seems to be taking a keen interest in you."

"It has nothing to do with me. My car was stolen and used in a robbery. They keep asking me about it."

"Why did they take your fingerprints?"

"Is that what he told you?"

"There's ink on your fingers."

Willa looked at her hands. Shit, he was right. She relayed what the last deputy had told her, concluding with, "It's nothing to worry about."

"If it's nothing to worry about, then why do you keep fucking up the orders?"

"It was only two."

"Don't forget about that chicken you dropped."

"I could have rinsed it off. I picked it up right away."

"Rinse it off?" Doran leaned forward, his face turning red. "Do you want people to get sick? They'll sue our asses off. Or worse, the health department will shut us down."

"Don't be such a drama queen."

"What did you say?"

"I said, chill out."

Doran leaned back and studied her face with his beady little eyes. Willa thought he looked like a possum. "Go home," he said.

"Am I being fired?"

"No." He smirked. "Just go home and 'chill out.' And I'm docking you for the chicken."

"What? Fuck you!"

"Okay, now you're being fired."

"You can't do that."

"I just did." He stood up. "Now please leave. Quietly. I don't want to have to call that deputy back."

***

During the entire half mile Willa walked home, she cursed the sheriff's department for taking her car. When she got there, she ripped off her

Speedy Chicken shirt and, using a pair of kitchen shears, cut it to pieces. That's what that bastard Doran got. Tomorrow she'd go to the restaurant, dump the pieces onto the counter, and give him the finger. Let him dock *that* from her pay.

She fetched a bottle of cabernet from the kitchen. Unscrewing the cap, she decided to drink the whole thing, then start in on another bottle. If she didn't have one, she'd go to the store and buy one. Maybe more than one.

When the bottle's last drop had trickled down her throat, she leaned back on her couch, closed her eyes, and felt the buzz hit her brain. No job, no money. Shit. Then an idea popped into her head. She took out her phone and placed a call. A man answered. "Hey, babe."

"I just got fired."

"No shit? Why?"

"Because my boss is an asshole, that's why."

The man laughed. "Aren't they all?"

"I need some money."

He didn't expect that. "Hey, I'm short of cash too."

"No, you're not," she said. "You're a millionaire. *We're* millionaires."

"You have to get that idea out of your head. Like I told you, we can't start spending that money for at least a year. People will notice."

"They're gonna notice a year from now, too."

"How many times do I have to explain this? We lay low for a year. In the meantime, I find us a place in another country. Once we move, you can spend as much as you want."

"What other country?"

"I'm working on that."

She bit her lip and thought. Could she wait? Unless she found another job in a hurry, she wouldn't be able to pay next month's rent.

And there weren't a lot of jobs to be found in Pinyon. Good ones, anyway.

"I need something now. Just enough to get me through this month." Her request was met with a long silence. "Did you hear me?"

"I heard you," the man said. "How about a thousand?"

She wanted to scream. Why was he being so cheap when he was sitting on a mountain of cash? "I need more than that."

"All right. But after this we're sitting tight for a while. Understand?"

"When will I get it?"

"Do you understand?"

He could be such a prick sometimes. "Yes. After this, we're sitting tight."

"Good. I'll bring it by tomorrow."

Chapter Sixteen

Cash hadn't planned a trip to Cavender's, but with the notion planted in his mind, he decided to go browse the store. As he pushed through the heavy wooden doors, he drew the attention of a staff member. She tensed as she registered his uniform. "Can I help you?"

"I'm just here to look."

Her face relaxed. "Let me know if you have any questions."

Cash strolled through the clothing section before spending twenty minutes browsing the boots. A pair of square-toed Black Jack dress boots tempted him, but after trying them on, he decided he couldn't justify the expense. Despite the raise he had received from Santos after breaking the case involving Jessica Patrice and Maurice Trahan, he couldn't afford to spend seven hundred dollars on footwear. Not when he already had four serviceable pairs in his closet at home. Instead, he satisfied himself with a long-sleeved snap shirt. Edie said he looked good in blue.

After leaving Cavender's, Cash drove to Torchy's on Spicewood Springs Road. Just as he was digging into an order of green chile pork tacos, his phone rang. "This is Cash."

"This is Frida. I have some news on the bullet that killed Slater Cobb."

"Yeah?"

"I should have checked this sooner, but I made the mistake of assuming Bergheim shot him. He didn't. You'll remember his Beretta uses nine-millimeter ammo. What I pulled out of Cobb is a twenty-two LR. That wouldn't fit in a Beretta."

"Which means that Bergheim didn't kill Cobb."

"Right. He was shot by the other robber."

"And Cobb shot Bergheim? His gun was a nine millimeter."

"Don't forget there was no gunshot residue on his hands."

"So the other guy shot them both?"

"Apparently. But he used two different guns. The one we found on Cobb and another one that's still missing."

Cash paused to ponder the new information. "This complicates things. Could there have been a third person?"

"I just analyze the evidence. You'll have to figure that out."

***

Cash wolfed down the rest of his tacos and drove back to Pinyon. He wanted to compare notes with the other deputies before making his next move. Had there been three intruders at Bergheim's? Why had one of them shot Cobb? Was Willa Dearborn as innocent as she claimed? And what was the deal with Kincaid? He had seemed hostile to Cash at his apartment. Shouldn't he want to help law enforcement catch his friend's killer? Or did he have something to hide?

Cash reached the department late in the afternoon. He found Santos in the lobby chatting with Vicky. "Can we talk?" he said, interrupting. He avoided looking Vicky in the eye.

"Let's go to my office," said Santos. He led Cash down the hall and shut the office door. "What's up?"

"Dieter Bergheim had over a million dollars hidden in that hole."

Santos let out a low whistle. "Holy cow."

"No kidding. He wants to know if we'll get it back."

"I'll bet he does."

"I also found out that Cobb didn't shoot Emil Bergheim."

"I know," Santos said. "Frida called me after she talked to you." He leaned back and stared at the ceiling. "Any ideas?"

Cash said, "Has Frida finished searching Willa Dearborn's car?"

"Yeah. There was a lot of mud on the floor in front of the driver but none anywhere else. Since it rained that night—"

"She told me. Probably no third person."

"At least not at the shop. There's still that other car we heard on the game camera footage."

"Has Deke checked in?" Cash asked.

"Yeah. He gave Dearborn's fingerprints to Frida. She's comparing them to the ones she took from the car. Cobb's too."

"And Hodge?"

"That's probably her coming now."

Footsteps approached and the door popped open to reveal not Hodge but Frida. Before Santos could ask what she wanted, she stepped into the office, shut the door, and pulled up a chair. "I'm glad I found you both here. I've got something new."

"Let's have it," Santos said.

"The car was wiped clean. I found Willa's prints in several places—after all, she's driven it since the attack on Bergheim—but little else."

"Little?" Cash said, picking up on the implication she hadn't come up empty.

"Our guy must have forgotten about the rear gate. Or maybe he just got careless. Anyway, I found a usable print on the release. It belongs to neither Willa nor Cobb."

"So, that's our shooter," said Cash.

"Could be. But we shouldn't jump to conclusions."

Cash's face turned red. For reasons he couldn't explain he wanted to impress his one-time babysitter. Now he felt like an idiot. "Right."

"One more thing." She held up an evidence bag containing a Jolly Rancher candy wrapper. "I found this under the driver's seat."

"I found one of those in Bergheim's workshop."

"The bastard likes his candy."

"Thanks, Frida," said Cash. "Anything else?" When she shook her head, he stood up.

"Where are you going?" Santos asked.

"Back to Willa Dearborn's."

***

Bernadette laid the menu on the table and frowned. "Are you saying I'm fat?"

Morgan pulled his gaze away from the cute server across the room at the Firewheel Café. She looked familiar, but he couldn't place her. "Of course not, babe. You're perfect. It's just ... that's a lot of calories."

Bernadette wanted a slice of cheesecake. Her boyfriend was buying, and dessert with a meal out was a rare treat for her. "Come on, I'll share," she said. "The blueberry cheesecake is out of this world."

Morgan broke into a smile. "Well, if we're gonna share."

"Ooh, they have whipped cream. Do you want that, too?"

Morgan didn't hear her. He had returned his attention to the hot server. Despite the unflattering blouse she wore he could tell she had a bod to kill for. As he ogled her, he noticed a loose strand of black hair hanging from the bun atop her head. That would look nice hanging in his face with her on top.

"I said, do you want whipped cream?"

His fantasy shattered, Morgan gave Bernadette an overly sweet smile. "Of course." He flagged down a server lurking nearby. Not the hot one, but an older one carrying thirty extra pounds. "One blueberry cheesecake with whipped cream. And bring two forks."

Once the server left, Morgan looked for the hot woman but she had disappeared. He wondered how he could finagle a conversation with her.

"Thanks," said Bernadette.

"Anything for you, babe."

"Do you think I'm pretty?"

"What?"

"I said, do you think I'm pretty?"

"Of course, I do. You're gorgeous." He winced at his white lie. Bernadette was pretty enough but not compared to the server.

Bernadette said, "I thought after we're done, we could walk around the square."

Morgan gave her another sweet smile. "I'd like that."

"We could hold hands. It would be romantic."

"We'll walk down to the river." He leaned across the table and whispered, "I know a place by the water where we can fuck each other's brains out."

Bernadette's face flushed. He sure knew how to get her juices flowing.

The server appeared with the cheesecake and two forks. "Bon appetít."

Morgan handed her two fifty-dollar bills. "I hope you can break that."

"No problem."

Morgan cut off a piece of cheesecake and held it up to Bernadette's mouth. She accepted it and moaned with pleasure. "That's good."

She used her fork to spear a piece and feed it to Morgan. "It tastes almost as good as you," he said.

The server returned with Morgan's change. He took a twenty from the wad and handed it to her. "Here you go."

"Gosh, thanks."

They left the restaurant. Morgan delivered a lingering kiss. Bernadette smiled and took his hand, but he slapped his jeans pocket and said, "Shit, I left my phone on the table. I'll be right back." Before Bernadette could respond, he hurried back into the Firewheel. He spotted the hot woman taking an order at a nearby table. When she was finished, Morgan stepped in front of her and said, "I know you. We met at Winkler's the other night."

"Yeah, I recognize you. Clint, right?"

"Right. And you're ..."

"Edie."

"Yeah, Edie. Do you go dancing a lot?"

"Every chance I get. There's nothing better than a cold beer and a good band."

"Hey, maybe we could go together sometime."

Her friendliness drained away. "I don't think so."

He flashed his most charming smile. "Are you sure? I'm a great dancer."

"Thanks, but no. Good seeing you."

Chapter Seventeen

Ellis Doran shook his head as Cash strode toward the counter. *What the hell is going on*? he wondered. *You'd think we're selling drugs instead of chicken.* "What can I help you with, Cash?"

"I need to talk to Willa Dearborn."

He knew he had been right to fire that bitch. "Well, you won't find her here. I had to let her go."

"You fired her?"

"Yep."

"Why?"

"She mouthed off one too many times. Told me to go fuck myself."

"Do you know where I can find her?"

"Sorry, I don't keep track of them once they're gone."

"Okay, thanks." He turned to go.

"Wait a second," Doran said. As annoying as the deputy's visits were, the guy was still a hero. "How about some chicken for the road?"

***

Willa eyed the man standing on her front porch and scowled. She leaned against the door frame. "Are you bringing my car back?" She lifted a wine bottle to her lips and took a slug.

"Sorry, no," said Cash. "You should get it tomorrow."

"I had to walk home from work today."

"I heard about that. Doran says he fired you."

"On account of you."

"That's not how he tells it."

"What do you want?" She swayed as she asked the question.

Cash removed his hat. "May I come in?"

Willa took another pull from the bottle. "You can ask your questions from there."

Cash could tell she was plastered. "All right. It's about your car. Who else's fingerprints would be on it? I'm talking about the outside."

She blew air through her lips. "Now, how the hell am I supposed to know that? Anybody can touch a car."

"Has anybody opened the gate over the past week other than you?"

"You're not serious."

"I am."

Her lips curled up into a sneer. "Go fuck yourself."

***

Cash's house rattled as he jerked the door shut behind him. The drive home had done nothing to soothe his irritation at Willa Dearborn. Where did she get off swearing at a county deputy?

He fetched a beer from the refrigerator and took a long pull. The ice-cold liquid dialed his temperature down far enough that he no longer felt like punching a wall. With his thirst quenched, he reopened the refrigerator and focused on his hunger. All he saw was a container of leftover spaghetti and a half-empty jar of sauce. He threw them together and slid the lot into the microwave.

As the pasta heated, Cash rummaged up some fresh spinach and heated it in a saucepan. Maybe the leftover pasta wasn't much of a meal, but at least he'd have something green and healthy to go with it.

His phone rang, and Edie's name appeared. "What's up?" he said.

"Maybe nothing, but something weird happened a little while ago at work."

"What?"

"Bernadette and her new boyfriend came in. I didn't wait on them—it was Sissy—but as they were leaving, he came over and hit on me."

"He did? Where was Bernadette?"

"She was outside. I thought he was just being friendly at first, but then he asked me to go dancing with him."

Cash felt his anger returning. "What did you say?"

"What do you think I said? I told him no. When he didn't give up, I had to be rude and shut him down."

"Is there anything you want me to do?" Cash knew what *he* wanted to do. He wanted to punch Clint Morgan in the nose.

"No. But I'd keep an eye on him."

"Believe me, I will."

Chapter Eighteen

"You want me to spy on him?"

Cash suppressed the urge to snap at his little brother. Why did he always have to make things so difficult? "No, I'm just asking you to get me something with his fingerprints on it. A glass, a Coke can, a bong. Something like that."

"Very funny."

"Give me a break. I've smelled your house."

"You gonna arrest me, Officer?"

"That's Deputy, smartass."

"Okay, Deputy Smartass. Is Eddie suspected of a crime?"

Cash didn't want to give details. He trusted Reid, but sometimes his brother let things slip out. "No, we found some prints on a car and need to be able to recognize his so we know which ones we can ignore. Will you do it?"

During the long pause Cash found himself humming the Willie Nelson tune "On the Road Again." He had a premonition about another trip to Austin.

"Tell you what. We're holding a practice tonight. Why don't you come? Then you can get whatever you need yourself."

"You're gonna make me drive all the way to Austin for a Coke can?"

"No, I'm gonna make you drive all the way to Austin so you can do your own damn spying."

"Come on, just something with his prints."

"We start at eight. You can have supper with Mom and Dad. Maybe you'll get lucky and Mom will make lasagna."

Cash loved his mother's lasagna, but if he was having supper in Austin, he'd just as soon go to Mighty Fine for a burger and chocolate shake. The fries were made in-house and they used Blue Bell ice cream for the shakes. "Yeah, maybe."

"All right. See you at eight. I'll get some Mountain Dew. Eddie sucks that stuff down like water. You'll be able to get all the cans you want."

Cash ended the call. Despite his irritation about the need to drive to Austin, his mouth watered at the prospect of a Mighty Fine chocolate shake. First, though, he needed breakfast. He got out of bed and made his way to the kitchen. There he scooped muesli into a bowl, cut a banana into it, and added milk. Before he could take a bite, his phone rang.

Thinking it was his brother calling back—maybe to tell him he'd get Kincaid's prints for him, after all—he flipped it over to look at the screen. It said, "Mom." He tensed. She never called this early.

"Hey, Mom."

"Hi, Adam. It's your mother."

"I know. That's why I said 'Hey, Mom.'"

"Don't be smart with me. I get all the sarcasm I need from your father." From her tone of voice, Cash knew she was kidding.

"What do you want, Mom?"

"Reid tells me you'll be coming to supper tonight."

Thanks a lot, Reid. There went Mighty Fine. No burger, no hand-made crinkle fries, no chocolate shake. "That's right. He said you might make lasagna."

She laughed. "You wish. I don't have time for that today. We're having leftover lentil bean soup."

Great. Cash hated lentil bean soup. It might be okay except for the mountains of kale his mother added to "make it healthy." Cash didn't like leaves in his soup. "Okay, I'll be there at seven."

"Make it six-thirty. Your dad will be a grouch if he has to wait any longer than that."

"Six-thirty it is." He reached for the "end call" button, then stopped. "Mom?"

"Yes."

"Do you have any Blue Bell ice cream?"

"I think so."

"What flavor?"

"Vanilla. We had apple pie last Sunday and I like it à la mode."

"What about chocolate syrup?" If he couldn't buy a chocolate shake, maybe he could make one.

"I haven't kept that around since you joined the army."

"Well, shoot."

"Tell you what. I'll pick some up at HEB before you get here. How's that?"

Good old Mom. "Thanks."

***

When Willa woke up and opened her eyes, her head exploded in pain and she slammed them shut again. She moaned and pulled a pillow over her face. *God, that hurts,* she thought.

The excruciating headache didn't surprise her. Drinking two bottles of wine was bad enough, but she hadn't stopped at two. She put away a third and started in on a fourth before slipping into alcohol-induced sleep. She passed a restless night on the couch, with only a thin throw blanket for warmth and a decorative pillow for head support. Her throbbing temples reminded her of the pulsating theme from *Jaws*. Her neck ached. She felt like throwing up. The sunlight penetrating the window's partially open blinds made everything worse.

Willa heard her mailbox lid squeak open and shut. A car started and drove away. It occurred to her that today was Sunday, and there should be no mail delivery. She rolled off the couch and staggered to her feet. She was too late to identify the car. By the time she opened the door, it had disappeared. She opened the mailbox and slid out an oversized envelope. After looking around to see if anyone was watching, she went back inside and ripped it open.

Inside was a thin bundle of bills held together with a paper clip. She removed the clip and fanned the bills. All hundreds. Ten of them. A thousand dollars. "That son of a bitch," she said, immediately regretting the noise, as it intensified the pounding.

Rage boiled in Willa's gut. Slater had died for that money. He had expected an even split. She didn't know how big the haul had been, but from the way Slater talked, it was way more than two thousand dollars. Now that he was gone, she deserved to receive his share. And she wanted it yesterday.

Willa wandered the den in search of her phone. She found it on the floor peeking out from beneath the couch. Yet her call went to voice mail. At the beep, she launched into a tirade. "Goddamn it,

Hooch. A thousand bucks? Is that a fucking joke? I make one call to the sheriff's office and you'll find yourself in some deep shit. I want what was coming to Slater. All of it. He told me it was supposed to be a fifty-fifty split. And forget about waiting. I want it now. So, call me back, asshole."

She killed the call, gritted her teeth, and let loose a muffled scream. Finding that insufficient, she hurled the phone against the wall. It bounced hard and landed face-up at her feet. Staring down at the shattered screen, she muttered, "Fuck it. I'll be able to buy ten more if I want."

Chapter Nineteen

On his way out of Pinyon, Cash stopped at Edie's to let her know where he'd be. He found her eating pancakes with Luke. "Let me get you a plate," she said as she ushered him into the kitchen.

"No, thanks. I already ate."

"What are you doing here?"

"I need an excuse to see my girlfriend?"

She smiled. "Of course not."

"I'm on my way to Austin for the day," Cash said. "Supper with Mom and Dad, then a band practice with Reid." He saw no point in explaining what he was after at the practice.

Edie's eyes lit up at the mention of the band practice. "Are you taking your guitar?"

He hadn't thought of that. He'd been practicing. But he had left his guitar at home. Too bad. Maybe he could have sat in with the band for a couple of songs. "No."

"I'm sure Reid has an extra one lying around. You should try playing with them."

"I'll ask him."

"Changing the subject, I was accepted at Texas Tech."

The unexpected news hit Cash like a horror movie jump scare. "You're moving to Lubbock?"

"Can I have another one?" Luke asked.

"No," said Edie.

"I want one!"

"Sorry, baby, I meant no to Cash." She slapped a pancake on his plate. "Here you go." To Cash, she said, "No. At least not yet. I'm still waiting to hear from UT."

Cash gulped. Everything seemed to be going so well. Now this. "You're going to nursing school." He said it flat, without emotion.

The lack of enthusiasm didn't escape Edie's notice. "Is that a problem?"

Cash tried to force a smile but couldn't. "It's not a problem. It's just ... it's a surprise. I can't say I'm thrilled at the prospect of you leaving."

"You mean like when you left to join the army."

"That was different. I told you at the time I wasn't ready to get married."

"I remember. You didn't want to get married, so you left."

This wasn't going well. "I had to. Do you know of any army bases in Pinyon?"

"Don't be a smartass. You could have gone to school. That's what we planned, remember? We'd go to college together? Instead, you ran away."

Cash squeezed his hands so hard they turned white. "Damn it, Edie, I didn't run away. I joined the army. To serve our country, mind you. You still went to school. But you quit and came back here. That was *your* choice."

"I came back here because I was running out of money."

"You would have run out of money with or without me. All I'm saying is that we're back together now and you want to split us up."

"To have a life!" Her face was red. "I don't know if you've noticed, but there are no nursing schools in Pinyon, either. And I'm coming back!"

"It just seems a bit selfish to me, is all."

Edie's mouth hung open. Her eyes narrowed as she slowly stood up. "I think you should leave now."

Had he really said that? What the hell was he thinking? "Edie, I'm sorry."

"Have a good time in Austin."

"I didn't mean that."

"Tell your mom and dad hi."

Uh-oh. This hole was too deep for a simple apology. Cash got up from the table and opened his mouth to speak. Edie cut him off with a curt, "We'll talk later."

"I'll call you," he said, grasping for a lifeline.

"Don't. I need time to think."

***

Cash climbed into his truck feeling sick to his stomach. Needing time to think sounded ominous. Had he blown it with her again? He pulled away from the curb cursing himself.

Soon the problem with Edie drifted from his mind. Cash was struck by an idea and turned his truck into the Dairy Queen parking lot. He pulled out his phone and checked the Houston Astros' schedule. Perfect. They had an afternoon game with the St. Louis Cardinals. Maybe he could hang out with Roy Baxter, watching the game on TV, before heading to his parents' house for supper.

Baxter picked up right away. "This is Roy."

"Hey, Roy. This is Cash. We met at—"

"You don't have to tell me! Big Astros fan, right?"

"Right. That's why I'm calling. I'll be in town this afternoon with nothing to do until this evening. I'm wondering if I could chill at your house for a while. The 'Stros are playing the Cardinals today. Maybe we could watch the game together."

"That would be great." He gave Cash his address.

"Better text it to me."

"Will do. See you soon."

"I'll bring a six-pack."

Baxter laughed. "Bring two. You might want some, too."

***

The conversation with Baxter lightened Cash's mood during the three-and-a-half-hour drive to Austin. When he arrived, he stopped at a grocery store and bought two six-packs of Firemans #4, the flagship beer of Blanco's Real Ale Brewing. He would have bought something from Steve's brewery but Steve hadn't yet been able to crack the Austin market.

Cash rang the bell at a modest brick house in the Milwood neighborhood. The door opened and Baxter pumped his hand. He ushered Cash into a dated but neat den with a large-screen TV mounted on the wall across from a cheap sofa. Fronted by a short counter was a small kitchen. The place had been decorated by someone who spent a lot of time in thrift stores.

"Are you hungry?" Baxter said as he stashed the beer in the refrigerator. "There's a great taco place nearby and DoorDash delivers."

"Sounds great."

Baxter came back into the den, holding two beers. He handed one to Cash and clicked on the TV. "Have a seat. The game starts in about ten minutes."

They settled on the sofa. "So, your parents live in Austin?" Baxter said.

"Yes, but I grew up in Pinyon. They moved here not long after I graduated from high school."

"What do they do?"

"Dad has an HVAC company. Mom helps keep the books."

"And you? What does Adam Cash do?"

Cash was surprised at the question. Baxter had seen him in uniform at Eddie Kincaid's apartment. "I'm a sheriff's deputy for the county."

Cash thought he detected disapproval on Baxter's face before his usual grin broke out. "Right. I forgot."

"I was only hired a few weeks ago."

"What brings you to town today?"

"I'm investigating a shooting. Also, dinner with Mom and Dad." He thought of the missed Mighty Fine opportunity. "Lentil soup."

Baxter inquired about the business end. "A shooting? Did it take place in Austin?"

"No, in Pinyon. But a person of interest lives here."

"Who's that?"

"Sorry, I can't discuss details."

As the game started, Baxter ordered the tacos. It was a good game, with the lead changing multiple times until Houston won in the bottom of the ninth on a bases-loaded single by third baseman Alex Bregman. Cash rose from the sofa. "I better get going. Thanks for letting me hang out."

"Any time. Hey, we didn't drink all of that beer. Want to take some with you?"

"You can keep it. I've got a fridgeful back home."

They shook hands. Baxter grinned. "I'll see you around, Sheriff's Deputy Cash."

Was Baxter making fun of his name? Cash was probably imagining it. "See you around, Roy."

Chapter Twenty

Cash spooned the leafy soup into his mouth and swallowed. "Great soup, Mom."

"Thanks, honey. The secret is the kale."

It's no secret, thought Cash. *There's a pound of it in my bowl alone.*

"How's the deputy business?" his mother said.

"Fine."

"Are they paying you enough?"

Even with his recent raise, Cash was finding it difficult to do more than meet expenses. Saving remained a pipe dream. But he didn't want his mother to know that. "I'm doing all right."

"Do you remember Tony Whitman?" his mother said, referring to a high school classmate of Cash's. "He just bought a house in Northwest Hills."

Cash gulped. Northwest Hills was an expensive neighborhood, made desirable by its central location. "Good for him."

"He's a lawyer, you know. He works for an oil and gas company downtown."

Cash knew where this was going. "I'd make a lousy lawyer, Mom."

"He's right," said Cash's father, Del. "He would be miserable cooped up in a downtown office. The boy loves the outdoors."

"All I'm saying is—"

"Stop it, Janet," Del snapped. "Adam is happy as a deputy. Aren't you, son?"

"Yes."

"I'm proud of you." He looked pointedly at his wife. "You should be, too."

Cash's mother seemed at a loss for words. Finally, she said, "Of course I am."

Cash knew she'd be a lot prouder if her son could afford a house in Northwest Hills. "Thanks, Mom."

His mother stood up and began collecting the dirty dishes. "Who wants a chocolate shake?"

***

Reid shared a rental house in with two of his bandmates, Travis Easterling and Roger Sanders. When Cash arrived, he found the three of them setting up their equipment in the garage.

"Do the neighbors ever complain?" Cash asked, noting the proximity of the houses on either side.

"Naw, they're cool," said Reid. He pulled Cash aside and lowered his voice. "I got the Mountain Dew. None of us can stand the stuff, but Eddie can't get enough. Once he leaves, grab as many empty cans as you want."

Kincaid arrived ten minutes later. As he walked up the drive, Reid called out, "Did you get your new kit?"

"Yeah!" said Kincaid. "Wanna help me unload?"

Sanders and Easterling followed him back to his car. Cash put a hand out to stop Reid. "He bought new drums?"

"Yeah, we've been ragging him about his crappy kit for a long time. He couldn't afford a new one until now."

"How much do those things cost?"

"He had his eye on a high-end Pearl set. I've heard those run around four or five grand."

Wheels turned in Cash's mind. "Where would he get that kind of money?"

"I don't know. You'd have to ask him."

"I will."

With the drum kit finally in place, Kincaid proved Reid clairvoyant by grabbing a Mountain Dew from an Igloo cooler and popping it open. While the other band members discussed the songs they would work on, he finished it and started another. Cash watched as he set the empty at his feet.

Over the next hour, the Whistling Armadillos ran through five songs. As the last notes of Reid's humorous "I'll Take Ugly over Stupid" reverberated around the garage, he announced a fifteen-minute break. He and his housemates wandered into the house in search of a bathroom. Kincaid stayed behind fiddling with one of the drums. Cash ambled up to him. "You guys sound good."

Kincaid didn't look up. "Thanks."

"Nice drums."

"They need breaking in, but they're coming around."

"Reid tells me it's a high-end set."

"To be the best, you've got to play the best."

"That's a good philosophy." Cash decided to risk a more direct question. "Can I ask where you got them?"

Kincaid shot a glance at Cash but didn't answer.

Cash hurried to explain. "I only ask because a friend of mine in Pinyon is a drummer. He's looking for an upgrade, too."

Kincaid grunted in understanding. "Guitar Center at Northcross Mall."

"I know that place. I bought a guitar there when I was in high school. A Yamaha A series. It took me two years to save up for it."

"Is that so?" Kincaid stood. "If you'll excuse me, I gotta go take a piss."

When Kincaid was gone, Cash put on latex gloves and slipped a gallon-sized Ziploc bag from his pocket. Three empty Mountain Dew cans were lined up next to the drums. He took out his phone and snapped a photograph before sealing all three cans in the bag. He had started toward his car when the voice of band member Roger Sanders stopped him. "What are you doing?"

Cash flashed a stupid grin. "Every litter bit hurts."

"What?"

"You know what Woodsy Owl says. 'Give a hoot, don't pollute.'"

Sanders pointed at a recycling bin. "There's the recycling."

Cash didn't want to launch into an explanation, so he deposited the bag in the recycling bin.

Sanders lost interest and began studying some sheet music. Kincaid and the other band member returned. Reid came into the garage with a guitar, which he held out to Cash. "Let's hear what you got."

Cash recognized the guitar. It was the Yamaha he had bought at Guitar Center. He had given it to Reid ten years ago when he left Pinyon for basic training. At the time, Reid didn't play, but Cash thought he detected an interest. Reid proved him right by taking to the instrument with passion. By the time Cash next saw his little brother, he had not only learned to play, he had surpassed Cash.

He took the guitar and draped the strap around his neck. He strummed a few chords.

"I tuned it," Reid said. "It's ready to go."

Cash started to demur, but by now Reid's bandmates were also urging him to play. With a sheepish grin, he said, "I don't know a lot of songs."

"Name one you do know," Easterling said.

"How about 'Folsom Prison Blues'?"

"You heard him, boys," said Reid. "Let's do it."

Cash played for half an hour. He was most familiar with older tunes such as "You Picked a Fine Time to Leave Me, Lucille" and "Up Against the Wall Redneck Mother." The band good-naturedly went along, even coaxing him into singing lead on "I'm So Lonesome I Could Cry." After accepting what he felt were unwarranted compliments, he said, "That's enough for me, guys. I'll sit and listen now."

Cash took a seat in a lawn chair and watched Eddie Kincaid. He could see why the others had recruited him for the band. Kincaid kept a strong, steady rhythm and didn't complain when his bandmates offered suggestions. He also kept pounding Mountain Dews. By the time the practice ended, he had deposited four more empty cans at his feet.

Band members began putting their instruments away. Cash waited for Kincaid to carry one of his drums to his car and swooped in with another Ziploc. This time, instead of heading for his truck, he hurried into the house and stowed the bag in Reid's bedroom.

When Kincaid left, Cash and the others gathered in the den. They killed two six-packs of beer before Sanders said, "Enough for me. I'm heading to bed." Easterling muttered about working in the morning and followed him out of the room.

Reid said, "You can sleep on the couch. I'll get you a blanket and pillow."

"Thanks."

When Reid returned, he dropped the bedding onto the sofa and said, "What's the deal with the can?"

Cash splayed his hands. "Like I told you, we just need to recognize his prints so we don't confuse him with somebody else."

"If that was true, you would have just asked him to give them to you."

Instead of answering, Cash began arranging the blanket on the sofa.

Reid said, "What the hell is going on?"

His brother could sure be a pest. "Sorry, I can't discuss it."

"So, yes, he is a suspect."

Cash slipped out of his jeans and lay down on the sofa.

"All right, be a jerk," Reid said. "But if you arrest Eddie, you better learn to play the drums."

Chapter Twenty-One

Cash stumbled into Reid's kitchen, gripping his head with both hands in a futile effort to stop the pounding. How many beers had he drunk last night? Three? Certainly no more than four. Yet here he was being savaged by a hangover like a teenager who broke into his parents' liquor cabinet. What a lightweight.

He glanced at a wall clock. Eight-thirty. He had intended to get an earlier start on the day. Not only did he need to find the Guitar Center clerk who sold the drum set to Eddie Kincaid, but he also had the drive back to Pinyon ahead of him. And today was Monday. He should be reporting to work about now.

Cash fished his phone from his jeans and called Santos. After explaining his whereabouts and plans for the day, he said, "I'll check in as soon as I'm back."

"You do that," Santos said. "And maybe next time let me know about your out-of-town excursions before you take them."

"Sorry, boss. Will do."

After ending the call, Cash found a bottle of painkillers in a kitchen cabinet. He swallowed three tablets with a swig of water. A pantry search yielded only an almost empty box of Lucky Charms. The thought of making a breakfast of the super-sweet cereal nauseated him.

Cash turned at the sound of pounding feet to see Reid bounce into the room. "Morning, big brother," he called with more cheer than Cash found acceptable.

"How can you be so cheerful?" he growled.

"Hair of the dog, eh? There's pain medicine in the cabinet."

"I already found it. Don't you have anything edible for breakfast?"

Reid pulled the Lucky Charms from the pantry. "Here you go. They're magically delicious."

"They're a barf-inducing nightmare. Do you have any muesli?"

"What the hell is muesli?"

"Never mind. I'll grab a breakfast taco."

"Suit yourself." Reid poured a bowl of the Lucky Charms, added milk, and sat at a small table.

Cash joined him. "Do you know what time Guitar Center opens?" he said.

"I think eleven."

"Good grief. Musician hours."

"What do you care?"

"I need to talk to the clerk who sold Eddie his drum set. I was hoping to get back to Pinyon sometime before Christmas."

Reid stopped eating. "Come on, Adam, tell me what's going on. What has you so hot and bothered by the best drummer we've ever had?"

"Okay, but you have to promise to keep your mouth shut."

"I can do that.'

"Yeah, right." He massaged his temples. The painkiller seemed to be kicking in. "Do you remember me telling you about Slater Cobb?"

"Yeah."

"Somebody was with him when he went to Bergheim's that night. I think it might have been Ringo."

"What? No way."

"If not, I can clear him easy enough. That's why I'm here. A game camera caught a guy coming out of the woods with a duffel bag. He opened the rear gate of his vehicle to stow it, leaving fingerprints on the latch. If they don't belong to Kincaid, I can eliminate him as a suspect."

Rather than respond, Reid spooned Lucky Charms into his mouth.

"There's more," said Cash. "Kincaid just bought a high-end drum set that, by your own admission, could cost as much as five grand. From what you've said, that's a ton of money for a guy strapped for cash. So the question is, where did he get it?"

"It's not like he's poverty-stricken. He has a job."

"Where?"

"At a retirement home. I think it's called Devonwick or something like that."

Cash snapped to full attention, forgetting all about his hangover. "Avonwick?"

"Yeah, that's it. He's a maintenance guy. Hangs pictures for the old folks, fixes leaks in their sinks, that kind of stuff. It's a part-time gig."

Wheels turned in Cash's head. Dieter Bergheim lived at Avonwick. Eddie Kincaid worked there. That's how he would have known where the money was. Dieter must have let it slip when Kincaid was around.

"You're freaking me out, man," said Reid. "What are you thinking?"

"Dieter Bergheim lives at Avonwick."

Reid's understanding of what that meant registered on his face. "I don't care. It's still not Eddie."

Cash looked up at the wall clock. Still only a quarter to nine. Guitar Center opened at eleven, meaning he had plenty of time to talk to Dieter until then. *Heck*, he thought, *I even have time for a breakfast taco.*

***

Cash rapped on Dieter's door and steeled himself for the angry shouts he figured that would bring. When none came, he pushed the door open and poked his head into the room. "Mr. Bergheim?"

Dieter sat at a card table with his back to Cash. He didn't move. Spread out on the table was a partially assembled jigsaw puzzle. Cash walked a wide berth around the old man and waved to catch his attention.

Dieter jerked in surprise. "Don't you knock?"

"I did. You didn't hear me."

"That's because I don't have my hearing aids in. You should have knocked louder."

"Sorry." Cash pointed at the puzzle, which depicted three overly cute kittens frolicking with a ball of yarn. Not the sort of puzzle he imagined Dieter would choose. "Looks like a fun one."

"Fun, hell. It's just a bunch of damn cats. I don't do them for fun. I do them because there's nothing else to do in this damn place."

"May I sit down?"

"Knock yourself out."

Cash pulled up a desk chair. "I wanted to talk to you about your missing money."

Dieter resumed scanning the puzzle pieces. "Did you find it yet?" His speech was better today. The Parkinson's meds must be working.

"No."

"Then what is there to talk about?"

"I'm getting closer. Do you know a guy named Eddie Kincaid?"

"Never heard of him."

"He works here at Avonwick. He's a handyman. Fixes things."

"So?"

Cash took a breath and told himself to be patient. "Has anyone come to your room lately to fix anything? A leaky pipe? Clogged vent? Anything at all."

Dieter's eyes narrowed as he contemplated the question. It occurred to Cash that his hard facial expression would have served well in business negotiations. The guy wouldn't blink first in a staring contest.

Without warning, the old man flung his arms out and swept the puzzle onto the floor. "That sneaky bastard," he said, his eyes flashing fire.

"Who?" Cash asked.

"I don't know his name. He was a young fella wearing a ponytail. He had more tattoos than Justin Beaver."

"Bieber."

"Huh?"

"It's Bieber. Justin Bieber."

"Who the hell cares? He was in here a while back to hang my TV. We got to talking and he made a joke about me having such a cheap-ass set. I told him I had plenty of money and could buy any set I wanted. He looked around the room and said, 'It doesn't look like it.' I told him he wouldn't say that if he knew what was in my tool shed back home."

Cash looked at the puzzle pieces strewn about the floor. In contrast to that mess, he felt like pieces were snapping together in his puzzle. He began scooping up the scattered cardboard.

"What are you doing?" said Dieter.

"I'm picking up your puzzle."

"What about my money?"

Cash dumped a handful of pieces on the table. "I'll keep you posted."

***

Cash hadn't been inside Guitar Center in years. A deathly quiet greeted him as he walked through the doors. The place had a distinct odor that he couldn't put his finger on. A combination of wood stain and paper. He found it pleasant.

There were no other customers, just a lone clerk arranging items on a wall display. Cash caught his attention. "Excuse me."

The clerk stuck a pack of guitar strings on a hook. He had long hair, a nose ring, and the bored expression of a musician trying to look cool. "What can I do for you?" he asked.

"I'm a deputy with the Noble County sheriff's department." Cash caught the guy examining his jeans and polo shirt. "Sorry, let me show you my badge." He pulled it from a pocket and held it out.

The clerk studied the badge longer than necessary. "Okay."

"I'd like to talk to someone about a recent drum purchase."

"I don't know. We sell a lot of drums."

"I should have said drum *set*. A high-end one. Pearl."

"Sorry, that doesn't ring any bells."

"Is there someone else I could ask?"

The clerk set a box on a shelf. "Let me check."

While the clerk was gone, Cash strolled over to admire a large guitar wall display. All of the big names were represented: Gibson,

Ibanez, Martin, Gretsch, and more. He thought of his old Yamaha and the session with Reid's band last night. It had gone better than he had expected. Moreover, he enjoyed himself. Maybe he should keep practicing and form a band in Pinyon. He could start by recruiting Steve.

"Sir?"

Cash turned to see a middle-aged woman in a black Guitar Center shirt a few sizes too small for her plus-size frame. "Jojo said you wanted to see me?"

Cash identified himself and flashed his badge. He asked her about a recent Pearl drum set sale.

"I do remember that. Youngish guy. Said he was in a band. The Whistling Pigs."

"Armadillos."

"Right. Armadillos. What about him?"

"Does he come here a lot?"

"He sure does. He'd been eyeing that set for at least a year."

"Besides the drums, does he ever buy anything else in the store?"

She scrunched her face in thought. "Not really. A piece of sheet music now and then. That's about it."

That's what he thought. "How did he pay for the drums? Credit card?"

"No, he said that was maxed out."

"He wrote a check?"

She scoffed. "Nobody under the age of forty knows how to write a check. He paid cash."

"Are you sure?"

"Of course. It's not every day somebody drops five grand in cash. I checked those bills for authenticity, you can be sure of that."

Cash nodded as another puzzle piece fit into place.

"Shit," said the woman. "Were they counterfeit?"

"Not that I know of."

"Then can I ask what this is about?"

He shook his head. "Sorry, no."

Chapter Twenty-Two

Cash drove as fast as he dared. He was eager to have Frida compare the prints on the Mountain Dew can with those on Willa Dearborn's car. If they matched, Eddie Kincaid had better have a good explanation. Otherwise, Cash would move him to the top of his suspect list.

Willa Dearborn also loomed large in his mind. She had seemed genuinely upset when she heard the news of her boyfriend's death, but she hadn't been eager to aid his investigation. And while her explanation of Cobb's use of her car without her knowledge was plausible, Cash sensed she was hiding something.

In addition to Willa, Cash wondered about Cobb's housemate Aiden Camp. He found it hard to believe Camp didn't have any idea of what was going down. He had been aggressive about distancing himself from Cobb's activities, denying involvement even before he knew what had happened. And he had no alibi.

Lingering in the gloaming was Hooch, the guy reported by Camp as having visited Cobb recently. Who was he? Without a last name to go on, Cash would have trouble tracking him down.

Finally, the mysterious Rick Smith, Dieter Bergheim's former business partner. Given how common the name was, finding the man in a state as large as California would be tough. Still, he had to try.

Cash's mind wandered to the recent spat with Edie. She said she needed time to think. About what? Was she reconsidering their relationship? Was she planning to dump him? Move with Luke to another city to attend nursing school? Where she would meet someone—probably a rich doctor—and disappear from his life forever? Contemplating such an outcome was too painful. Edie was the woman for him, he was convinced of that. But was he the man for her?

Cash reached the station at four. He rushed to Frida's office, but she was out. So he called her. "Frida, it's Cash. I mean Adam. I have some drink cans that need prints lifted. They're from Eddie Kincaid."

"Who's that?"

"The drummer in Reid's band. Also, a friend of Slater Cobb's."

"I'll be there in ten minutes."

She made it in five. As Cash handed her the evidence bag, he said, "How fast can you compare these to the prints on the car?"

"Give me an hour."

He left her office in search of Santos. The sheriff wasn't in, but when Cash entered the lobby to ask Vicky about him, Santos strolled through the front door. "I've got news," Cash said.

Santos pointed at the hallway. "So do I." He led the way to his office. "Yours first," he said when they had each settled into a chair.

Cash told him what he had learned in Austin from Dieter Bergheim and the manager at Guitar Center.

"Good work," Santos said. "Kincaid is beginning to look like our man."

"I brought back a Mountain Dew can with his fingerprints on it. Frida is comparing them to the ones on Dearborn's car."

"If they match, we'll arrest him."

"Would we have enough for that? A good lawyer could argue that prints on the car don't prove he was at the scene."

"Okay, but it's certainly enough to bring him in for questioning. We'd give him a chance to explain. We'd also search his car and apartment. Of course, that would require a search warrant." He gave Cash a knowing look.

"Right," he groaned. "Judge Mixon."

He and Judge Barbara Mixon hadn't seen eye to eye the only other time he had asked her for a warrant. On that occasion, she angered him by suggesting the request looked like a fishing expedition. He made the mistake of firing back with a sarcastic remark about her sense of justice. She lit into him, warning him to keep such sentiments to himself or face unpleasant consequences. As he slunk out of the meeting, he felt like a chastened schoolboy leaving the principal's office. Since then he had stayed away from her.

"Now for my news," said Santos. "This morning I sent Hodge to another domestic disturbance call. It was at Bernadette's house."

"Was it Morgan?"

"I think that was the guy's name. Hodge said it was her boyfriend. When she got there, they were out on the driveway screaming at each other."

"Where was her mother? She lives there too."

"Inside with your daughter. She said the argument started when Morgan wanted Bernadette to call in sick so they could go riding on his motorcycle. Emma started crying and they went outside. Emma's fine, by the way."

Emma might be fine, but once Cash found Morgan, that asshole might not be. First, though, he needed more information.

"Frida said she'd be an hour to work on the fingerprints. Is it okay if I go talk to Bernadette?"

"Sure, no problem."

Cash stood up.

Santos said, "Take a deep breath before you see her."

***

How Bernadette had hung onto her job with Dr. Manor during her earlier days of weed and booze, Cash had no idea. She cleaned up her act after he caught her partying with some shady characters at Roadrunner Pete's gun range. If this morning's fight with Morgan was triggered by her refusal to skip work, that was a good sign.

Dora pointed toward the back when Cash entered the lobby. "She's cleaning room two. She wasn't happy when she got here this morning."

"That's what I'm here about. Is it okay if I talk to her? I don't want to get in the way."

"No problem. There aren't any patients here."

Cash walked down the short hall to the exam rooms. A strong odor of animal urine hit him as he reached room two. Bernadette was on her knees, wiping a wet spot with a rag.

"Fido had an accident, eh?" Cash said after rapping on the door frame.

Bernadette looked at him and set her jaw. "I don't want to talk about it."

"Talk about what?" He stepped into the room and shut the door.

Bernadette flung the rag against the vinyl floor and stood up. "You know damn well what about. All we were doing was having an argument. Couples do that all the time."

Cash winced. He and Edie were proof of that. "It was loud enough that your neighbors called us."

"I know. That Black lady came out."

"Her name is Deputy Hodge."

"Okay, Deputy Hodge. She gave us a talking-to and told us to keep it down."

"So, everything's okay between the two of you now?"

"It is if everybody would just leave us alone."

Cash sighed. "Bernadette, we have to think about Emma. What kind of environment is that for her with you two screaming at each other?"

"Emma's fine."

"Physically, maybe. But how about her emotional health?"

"What are you saying?"

He exhaled sharply, irritated that she wouldn't concede the point. "All I'm saying is that if you guys are going to fight, you shouldn't do it in front of her."

She scoffed and rolled her eyes. "Thank you, Dr. Phil."

"You know who Dr. Phil is?"

"Mother watches his show. Is there anything else you want?"

"No." He started to leave and caught himself. "I heard he wanted you to skip work. I'm proud of you for refusing."

She opened the door. "I don't need that from you."

Chapter Twenty-Three

By the time Cash returned to the station, he still hadn't heard from Frida. As he stepped down from his truck, a squad car pulled in next to him. Hodge got out and waved to get his attention. "I saw Bernadette today."

"So I heard."

"That boyfriend of hers is a piece of work."

"Did he hit her?"

"If he did, I didn't see any evidence. It looked like he pushed her down, but I couldn't swear to it."

"Whether he did or not, that guy is bad news."

Hodge nodded. "Agreed. What are you going to do?"

"I'm gonna have to think on that. Bernadette doesn't want me to get involved."

"Let me know what I can do when you don't get involved."

Cash laughed. "You know me better than I thought." He started toward the building. "There *is* something you can do for me."

"What? Beat that guy up?"

"I wish. No, Dieter Bergheim used to work with a guy named Rick Smith. He's from California. Middle-aged or older. I need you to track him down."

She gave him a wry look. "Are those the only clues I get?"

"I know," he said. "It's asking a lot. But a lot of those online directories show places where people have lived in the past as well as where they are now. Maybe you'll get lucky and find a California Rick Smith who used to live in Austin."

"You know I love homework. I'll work on it tonight."

"Thanks."

"By the way," she said with a grin, "I'm ready to kick your ass on the basketball court again whenever you're ready."

"Soon."

Hodge drove away in her white Corolla Cross Hybrid. Cash was idly wondering what kind of gas mileage she got in the vehicle when his phone buzzed. It was Frida. "What did you find?"

"Your hunch was right. Kincaid's prints match those on the car."

"Son of a gun. Thanks, Frida."

Cash couldn't wait to share the news. Had Santos gone home already? No, he was still sitting at his desk. "Do you ever get out of the office?" he said as he dropped into a chair.

Santos flashed a disgusted look. "Don't remind me. I've been working on a presentation to the commissioners' court asking for permission to hire another deputy. I know I can count on Fred Uecker's vote but the rest I'm not so sure of. Not to mention the head honcho, Judge Mixon."

"Speaking of Judge Mixon, I *will* need to ask her for a warrant to search Eddie Kincaid's apartment and car."

"I take it the fingerprints match?"

"They do."

"She'll want to know what you're looking for."

"I know," Cash said, determined. "The gun used on Bergheim, for one. A big stash of hundred-dollar bills, for another. And I want to get his boots and compare them to the casts Frida took."

"I thought she said those weren't definitive."

"Yeah, but a match would support our case. I was thinking of calling Mixon this evening."

"Don't," Santos said, shaking his head. "This isn't all that urgent and you'll just piss her off. That will hurt both our causes."

"Got it. Is it okay if I take Hodge with me on the search?"

"Take Deke. He's been complaining that all he ever gets to do is write speeding tickets."

"I thought he liked writing tickets."

"He does, but he's jealous of you and Hodge getting to do what he calls 'all the fun stuff' while he sits in his car on the interstate. Now that he's healed up from being shot, he wants to be more involved."

Cash let out a sigh.

"Is there something wrong?"

"No, I'm just not relishing all that time in a car with him. His conversational abilities extend to only two topics: women and goats. Beyond that, he's got nothing to say."

"Says the man who can't shut up about the Houston Astros."

"That's not true."

Santos rolled his eyes. "Tell me you don't know their exact record, their schedule for the next week, and the stats of every player on the team."

"I'll let you know what Mixon says," Cash said, standing up. "And I'll admit that I know they have seventy-seven wins, fifty-nine losses, three away games with the Mariners this week, then three back home with the Angels. But I don't know all the stats." He grinned. "Except for the important ones."

Chapter Twenty-Four

Cash handed the warrant application across Judge Mixon's desk and settled back in an ancient padded chair. The judge reached for a pair of cat-eye glasses, which transformed her countenance from imposing to downright scary. Her face betrayed nothing as she read.

Cash kept his hands in his lap and looked around the room. He had vowed to keep his cool no matter what the judge said. His gaze took in various framed diplomas and proclamations as well as photographs of Mixon with state legislators, governors, and—for some reason—former Dallas Cowboys quarterback Tony Romo. On her desk was a picture of her and Mr. Judge Mixon on a cruise ship. Her smile made her look almost human.

Mixon cleared her throat. "What precisely would you be looking for?"

He explained, ending with a summary of how his findings would bolster the case against Kincaid. Mixon grunted and kept reading. Cash took a deep breath and reminded himself to keep his emotions in check.

"How strong a suspect is this man?"

A softball question. "He's our main suspect. Unless he can explain why his fingerprints are on the car used in the robbery, he's as guilty as hell."

The stern look she gave him with his use of the mild expletive sent a shiver down his spine.

She reached for a pen. "All right, I'll approve this." She signed the paper and slid it across the desk.

"Thank you, Judge."

"I'm pleased to see you've matured in your attitude toward this office. It will serve you well."

Cash froze, not knowing how to respond.

Mixon removed the glasses and gave Cash an indulgent half-smile. "You can go now."

***

Cash drove the squad car while Conrad munched potato chips in the passenger seat. "I'm telling you," Conrad said, "goat meat will be more popular than beef someday. It's lower in fat and cholesterol than beef or pork. Plus, it's the most common meat eaten by eighty percent of the world's population."

Cash kept quiet. He didn't want to encourage his loquacious colleague.

"I've got forty-two Boers, sixteen Kikos, and a dozen myotonics."

Cash had to ask. "What's a myotonic?"

"You know, the fainting goats. Give them a scare and they drop like a shot hog. It's funny as hell."

"How does that work out for them if a coyote pays a visit?"

Conrad stopped eating. "I don't know. I never thought of that."

"Listen," Cash said, wanting to change the subject, "I've been meaning to ask. How are you doing?"

"Me? Great."

"I mean after being shot last June. Are there any lingering effects?"

"Naw." He pounded his chest. "I'm fit as a fiddle."

"Glad to hear it."

Conrad slid a chip into his mouth. He chewed a bit and then reached a conclusion. "You know what would go good with these? Goat chili."

***

The Madrone Field Apartment complex was a U-shaped two-story building in East Austin, bordered by a drainage ditch on one side and a shuttered convenience store on the other. A row of sickly privet bushes ran along the front, their leaves brown and curled for lack of water. The building's bricks had once been white, but years of accumulated grime had washed them gray. A handwritten sign posted by the entrance drive warned residents: "Excessive noise after 10 PM will not be tollarated."

As Cash got out of the squad car, he noticed the gleaming four-story glass and steel apartment complex across the street. The sign in front of Whitfield Lofts promised "Luxury Living at Its Finest" and lured prospective tenants with free Wi-Fi, a fitness center, and a lap pool. Conrad noticed Cash staring at the building and said, "I'd rather live in that one."

Cash jerked a finger at Madrone Field. "That one isn't long for this world."

"What do you mean?"

"Gentrification. I'm sure developers are already drooling over this property."

Stepping with care on the uneven sidewalk, Cash and Conrad made their way toward the manager's office inside the U. Dead weeds protruding from baked earth surrounded a walkway around a postage-stamp–sized pool. At least the complex kept the pool and walkway clean.

The manager, a heavy-set man sporting a cheap jacket and tie, greeted them with raised eyebrows. "Ben Pugh. What can I do for you gents? You don't look like you're here to rent a room."

Cash explained the purpose of their visit. He handed Pugh the signed warrant and said, "Do you know if Eddie Kincaid is here?"

"Today's Tuesday. He should be at work," Pugh said. "Wait a minute, this is from Noble County. It's no good here."

"Search warrants signed by a judge are valid throughout the state. Now, please let us into his apartment."

"Are you sure about that?"

"Are you sure all of your units are up to code?"

Pugh frowned, defeated. "What's this all about? Is he wanted for something?"

"Sorry, we can't discuss an ongoing investigation."

"Is he selling drugs? Running a meth lab? If so, I want him out of here."

"Seriously, I can't give you details. I *can* tell you I'm not aware of any reason for you to be worried."

Pugh stared at Cash for several seconds before fishing a set of keys out of a desk drawer. "Follow me."

Cash hadn't noticed this on his first visit, but the apartment struck him as well-kept by young bachelor's standards. The floor and counters were clear of clutter. There were no dirty dishes in the sink, no empty ramen wrappers on the counter, no pizza boxes on the coffee table. Even the lone couch pillow leaned neatly against the armrest.

Pugh settled into a lounge chair. He caught Cash looking at him and said, "I'll stay out of your way."

Cash pointed at the kitchen. "Start in there, Deke. I'll take the den." He donned a pair of gloves and began his search. Ten minutes later, he hadn't found anything of note. As he walked into the kitchen, Conrad was dumping a drawer full of flatware onto the counter. "Easy there, Deke. We need to leave the place like we found it."

Conrad's protest was cut off by the sound of the apartment door opening. Cash hurried into the den, and Kincaid recoiled at the sight of him. "What are you doing?" Kincaid asked.

"We have a warrant," Cash said. He showed it to him.

"Why are you searching my apartment? I didn't do anything."

"Have a seat."

Kincaid sat on the sofa. Cash looked at Pugh and said, "We can take it from here."

Thought reluctant, Pugh left. Conrad came into the den and sat in the lounge chair. Cash fetched a chair from the kitchen for himself and positioned it to face Kincaid. "Where did you go after you left the dance hall the night Emil Bergheim was shot?"

"You asked me that already. I got into my car and drove back here."

"We found your fingerprints on the gate lift to Willa Dearborn's car. That's the same car used in the robbery."

Kincaid's eyes flashed white heat. "You son of a bitch. When did you—?" He caught himself. "The rehearsal. That's why you were there, wasn't it?"

Cash shrugged. "Tell us about the fingerprints, Eddie."

Kincaid had to recollect. "I know. I stayed with Slater the night before the gig. When we got to Winkler's, I realized I left my cymbals at his house. He hadn't arrived yet—he said he had an errand to run—so Willa let me use her car."

"Why didn't you use your own?"

"I still hadn't unloaded it. She said she'd do that while I got the cymbals."

"Cut the bullshit," Conrad snapped. "We've got you red-handed."

"It's no bullshit!" said Kincaid. "I didn't do anything."

Cash held up a hand to quiet Conrad. "Do you recall hanging a TV for Dieter Bergheim at Avonwick?"

"Who's Dieter Bergheim?"

"Emil Bergheim's brother. He's a resident where you work."

"I hang a lot of TVs."

"You made a crack about him not being able to afford a new one. He said you wouldn't say that if you knew what was in his tool shed."

Kincaid scoffed. "Do you think I remember every crazy thing one of those old farts tells me?"

"So you don't remember him saying that."

"No. What I do remember is the guy was grouchy as hell. I couldn't wait to get out of that room."

Cash tapped the pocket containing the search warrant. "This says we can search your car."

"Be my guest."

Cash and Conrad followed Kincaid into the parking lot. Kincaid pointed at a late-model Buick Envista. "Knock yourselves out."

Cash didn't expect to find anything in the vehicle. He figured once he had searched it, he and Conrad would resume going through the apartment, which is where he suspected anything relevant would have been stashed. He was therefore surprised when he peeked beneath the driver's seat and saw a gun. Using a gloved hand, he pulled it out into view.

"That's not mine," Kincaid protested, unable to hide the panic in his voice.

Cash said, "That's a Smith & Wesson logo." He removed the clip. "Looks like a twenty-two. That would match a gun that fired the bullet Frida pulled out of Cobb."

"I didn't shoot Slater," Kincaid said. His breaths were coming hard and fast.

"What do you think, Deke?"

"I think it's mighty suspicious."

Kincaid began pacing back and forth, gesticulating with his hands. "I can't believe this. Somebody put that there. I don't own any guns."

"Who else has access to your car?" said Cash.

"Nobody." He was near tears.

Cash stowed the gun in an evidence bag. He and Conrad finished searching the car and found nothing more. Cash said, "Let's go have a chat, Eddie."

Back in the apartment, Kincaid sat hunched over on the sofa, wringing his hands. "I swear, I've never seen that gun before. Slater and I were old friends. I didn't shoot him."

Conrad said, "Give it up, Eddie. That's the gun that killed Slater Cobb."

"It *could* be the gun that killed Cobb," Cash qualified. "We'll need a ballistics test to verify that."

"Right," said Kincaid. "You don't know it's the one."

"But you have to admit, it doesn't look good."

Kincaid sucked in a deep breath. "All I can tell you is I didn't do it. I played the gig, loaded up my stuff, and drove back to Austin. That's it. I've never heard of Emil Bergheim and don't know shit about Slater getting shot. And that is definitely *not* my gun."

The vehemence in Kincaid's voice suggested sincerity to Cash. Nor did he show any of the usual tells of someone lying. "You can see our dilemma, can't you?" Cash said. "What would you suggest we do?"

"I don't know," said Kincaid. "Run your ballistics test. Talk to your brother. He'll tell you I didn't do it."

"Did anyone see you loading your drums when you left Winkler's?"

A monotone. "No."

"Speaking of drums, where'd you get the money for a new kit? That's an expensive set you bought. I checked with the store."

Kincaid shot Cash a defiant look. "I saved up for it. Took me three years."

"Why'd you pay cash?"

"I don't have a credit card anymore. The one I had was canceled. And before you ask, I don't have a checkbook, either."

"Did anyone see you back here at the apartment? Is there anyone that could vouch for you being here?"

Kincaid hung his head. "No."

"Did you stop anywhere along the way? Maybe fill up your car or get a cup of coffee?"

"Yeah!" His face brightened. "I did."

"Where?"

"I'm not sure. Before I got to Fredericksburg."

"Had you already gone through Junction?"

"Yeah. Maybe a half-hour earlier."

Cash opened the maps app on his phone. He pulled up the route from Junction to Fredericksburg and showed it to Kincaid. "That would put you near Harper. Does that ring a bell?"

"Maybe. I know it was a Valero station."

"Did you pay cash or with a credit card?"

"Cash. Like I told you, I don't have a card."

"Do you have a doorbell camera here?"

"No."

"Is there a security camera in the parking lot?"

Kincaid seemed annoyed. "I don't know. You'd have to ask the manager."

Cash stood up. "We will."

"Aren't we going to arrest him?" Conrad said.

Cash jerked a thumb at the door. "Outside."

Out in the parking lot, Conrad threw up his hands and said, "Jesus Christ, why aren't we bringing him in?"

This was why Cash didn't want to bring him. "We found a gun. It could be the one that was used to kill Cobb but we don't know that for sure. If the ballistics match, we'll arrest him then."

"He could bolt."

"He might. But he doesn't strike me as the kind that would be able to hide for long. In the meantime, we need to find that Valero station."

Before starting the drive back to Pinyon, they stopped at the manager's office and asked Pugh about a surveillance camera in the parking lot. "We had one," Pugh said, "but kids kept spray-painting over it so I said 'the hell with it.'"

"They make smaller cameras now that are hard to see."

Pugh shrugged. "Yeah, I should get one of those."

***

"There are three Valero stations between Junction and Fredericksburg," Conrad said, studying his phone screen.

Cash said, "Which ones are halfway in between?"

"The ones in Harper."

"Harper has more than one?"

"Yeah, there's two. But only one of them is open late."

They stopped in Fredericksburg for barbecue, which they ate in the car as Cash drove. "Sorry they didn't have any goat," Cash said as he finished wiping grease from his chin.

"They're missing out."

Stan's Valero station was a nondescript tin building with two gas pumps and a convenience store. Cash and Conrad found a lone clerk behind the counter reading a book, which she closed as they approached her.

After identifying himself, Cash said, "Do you have video surveillance?"

"We do. Inside and out."

"May we see it?" He gave her the date. "It would be late. Probably around two a.m."

"We close at two. But the pumps operate twenty-four hours."

"The guy we're interested in said he paid cash, so it would be when you were still open."

She led them to a back room and powered up a laptop. After a few mouse clicks she said, "Here you go. Fast forward here. Stop here. And that's rewind."

Conrad leaned over Cash's shoulder as he pushed play. He sped up the replay until he saw a customer enter the store. It was an old man. "That's not him." Three more customers came and went. None were Kincaid.

Conrad said, "He was lying."

Another customer came in. "I don't think so," said Cash, recognizing Kincaid. He came to the counter and handed over several bills. He received his change and left. Cash straightened and touched his hat brim. "Can we get a copy of that?"

"Sure, if I had a memory stick."

"You don't have one?"

"We sell them."

"Sell me one, then."

Soon enough, the clerk returned with a package that she cracked apart. After copying the surveillance file, she handed the stick to Cash.

"Thank you, ma'am," Cash said.

"It's six ninety-nine. Plus tax."

Cash pulled out a credit card. "I'll need a receipt."

***

Back on the road, Conrad said, "Maybe he went to Bergheim's and then drove home."

"That doesn't work. Bergheim called nine-one-one at three. The station had been closed for an hour."

"If it wasn't Kincaid and the ballistics match, how did that gun get in his car?"

"That's a good question." Cash recalled his ordeal when the reputed murder weapon was found in his car after Griff Turner's murder. "Either he's an idiot and left a murder weapon in his car, or the real killer planted it there. I'm leaning toward number two."

"Speaking of number two," Conrad said, "can you stop at the next gas station?"

Chapter Twenty-Five

Cash shielded his eyes from the late afternoon sun blasting through the conference room window. "Let me guess," he said, squinting. "The ballistics tests match."

"They do," said Frida.

"And I'm guessing you didn't find any fingerprints on the gun."

"No, I didn't."

Santos said, "Assessment?"

Before Cash could respond, Conrad said, "The guy's guilty as hell. You should have seen his face when we found the gun."

"How do you explain the gas station surveillance footage?"

"What does it matter? The murder weapon was in his car."

"Cash?"

Cash didn't want to offend Conrad, but he needed to keep the investigation on target. The problem was, at this point he couldn't identify a target. "I can't agree. Unless Kincaid had some way of altering the time stamp—and I can't imagine how he could have—the video places him at the gas station at two a.m. He left Winkler's at twelve-thirty. Bergheim made his call around three. There's no way Kincaid could have driven to Bergheim's, robbed the place, and made it to Harper by two."

"So how did his prints get on Willa Dearborn's car?"

Cash relayed what Kincaid had told him about using the vehicle to fetch his cymbals.

"It's plausible," said Santos. "Where does this leave us?"

"Back at square one," said Cash. "I was beginning to see Kincaid as the killer, but now I'm not sure who did it."

"Who else is there?"

"Willa Dearborn?"

"That doesn't look like her on the game camera."

"Well, Cobb's roommate Aiden Camp doesn't have an alibi."

"Do you have anything definite that implicates him?

"No." Cash chewed his lower lip. "That leaves only mystery men Hooch and Rick Smith."

"Who's Rick Smith?"

Cash explained Dieter's suspicion about his one-time business partner. "Hodge is trying to find him."

"Until she does, we're spinning our wheels, aren't we?" said Santos. He paused to think through what they knew. "We've got the boot prints to work with. Cobb was wearing sneakers. Willa could have been wearing boots since she was at the dance. But she'd have to have awfully big feet for those to have been hers."

"Easy enough to check," said Hodge, speaking up for the first time.

"We need to knock on some doors," said Cash. "See if anyone in her neighborhood saw her car coming or going that night."

"While you're at it, squeeze Aiden Camp," said Santos. "And find this guy Rick Smith."

***

Camp answered the door wearing jeans and his Sonic work shirt. "May I come in?" Cash asked. "I have some follow-up questions about Slater."

Camp frowned. "Can we make this quick? I was about to leave for work."

"It won't take long."

Camp motioned Cash inside. After closing the door, Cash said, "Tell me everything you know about Slater."

A puzzled look appeared on Camp's face. "Like what?"

"What was he like? Who were his friends? Did he have any hobbies? That kind of thing."

"Like I already told you, we weren't close."

"When did you become housemates?"

"Two, maybe three months ago. One day at work I told him I was having trouble paying my rent, and he said I could live with him. Sonic doesn't pay shit, so I said yes."

"Did you guys ever do stuff together?"

"Not really," Camp said warily. "Sometimes we'd share a joint, but that's about it. He spent most of his time with Willa. They used to—"

"Bang like rabbits. You told me. Do you own a gun?"

"Why are you asking me that? Do you think I killed him?"

Cash decided to come clean. "It's like this, Aiden. Your ex-housemate turned up dead at a robbery. We know he was shot by his partner. And you don't have an alibi."

"It wasn't me." Camp sounded desperate." I'd never kill anyone. Ask anybody. I've never even been arrested."

Cash knew that. He had checked before coming over. "All right, Aiden." He removed one of his cards from his shirt pocket and handed it to Camp. "I'll let you get to work. But if you think of anything that might help—"

"I know. Believe me, I'll call you."

***

Cash found no one home at the first two doors he tried on Slater Cobb's street. A stocky older man answered the third.

"Mr. Anson," Cash said, surprised. Will Anson, one-time Houston Oiler and owner of Will's Attic, an antique shop on the square, had known Cash since he was a baby. He still had a framed, autographed photo of Anson in his Oilers uniform in his closet. "I didn't know you lived here."

Anson smiled. He had always been friendly, even when as a boy Cash threw a rock at Steve and cracked one of the antique store's windows. Cash worked for Anson after school for a month to pay for the damage. During that time he developed a fondness for the older man. "Everybody has to live somewhere," Anson said. "Want to come in?"

Cash followed him into a tidy den that looked like a wing of the Pro Football Hall of Fame. Plaques, helmets, signed footballs, and more drew his attention away from the purpose of his visit. Judging from the preponderance of items bearing the Oilers logo or that of the Texas Aggies, Cash figured the display reflected the former athlete's playing career rather than an interest in sports memorabilia.

"Wow," Cash said. "This is an amazing collection."

Anson picked up a football and tossed it to Cash. "Read the name on that."

Cash studied the signature. "Holy cow, Earl Campbell!" Campbell had won the Heisman Trophy at the University of Texas before a Hall of Fame career in the NFL.

Anson said, "Earl ran eighty yards for a touchdown against the Dolphins on *Monday Night Football*. I threw a key block for him and he gave me this ball."

Cash returned the ball. "Mr. Anson, as much as I'd like to spend all day looking through your collection, I'm here on official business."

Anson gestured for Cash to sit and settled into a chair, "What brings Pinyon's most famous deputy to my house?"

"I don't know about that."

"Don't kid yourself. You made newspapers around the state."

Cash ignored the comment. His time on the run while trying to solve Griff Turner's murder was not what he wanted to be remembered for. "I'm investigating a neighbor of yours, Slater Cobb."

"Ah, yes, good old Slater. Not my favorite neighbor. When he's not high, he's drunk. What did he do this time?"

"He's dead. Somebody shot him while he was trying to rob Emil Bergheim at his ranch."

Anson snapped to attention. "Is Emil okay?"

"Yes. He took a bullet but will recover. How well did you know Cobb?"

"Not very. We'd nod to each other but didn't talk much."

"Do you know what he did for a living?"

"The last I heard, he was working at Sonic. I'd see him wearing their shirt when he left for work."

"Did he have many visitors?"

"Not a lot. Mostly a young lady. I think it was his girlfriend. A real good-looker. Oh, and there was this big guy that came by a couple of times last week."

Rick Smith? "Do you know his name?

"Sorry, no."

"What did he look like?"

"Hard to say. I didn't pay him much mind. Tall. Close-cropped hair. No beard or mustache. Wore a black cowboy hat."

A lot of men wore black cowboy hats in Noble County. "How old was he?"

"I don't know. Thirty? Forty?"

That gave enough for at least a basic description. "What can you tell me about Aiden Camp?"

"Who?"

"Slater's housemate."

"To tell you the truth, I didn't know he had one."

Cash stood up. "Thanks, Mr. Anson. I'll get out of your hair now."

"Wait a second," said Anson. "You asked about his job. Besides working at Sonic, he picked up weekend work, too. Most recently he was helping Emil build fences. You used to do that, right? Anyway, I thought you'd want to know."

Cash shook the old man's hand. "I do. Thanks again."

Chapter Twenty-Six

Cash gained no new information from Anson's neighbors. A young woman said she had seen a man in a black cowboy hat once, but couldn't give any more of a description than Will Anson had. A teenage boy confirmed that Cobb had worked at Sonic. That was it.

Back in his truck, Cash called the hospital in Junction and asked for Emil Bergheim's room. He picked up on the first ring. "Hello."

"Mr. Bergheim, this is Adam Cash. How are you doing?"

"I'm bored out of my mind. A man can only watch so much TV."

"I'd like to come see you tomorrow morning. Do you know if you'll still be there?"

"I haven't been paroled yet. Of course, them doctors don't always let me in on their plans."

"Great. Is nine o'clock okay?"

"I'll check my appointment calendar and let you know."

When had Bergheim gained a sense of humor? "Okay," said Cash. "I'll see you then."

Cash called Edie. "Hey," he said.

"Hey."

"Is now a good time for me to come by? We need to talk."

"Give me an hour. I need to get Luke to bed."

With an hour to kill, Cash drove to the Dizzy Dillo for a beer and a bite to eat. It was his first time in the place since the night of Griff Turner's murder. Cash had just lost the sheriff's race to Turner and went to the Dillo to drown his sorrows. Deputy Sheriff Clovis Ward showed up and bought Cash several beers. After Cash left, Ward took one of Cash's bottles and planted it in his car to frame him for Turner's murder.

One beer and a cheeseburger later, Cash returned to his truck. Before he could climb in, a woman called his name. Judge Mixon was coming out of Chez Abby. "Just a minute, Deputy," she said, hustling toward him.

A man who looked her age accompanied her. He frowned like he was being dragged along on a women's shopping trip. Judge Mixon said, "Deputy, this is my husband, Jake."

Cash shook the older man's hand. What did Mixon want?

"I was wondering," she said, "what was the outcome of that search I authorized?"

So, that was it. "We found a gun in his car. The ballistics match the gun that killed Slater Cobb."

"Did you arrest the man?"

"No." Cash flinched at the steely-eyed look she shot him. "He said he was at a gas station in Harper at the time of the shooting. Deputy Conrad and I went there, and they had a surveillance video that backed up his story."

"How do you explain that?"

"Somebody must have planted the gun in his car."

"Shouldn't you have known about the surveillance video before you asked me for a warrant?"

Good grief. Would that have changed anything? After all, they did find the potential murder weapon. "We didn't know he'd been there."

"You mean you didn't ask him."

Cash gulped. "Yes, ma'am."

"You did ask him?"

"No—I meant yes, ma'am, we didn't ask him. At least not until we served the warrant."

She studied him in excruciating detail before saying, "I'll say this. For all his deficiencies, Sheriff Turner never asked me for a warrant without having all the information it was possible to have ahead of time."

Cash couldn't believe she was finding him lacking compared to that arrogant asshole Turner. "Yes, ma'am."

She flashed a thin smile that conveyed anything but warmth. "Come on, Jake. Let's go home. I'm tired."

Jake said, "It was nice to meet you, Deputy." He jerked a finger at Chez Abby. "You should try the beef tenderloin. It's out of this world."

As they walked away, it occurred to Cash that the chances of being able to spring for beef tenderloin at Chez Abby were also out of this world. It was the only special-occasions restaurant in Pinyon. White tablecloths, live piano music, and servers dressed in black gave the place an upscale atmosphere. He had been hoping to take Edie there for her birthday. If he could afford it.

Cash climbed into his truck fuming. What did Judge Mixon have against him? She could have asked him if Kincaid had an alibi before she signed the warrant. And they did find the gun. Wasn't that worth her signature?

As he pulled up to Edie's house, a light shone in the kitchen window. His heart thumped like an impact drill as he knocked on the door. He gasped when Edie opened it wearing a skirt and form-fitting blouse that triggered a familiar stirring down below. With makeup and beautifully coifed hair, she looked ready for the nightclub scene.

"You look great," he said.

"You look ... tired."

She led him to the kitchen table. "Want a beer?"

He didn't want a beer. He wanted to rip her clothes off and carry her to the bedroom. "No, thanks."

Edie informed him, "I've got fifteen minutes before Julie shows up."

"You're going out?"

"Do you remember Georgeann from high school? She and her sister are in town from St. Louis. We're going to Chez Abby. Julie's watching Luke."

Chez Abby? Son of a bitch.

"What's on your mind?" Edie asked.

"I just wanted to say I'm sorry. I was out of line."

She nodded. "Thanks. I could have handled things better too."

Was that an apology? "So, we're good?"

She studied his face. Cash knew he was a lousy poker player.

"Are you afraid you're going to lose me?" she asked.

Cash gulped. Afraid? He was terrified. "It happened once. I don't want to blow it again."

"I appreciate that. I like us being together. But if you're going to get the vapors at the thought of me leaving town to get a nursing degree, I'm not sure we're on solid enough ground for a long-term relationship."

Bam. She was breaking up with him. "You're right." He prepared himself for the worst.

"I need support from my partner, not conflict."

A glimmer of hope. "You've got it."

"Do I?"

He took her hand. "You do."

The doorbell rang. "Oh," Edie said. "Julie's early."

Cash stood up. "Have a good time tonight."

"Thanks." She rose and pecked his lips.

"You really do look great."

"And you still look tired." She leaned in for a longer kiss that left Cash wanting more. "I'll see you soon," she said.

"I'll look forward to it. Enjoy Chez Abby. I've been meaning to take you there."

"I'd like that."

Chapter Twenty-Seven

Emil Bergheim picked at the pancake on his plate. "I don't know anyone by the name of Slater Cobb."

"Will Anson told me he built fences with you," said Cash.

Bergheim's eyes filled with recognition. "Come to think of it, he did. That kid was a sorry piece of work. Lazy as all get-out. Argued about every little thing. A couple of weeks ago I sent him home and told him not to bother coming back." He gave Cash a quick smile. "If you ever need any extra money ..."

"Thanks, but I'm busy enough being a deputy."

"Too bad."

"Something's been bothering me, Mr. Bergheim. How did those people know about the money at your place?"

"How should I know? I told you before, I didn't even know it was there. Did you ask Dieter?"

"I did," Cash said. "He said he let it slip to a maintenance man at Avonwick. The guy's name is Eddie Kincaid. Does that ring a bell?"

"No."

"When you were shot, though, Kincaid claimed he was driving to Austin from Pinyon. We found a gas station video that backs him up."

"I guess it wasn't him."

"Did you know Dieter's former business partner? His name is Rick Smith."

"I heard the name a time or two but never met him. Dieter and I didn't see much of each other back then."

"He thinks Smith might have been involved."

"I wouldn't know about that."

"Is there anything you do know about him? Maybe where he's living now?"

Bergheim shook his head. "No."

Another dead end.

"You're not going to be able to find them fellas, are you?" Bergheim said.

"I'm not ready to give up yet."

"I appreciate that. Without the money Dieter can't afford that fancy place he's living in."

His brother had said the same thing. But something didn't add up for Cash. "About that. If you didn't know that money was hidden in your tool shed, and Dieter's living in a retirement facility in Austin, how *was* he paying those bills? Somebody had to be fetching the cash for that to work."

Bergheim stared out the window for a long time. Cash kept quiet, knowing his question had stumped the old man. "All right," Bergheim said at length. "I did know about it."

"Why didn't you tell me?"

"I was afraid you'd think I stole it."

Cash had always tried to keep an open mind to all possibilities, but he had a hard time pegging Emil Bergheim for a thief. He had once seen him apologize to a landowner because the price of fence staples had jumped twenty-six cents, meaning that the final bill for the man's fence was three dollars more than Bergheim had quoted. "Don't worry, Mr. Bergheim," Cash said. "You're low on my list."

***

Willa heard a car pull into her driveway and rushed to the window. It was him. About damn time.

She'd met him while working late one night at Speedy Chicken. At five before nine, he came waltzing in like it was no big deal to order a meal as they were about to close. She tried to tell him he was too late, but he ignored her and said, "This is my lucky night, finding a hot babe like you behind the counter."

"Is that so?" she said, intrigued but still annoyed.

"Yeah. Most of the women working here look like they've been helping themselves to too many fries, if you know what I mean. You, on the other hand ..." He let out a low whistle. "Hot damn."

He was a good-looking guy or she would have told him to go fuck himself. "What's your name?" she said.

"Hooch."

"Hooch? You mean like booze?"

"You don't like it?"

"I didn't say that."

She took his order and told Ellis he could go close out the books and she'd take care of the food. When she gave the guy three extra pieces of chicken and a double order of fries he said, "Damn, that's enough food for two."

"I thought you'd never ask," she said, proud of herself for being so clever.

She ate with him at a booth in the dining room. "Don't you need to clean up?" he asked with a sly smile.

"Later," she said.

"What about your boss?"

"Screw him. I can do it after he leaves." An idea formed in her head. Hooch was hot. She wanted him. "Wouldn't it be great to do it in his office? I mean, right on top of the stupid fat fuck's desk? That'd show him."

Hooch's smile returned. "Are you talking about what I think you're talking about?"

She slipped off a shoe and lifted her foot between his legs. "I don't know. What do you think I'm talking about?"

They finished the chicken. Willa told Hooch to wait and went to check on her boss. She found him just stepping out of his office. "Are you finished out there?" he asked.

"Almost. You can go home. I won't be long."

After he left, she returned to Hooch and led him back to the office. He watched her strip, then allowed her to undress him. Doing it on top of a desk was more awkward than she had imagined. The hard surface dug into her back and her head bounced against the wall each time he thrust. But the rough ride was worth it for the feeling of power it gave her. The next time her boss got all high and mighty with her, she'd just remind herself of this sex fest. Who knows, maybe they'd make it a regular thing.

He waited while she got dressed and closed the restaurant. Then they went out back and smoked a joint. After that, he followed her home and they did it again, this time in the comfort of a bed. He spent the night. They did it twice more before he left the next morning.

They saw each other regularly after that. She had to be careful so Slater wouldn't find out. Slater was sweet, but this new guy was a lion.

Eventually, she'd work up the nerve to tell Slater to take a hike, even though she suspected Hooch didn't limit his carousing to her. At first that bothered her, but when she'd bring it up he'd start kissing her and massaging her breasts, and soon she'd forget about being angry. Then he told her about a fortune in cash buried at some old guy's place out in the country, just waiting for someone to come and get it. He had learned about it from Slater. "He never told me that," she said.

"I guess he didn't want to share. Anyway, we're gonna go get it."

That sounded exciting. "I have an idea. When you're done, you and me can go somewhere fun."

"What about your boyfriend?"

She touched his crotch. "What about him?"

A few nights later, the two thieves drove to the old guy's place. Only one of them came back. It was too bad about Slater, but, according to Hooch, he panicked and brought his death on himself. Now Hooch had a mountain of money, half of which was supposed to have gone to Slater. She wanted his share. Hooch said she'd get it but she'd have to wait. Well, she was tired of waiting.

A car door slammed outside. Willa went to her bedroom and removed a .38 Special from her bedside table. She wouldn't shoot him, but if the money wasn't forthcoming, she'd show him the gun to scare him straight. The feel of the weapon in her hand made her horny. Once Hooch came to his senses, maybe she'd give him a blow job as a show of gratitude.

She stuck the gun behind her back and opened the door. She noticed the lack of cash in his hands. Maybe he had the money in his car. She'd give him the chance to say so before pulling the gun.

"Where's the money?" she said as she shut the door.

"I didn't bring it. I've told you a hundred times, it's too soon. If you go flashing money around town now, somebody will figure things out."

"I wouldn't spend it in town. I figure we'd go on a trip. Hawaii or maybe Australia."

He scowled. "We're not going anywhere. Don't you get it? Slater's dead and I had to shoot the old man. We need to let things settle down."

"I told you I got fired, right? I need money. Now."

"Is it my fault you got your ass fired? Just find another job."

Her mouth fell open. "Find another job? Look around you. We live in Pinyon. There aren't any jobs in this town."

He dropped onto the couch and pulled a joint from his pocket. "You haven't even tried yet. There's gotta be something out there. Now come on, let's get high."

She knocked the joint from his hand. "Fuck you. I want my money."

He leaned over and nonchalantly picked up the weed. She wanted to hit him. Instead, she slipped the gun from her waistband and pointed it at him. He stood up.

"What the hell is this?" he said.

"I'm serious. I want that money now."

With lightning quickness he swatted her hand and sent the gun clattering to the floor. She froze momentarily, then made a move for it. He beat her to it.

"You were gonna shoot me?" he said, his eyes dancing. "You stupid bitch."

"Half of that money is mine."

"I don't think so. You didn't do jackshit."

"Slater was my boyfriend. He died for that money."

"That's rich. If he was your boyfriend, why did you spread your legs for me every chance you got?"

"You owe me."

"Fuck you!" he shouted, sending a spray of spittle into her face. "Slater was an idiot. He was never getting half of that money. I did all the work. All he did was drive the car."

"What do you mean?"

"Don't you get it? I killed the motherfucker."

She lunged for the gun. He stepped back and swung it against her face. Feeling a white-hot blast of pain, she dropped to her knees and swayed like she was going to drop. He swung again and she crashed to the floor. She faintly knew her blood was spilling onto the carpet. She looked at him with uncomprehending eyes. Why? She had only wanted what was fair.

"I thought you loved me," she said, her voice weak.

He laughed. Spying her phone on an end table, he grabbed it and stuck it in his pocket. "Dream on, bitch."

"That's my phone."

"I'm borrowing it."

"You killed him."

"Yep," he said, dragging her to the couch. He hoisted her limp frame onto the cushions and pressed the barrel of the .38 against her temple. "All you had to do was wait."

Chapter Twenty-Eight

Hodge knocked on Willa Dearborn's door knowing she didn't have much of a plan. Her goal was to get a look at Willa's feet so she could estimate her shoe size. Ideally, she'd get a peek at any boots she owned, but that was a long shot.

No one came to the door. Hodge rapped again, this time louder. Again, there was no response.

Was Willa ducking her? Hodge knew from Cash that she wasn't happy with the sheriff's department. She blamed Cash for losing her job. Having her car taken away to be searched was a sore point as well. That had been returned, but the hard feelings likely lingered.

Recognizing Willa's Encore in the driveway, Hodge concluded she was home but refused to answer the door. She stepped to a window and peered into the den through a sheer curtain. Was that her asleep on the sofa? If so, how could she sleep in that position? She would wake up with a terrific neck ache. Wait, what was that dark stain on the carpet?

Hodge returned to the door and turned the knob. She pushed it open and called out. "Willa, are you there? It's Deputy Hodge with the sheriff's department." Receiving no response, she stepped inside.

***

"It looks staged," Hodge said, eyeing the bloody scene in Willa's den.

"I agree," said Cash. "The bloodstain on the carpet is out of the line of fire. And look at the cut on her forehead. Somebody hit her before she was shot."

Willa's lifeless body sprawled awkwardly on the couch. Her feet were splayed on the floor, her torso leaned to one side, and her head angled sharply onto the armrest. A gruesome circle of coagulated blood ringed her matted hair. Blood also seeped from a deep gash above her left eye.

A .38 Special rested in the palm of her right hand, the fingers curled around the handle. A line of blood spatter fanned out from the sofa toward the opposite wall, the one away from the stained carpet.

"I'll bet there won't be any prints on the gun," said Hodge.

"Just hers, if the killer is smart. The question is, was he smart enough to fire the gun with her hand after he killed her?"

"We'll know soon enough. Frida is on her way."

***

Cash and Hodge knocked on every door on Willa's street. Only one person was home, an elderly woman who was hard of hearing. Not surprisingly, she hadn't heard the gunshot. Nor had she seen anyone coming or going at the house. At each door, Cash looked for a doorbell camera, but apparently, no one on this street had received the memo about that particular technological breakthrough.

They returned to Willa's house. Frida was just finishing up her examination of the scene. "I agree with you," she said. "The killer hit her over there. She was probably unconscious when he dragged her to the couch. That's where he shot her. I'll test for gunpowder residue but, either way, it wouldn't change my mind about this being staged."

"What about the gun?" Cash said.

"I'll check for prints. Again, the results won't change my interpretation. Maybe we'll get lucky, though, and the killer didn't wipe it down."

Hodge pointed out one bright spot. "I guess we can rule her out as a suspect in Cobb's death."

"Just a minute," said Cash. He went down a hall and reappeared with a pair of cowboy boots. "These are the only boots in her closet. They're way too small to match the cast Frida made."

"Couldn't you tell that from the feet?" Hodge said, pointing at the body.

"She could have worn bigger boots to throw us off. If so, I thought they might still be in her closet." He rested his hands on his hips. "I'll tell you one thing for sure. We really need to find Hooch and Rick Smith."

***

They returned to the station. Entering the lobby, Cash said, "Keisha, you get back to work finding Rick Smith. I'll brief Santos."

"What about Cobb's housemate?" she asked. "Did you find anything on him?"

"No," Cash said with a head shake. "He's not in the clear, but without anything specific, we're nowhere with him."

Cash found the sheriff with Conrad in the conference room. He explained what he and Hodge had discovered, concluding with, "It wasn't suicide."

"Somebody's covering their tracks," Santos said.

"Or decided they didn't want to share the money they stole."

Conrad said, "I still think that guy Kincaid is involved. He looks shady to me."

"Could be," said Cash. "But my money is on Rick Smith."

"Let's focus on the money for a second," said Santos. "Deke, check around town. See if anyone's been flashing a lot of cash lately."

"Kincaid has been." When Santos raised an eyebrow, Conrad added, "He just bought an expensive drum set. Which he paid cash for."

"That's true," said Cash. "He said he's been saving for several years. My brother said the same thing."

"Even so," said Santos, "let's get his bank records."

Cash groaned inside. Another trip to see Judge Mixon. "I'll write up a warrant."

"Or, you could just ask Kincaid to see them. If he's innocent, he should be eager to show them to you."

"Good point. I'll call him."

An exuberant shout sounded in the lobby. Then Hodge burst in. "I found Rick Smith." She flashed a triumphant grin around the room.

Conrad said, "Are you going to tell us who he is, or are you going to make us play charades?"

"Ooh, that would be fun."

"Just spit it out."

"Okay," said Hodge. "I've been assuming that Rick was short for Richard."

"It is," said Cash.

"True, but I was getting nowhere that way. Then I asked Mr. Google what other names Rick could be a nickname for. It turns out there's a lot of them."

"Like what?"

"Derrick, Patrick, Frederick, Roderick, even Enrique."

"With a name like Smith, it's probably not Enrique."

"Right," said Hodge. "Anyway, I started searching names in California using some of those other names. Know what I found?"

"Come on," said Santos. "You're killing us."

"There's a Roderick Smith, age sixty-three, who used to live in San Marcos," she said, referring to a town south of Austin. "He moved to California for a long time. Then, two years ago, back to Texas. More specifically, to Austin."

"Did you get an address?" said Cash.

"Yep. 4719 Galindo Street."

"Galindo Street," Cash repeated. "That sounds familiar." He pulled out his phone and scrolled through his texts until he found the chain with Roy Baxter. His heart sank when he read the latest message. "This is Roy. My address is 4719 Galindo. See you soon."

Roy Baxter couldn't be Rick Smith, could he? Maybe two people were living in the house. But Cash had seen no evidence of that.

He recalled the shabby furniture and cheap decor in the house. Clearly, its occupant had little money. If Rick Smith had sold out right before Dieter Bergheim hit it big, he could have resented Dieter's success enough to rob him. What about murder? Men had killed for far less than a million bucks.

Cash said, "I can't believe this."

"Believe what?" said Santos.

"I know him." He told of meeting the man he now believed was Rick Smith at Winkler's. "He's Eddie Kincaid's grandfather."

"I knew it," said Conrad. "I knew Kincaid was dirty."

"Let's not forget Kincaid's presence at the gas station," Cash said. "And we don't know yet whether Smith is guilty of anything."

"Come on. How can you not see it?"

Santos said, "Cash, you'll call Kincaid?"

"Yes."

"Let me know what he says. What about Smith?"

"I'll go see him."

"You could call him, too."

"I don't want to spook him," Cash said. He didn't relish the thought of yet another solo drive to Austin. "Do you want to come?"

Santos shook his head. "I can't. I've got a meeting with the commissioners this afternoon."

"Are they going to give you the go-ahead to hire another deputy?"

"We'll find out."

"I'll go with you," said Hodge.

That was the person he wanted to answer. Cash stood up. "Let's roll."

***

First they swung by the Firewheel for some sandwiches to take on the road. As they waited for their order, Cash's phone rang. It was Wanda Fenster.

"What's up, Wanda?" Cash said.

"You've got to get over here." Her voice sounded urgent.

"What's up?"

"It's that bastard Clint Morgan. He hit Bernie."

Rage flooded Cash's mind. "Is she okay?"

"Yeah, but she's in her room bawling her eyes out."

"Where's Emma?"

"She's with me. She's fine."

"And Morgan?"

"The son of a bitch took off when I fetched my shotgun."

Cash had seen Wanda with that shotgun. He didn't doubt she had scared him off. "I'll be right there."

He ended the call. "I'll be right back," he said to Hodge. Before she could react, he dashed out of the restaurant.

Wanda opened the door still holding the shotgun.

"You can put that down now," said Cash.

"I was afraid he might come back," she said. She stowed the weapon in a closet. "He said he was going to kick my ass."

"Tell me what happened."

Wanda heaved an impatient sigh. "They was fighting again. Shouting loud enough to wake the dead. Don't ask me what it was about because I don't know. Anyway, I was in the kitchen and I heard a loud smack. I come running to find Bernie on the floor crying, with that bastard standing over her like he was Muhammed Ali. 'Did you hit her?' I said. He told me to mind my own business. I asked him again and he said, 'Do you want a taste of this, too?' That's when I fetched the shotgun."

"And he left."

"You're damn right he left. Elsewise he'd be picking buckshot out of his belly for the next year."

"He would have deserved it."

They both turned to see Bernadette in the doorway.

"Are you all right?" Cash asked.

She nodded and wiped her nose. "I'm fine."

A cry from Emma rose from a back bedroom.

Wanda said. "I'll go settle her down."

Cash walked up to Bernadette and put his hands on her shoulders. As he studied her face, he said, "I don't see any bruises."

"That's because he slapped me. He's smart enough not to use his fist, I guess." She pulled away and sat on the couch.

Cash sat down next to her. "Bernadette, I'm sorry."

"Why? It ain't your fault."

"You can't see him again."

"I know. He can go to hell for all I care. But what if he comes back?"

He took her hand. "I'll make sure he doesn't."

She regarded him with curiosity. "How are you going to do that? Beat him up?"

"I'll talk to him. Make him understand that you two are through."

Her resentment flared again. "You don't have to do that. I can tell him myself."

"I'm doing this for Emma, too." He paused, trying to come up with a diplomatic way of saying what was on his mind. "I should take you to the station so you can file a complaint."

"Please, don't," she said. "I don't want a bigger mess than it already is."

"Bernadette, you've got to. Without it—"

She stopped him with an upraised hand. "All I care about is that I never see him again. I don't want to see him go to jail."

"He might hurt somebody else."

"That somebody could be me if I make a fuss." She pinned him with a look and added, "Or Emma. You can't make me do it."

She was right. He couldn't force her. And if he tried he risked damaging his access to his daughter. He let go of her hand. "All right. Text me his address. And if he comes here again, you call me right away."

"I will."

He stood up. She followed suit and offered another way out. "I don't want him to go to jail," she said, "but I wouldn't complain a bit if you put him in the hospital."

Chapter Twenty-Nine

Hodge scowled at Cash when she saw him enter the Firewheel. She handed him a wrapped sandwich, announcing, "Honey mustard chicken. Extra pickles."

"Where's yours?" he said, glancing at her empty hands.

"I ate it."

"Sorry I left you hanging. I'll explain in the car."

Hodge drove so Cash could eat. "What's your plan with the guy?" she asked.

"I'm still thinking it through," Cash said, arranging the sweet pickle chips on his sandwich. "I can't arrest him because Bernadette won't file a complaint. I can make his life miserable, though, if he doesn't stay away from her."

"You could make him leave."

"Make him leave Pinyon?"

"Yeah."

"How?"

"Like you said, you can make his life miserable. Tell him you'll make that your life's mission if he doesn't get out of Dodge."

Cash chewed a bite of the sandwich which, with the pickle chips, was a perfect blend of sweet and savory. "I'd enjoy making his life miserable."

"All right, then. There you go."

As the miles drifted by, Cash remembered Kincaid. "I'm going to call the drummer. We could swing by and see him after talking to Rick Smith."

Kincaid answered on the third ring. "This is Eddie."

"This is Adam Cash."

Kincaid was under no delusions about the reason for the call. "Was that the gun used in the robbery?"

"We think so."

"Are you going to arrest me?"

"You can relax. The gas station's surveillance video backed your story."

"Thank God."

"I need to ask you about something else."

"What?"

"It's about you paying cash for the drums."

"I told you, man, I saved up for three years."

"I know," Cash said. "I just need some proof. Other people in the department still think you might be involved."

"What kind of proof?"

"Bank statements showing your savings ought to do it. Can you show them to me?"

"Do you have a warrant?"

"No, but I can get one. That will take time, though. I'm trying to get you cleared as quickly as possible."

"Doesn't the video do that?"

"Let me see the statements and we're done."

"I'm not giving you my login information," Kincaid said.

"I'm not asking for it. I'll be in town later this afternoon. I could come by your place and you can show them to me."

"What time?"

"How about six?"

"See you then."

***

Baxter opened his door and, at the sight of two uniformed deputies, stuck out his hands. "I'll come peacefully, officers," he said with a grin.

"We need to talk," said Cash in an unfriendly tone.

Baxter's grin faded. "I'm kind of busy at the moment. I'm on hold with my credit card company. The bastards charged me twice for the pizza I had last week."

"It's about Rick Smith."

The color drained from Baxter's face. "I don't know a Rick Smith."

"Are you sure? He's a friend of Dieter Bergheim's."

Baxter swallowed hard. Without a word he ended his phone call and nudged the door all the way open.

The deputies followed Baxter inside, and he invited them to sit. Cash said, "We know that you're Rick Smith."

"That's right," said Baxter. "What about it?"

"Why the name change?"

"My full name is Roy Roderick Baxter-Smith. Dad was a Smith, Mom was a Baxter. I hated that name growing up. The other kids were ruthless, and I got picked on a lot. A few years ago, I had my surname legally changed to Baxter. My dad was an asshole, so I wasn't sorry to ditch his name."

"Why change Rick?" Cash asked.

"I figured as long as I was remaking myself, I might as well go all the way. And I liked the sound of Roy Baxter better than Rick Baxter."

Hodge said, "You used to be Dieter Bergheim's business partner, right?"

"I'm sorry," Baxter said. "I didn't catch your name."

"Deputy Hodge. Tell us about your association with Bergheim."

Baxter leaned back and blew a long breath. "Dieter Bergheim. Not my favorite person in the world."

"Were you his partner?"

"Yes. Everybody makes mistakes."

Hodge started to speak, but Cash raised a hand to stop her. Baxter went on, "At first he seemed like a great guy. Smart, hardworking, fair even. And he had a terrific business model. He saw a niche no one else was taking advantage of."

"What was that?" Cash asked.

"Industrial insulation. Boring, right? That's why nobody else was doing it, I guess. He brought me in due to my background in materials science. I'd take one of our products, study it, and refine it to make it better. Cheaper, too. We were going to make a ton of money."

"If that's the case, why did you sell out?"

"I should say, we *thought* we were going to make a lot of money. Dieter began pushing the market too hard. We had more orders than we could possibly fill. I figured I'd get out before everything came crashing down."

"But that didn't happen," Cash said, nodding. "Did it?"

"No. The son of a bitch had figured out a way to extend our manufacturing to a plant in China. He didn't tell me about that. I should have suspected something when he was so willing to buy me out. He didn't squawk at all."

"He didn't try to convince you to stay?"

"Not for a second. He suggested a price and I took it. I felt like I had to get out of Texas. I moved to California. That's where I'm from. I kept my eye on the company, though, mainly out of curiosity about how long he could hold on. The next thing I know, he's swimming in profits."

"And you didn't like that."

"Of course I didn't like that," Baxter said, his voice rising. "Would you?"

"I suppose it made you pretty mad."

"Mad? It made me furious."

"So furious that you went to see him."

"Yes, I went to see the old cuss." He took a deep breath and lowered his volume. "I thought maybe he'd see the fairness of cutting me in again. After all, the product he was selling was stuff I came up with."

"But he didn't see it that way."

"No, he did not. He's the same ornery bastard he always was. Maybe more so." Baxter waved a hand at the room. "Look at this place. Decorated with cheap crap I bought at Goodwill. I could be living on Lake Austin with the money I was due. Hell, I could be Matthew McConaughey's neighbor."

Cash cleared his throat. "Did you know that Dieter squirreled his money away on the ranch he shared with his brother?"

Baxter scoffed. "That's no surprise. He hated banks. Didn't trust them. Can you imagine that? A businessman not wanting to use banks?"

"Somebody stole that money. They shot Emil Bergheim in the process."

"All of it? They didn't leave anything?"

That was an odd question. Since when did robbers leave anything behind? And he led with that instead of asking about Emil's health? Cash said, "Didn't leave a dime."

"I heard about that," Baxter said. "My grandson told me. He said you tried to blame him." He gave Cash a sharp look. "Now you're after me."

"You've got to admit you had a motive."

Baxter stared long and hard Cash. "It wasn't me."

"Who, then? Help us out here."

"How should I know?" He threw up his hands. "Serves the bastard right, though."

"Do you mind if we have a look around?"

"Hell yes, I mind. Do you have a warrant?"

"What are you hiding?"

"Not a damn thing." Baxter stood up. "I think this is enough. Please get out of my house."

Cash wasn't finished. "If you had to get out of Texas so bad, why did you come back?"

"On account of Eddie. He's an only child. His father was killed in Afghanistan. His mother, my daughter, died of a brain tumor a year ago. Before she died, she begged me to move to Austin and keep an eye on him."

A wave of sympathy coursed through Cash. He had served in Afghanistan. He knew a lot of good people there who had come back home in a box. And a brain tumor? What a nightmare.

Cash motioned to Hodge and stood up. He handed one of his cards to Baxter. "We may have more questions."

"Then run them through my lawyer."

"Who's your lawyer?"

"At the moment I don't have one." He strode across the room and opened the door. "But that's about to change."

Chapter Thirty

They had an hour to kill before meeting with Kincaid, so Hodge suggested they grab a quick bite at the Texas Chili Parlor in downtown Austin. She ordered a bowl of habanero red. Cash went with black bean and Elgin sausage, mild.

"What's the matter?" Hodge said when the server left. "Can't you take the pain?"

"I've always thought eating should be a pain-free experience."

"And here I thought you country boys were tough."

Cash let that ride. His toughness wasn't the main issue on his mind. "On another note, what did you think of Roy Baxter?"

She opened a packet of crackers and shook one into her hand. "It's hard to ignore his motive. As well as him visiting Dieter not long before the attack."

"We've got nothing that puts him at Emil's."

"Don't forget that second vehicle on the game camera."

"Right. So, how do we rattle his cage?"

"First off," she said, "we should ask Kincaid about him. Clearly, they communicate. At the very least, Kincaid would let his grandfather know we're sniffing around. That will make him nervous and nervous people make mistakes. And I don't think Kincaid is completely in the clear yet. He could have been involved in the planning without going to the actual robbery."

"Good point."

Their food came. As Hodge prepared to dig in, Cash said, "Seeing as how you like pain with your food, I could kick your leg with each bite."

"Or, I could flick a spoonful into your eye."

Cash recoiled in mock surprise. "All right, then. Enjoy setting your mouth on fire."

"Enjoy being a wimp."

***

"What happened to that other deputy?" Kincaid said, standing in the doorway.

"He's chasing bad guys back in Pinyon," said Cash. "May we come in?"

Kincaid motioned them inside. They followed him to a bedroom furnished only with a desk and a laptop. Kincaid rolled a desk chair over and sat down. "Give me a second." He entered a few keystrokes. "Do you mind? I need to type my password."

Cash and Hodge turned around.

"Okay, I've got it pulled up. What do you want to see?"

They peered over his shoulder. Cash said, "Starting three years ago, let's see your bank statements from every fourth month."

"I made a separate account for the drums," Kincaid said. "It's pretty much drained now, but this will show you how I saved up to buy the kit." He pulled up the first statement. "See there?" he said, pointing with the mouse. "A hundred bucks that month."

Cash studied the statement. The only transaction for the month was a deposit of a hundred dollars. There were no withdrawals. "Let's see another."

Kincaid typed. "This month wasn't so good. Only twenty-five bucks."

Again, the deposit was the only transaction on the statement. "Keep going," said Cash.

Kincaid took them up through the present, jumping ahead four months each time. Except for the dollar amount of the deposits, each statement was identical, with only a single deposit and no withdrawals. As he opened the most recent statement, Kincaid said, "This is where I took out the money to buy the drums." Cash noted a withdrawal of five thousand dollars, which left just under two hundred in the account.

Cash was satisfied that the bank records backed Kincaid's story. One deposit a month ranging from twenty-five to a hundred ninety-five dollars. Then a single withdrawal of five thousand dollars when he bought the drum set. Now Cash wanted to see what Kincaid could tell him about his grandfather. "Let's go talk."

Kincaid closed the laptop and led them back to the den. Once everyone was seated, Cash said, "All right, I can see you were saving money for the drums. And we know you couldn't have been at the robbery scene."

"So, I'm in the clear?"

Cash held up a finger. "Probably."

"Probably? What the hell does that mean?"

"It means we have a few more questions," said Hodge.

"Son of a bitch," Kincaid said, exasperated. "What now?"

Cash said, "We know your grandfather was once Dieter Bergheim's business partner. Were you aware of that?"

"Yeah, I knew that. I'm the one who told him the old man was in Avonwick."

"Then why did you tell me earlier that you didn't know who Dieter was?"

"What are you talking about?"

"I asked you if you hung a TV for Dieter Bergheim and you said, 'Who's that?'"

"Yeah, well, I guess I forgot."

"Okay," said Cash, "you forgot. What can you tell us about your grandfather?"

"What do you want to know?"

"I want to know if he shot Emil Bergheim and stole a million dollars from his brother."

Kincaid reared back in his seat. "Not that I know of. Doesn't sound like something he'd do."

"How did he get back from Pinyon the night of your gig at Winkler's?"

"Drove, I guess."

"Why didn't he ride with you?" Cash asked.

"There was no room in my car. Too many drums."

"Why did he go to Pinyon in the first place?"

Kincaid brushed a lock of hair out of his eyes. "I wondered the same thing. My mother had cancer. Before she died, she told me she would ask him to keep an eye on me. I guess that's what he's doing."

When Cash paused to plan his next question, Hodge jumped in. "Did your grandfather know Slater Cobb?"

"Not that I know of. You could ask Willa."

Hodge gave Cash a look that begged for help.

"She's dead," said Cash.

Kincaid's head jerked up. Was that genuine surprise? Or was he merely a good actor? "What are you talking about?"

"We found her dead in her house. Beaten and shot. Whoever did it tried to make it look like a suicide."

Kincaid opened his mouth but no words came out. He shook his head and finally managed to say, "Who did it?"

"You tell us."

"How should I know?"

"Let me put it this way, Eddie. You work at Dieter Bergheim's retirement home. You told your grandfather that Dieter lives there. He goes to see his old business partner because he thinks he pulled a fast one on him. Not long after that, two men, one of whom is your pal Slater Cobb, steal Dieter's money. But Cobb's partner gets greedy and kills him. Later he kills Cobb's girlfriend Willa, presumably to keep her quiet. We found the gun that killed Cobb in your car. Since you couldn't have been at the robbery, we have to assume the killer planted it there. Or maybe you were hiding it for him. It's hard not to see Grandpa as the killer and you, at the very least, trying to help him hide that fact."

As Cash spoke, Kincaid sank lower and lower in his chair. When he could go no lower without slumping to the floor, he said, "All I can tell you is, I don't know who robbed old man Bergheim, I don't know who shot Slater, I don't know who killed Willa, and I don't have any fucking idea how that gun ended up in my car." He closed his eyes. "Are you going to arrest me?"

Cash stood up. Hodge followed suit. Cash said, "No, Eddie, I'm not. But if you're hiding something, if you're protecting your grandfather, we're going to find out. Then we'll be back with handcuffs."

***

Cash asked Hodge to drive so he could check in with Frida. When his call went to voice-mail, he hung up and called again. She answered on the first ring. "This better be an emergency," she said. "It's seven-thirty."

"What, you have a hot date?"

"Yeah, with Netflix, a glass of wine, and Buster the cat. What do you want?"

"I was wondering if you checked the magazine of the gun we found in Kincaid's car."

"I was going to find you first thing tomorrow," she said. "I pulled a print from one of the bullets. It doesn't belong to Kincaid."

Cash said, "Maybe it's his grandfather's."

"Why would it be his?"

He explained Roy Baxter's connection to Dieter Bergheim. "He thinks Dieter cheated him."

"Can we get his fingerprints for comparison?" Frida asked.

"We'd probably need a warrant. He's hiring a lawyer."

"I could check with the State Identification Bureau."

"Don't bother. I'll do it in the morning. You can finish your movie. What are you watching?"

"Game of Thrones."

"You know everyone dies, right?"

"Good night, Cash."

Chapter Thirty-One

Cash awoke the next morning eager to set Clint Morgan straight. He inhaled a granola bar and chocolate milk for breakfast and drove to Morgan's house, located on an unfenced property a mile south of town. He cringed at seeing dozens of cedar saplings sprouting up in the field leading up to the one-story house. Left unchecked, the cedar would eventually kill off the grass.

Morgan's car, a late-model Ford Ranger pickup, was parked on a cracked patch of asphalt at the end of the drive. Cash parked behind it and checked the load in his Ruger. He didn't expect trouble, but Morgan's recent behavior painted him as a loose cannon. And no one would be happy to see a county deputy at their door at seven a.m.

Cash rang the doorbell. He stepped to one side and waited. When no one answered, he banged the door hard enough to rattle it in its frame.

"Who's out there?" Morgan shouted from within.

"It's Adam Cash with the sheriff's office."

The door opened, exposing a scowling Morgan wearing only a pair of boxers. "Cash! What's up?"

Cash stepped past him into a disheveled living room.

"What's going on?" Morgan said.

"Sit down."

"Not until you tell me what you're doing here."

"I said, sit down."

Morgan grunted and shuffled to an easy chair. "Okay, I'm sitting."

"I'm here to tell you that it's over with Bernadette."

"I guess you heard about yesterday."

"'I did. Bernadette says you hit her."

Morgan covered his face with his hands. "I did. I feel terrible. I wish there was some way I could take it back."

"You're lucky I'm not here to arrest you. Bernadette asked me not to."

"You'd have every right to. God, I can't believe I did that." He looked up. "Will you tell her I'm sorry?"

A female voice interrupted from behind Cash. "Who's Bernadette?"

Cash turned to see a sleepy-eyed woman with stringy hair wearing a knee-length T-shirt.

"Nothing, baby," said Morgan. "Go back to bed."

Cash headed to the door. "Remember, leave her alone. Don't let me hear that you're trying to patch things up with her. And don't hit any more women."

The woman said, "Clint? Who did you hit?"

"I'll tell you later," said Morgan.

Cash felt sorry for her. "You can do better."

***

Coffee sloshed over the side of his cup as he set it next to the laptop in the department conference room. Cleaning up the mess could wait. He was anxious to find fingerprints for Roy Baxter, a.k.a. Rick Smith.

It occurred to him that Baxter might have a criminal record in California. He called the state Department of Justice and, after being passed around to several offices, learned about the California Law Enforcement Telecommunications System, a statewide computer network that allowed law enforcement agencies to access information about individuals with a record in the criminal justice system. "Could you look up a name for me?" he asked a polite woman on the other end.

"What department did you say you're with?"

"The sheriff's department in Noble County, Texas."

"Are you there now?"

"Yes."

"I'll call you back."

"Why?"

"Policy."

The line went dead. Cash reckoned the policy was in place to guard against unauthorized access to the system. He pocketed his phone and rummaged in the cabinets for paper towels to clean up the spilled coffee. As he wiped the counter, Vicky appeared in the doorway. "There you are," she said. "Some lady from California wants to talk to you."

Cash pointed at the office phone by the laptop. "Put her through."

Vicky left, and then the phone rang. "This is Deputy Cash."

"This is Barbara. I believe we were just speaking."

"Yes. Can you check that name for me?"

"Of course."

Cash gave her what he had on Rick Smith.

"I'm going to put you on hold," she said.

He wadded up the soggy paper towel and tossed it at the trash can. It missed. "Damn it."

"Pardon me?"

"Sorry, ma'am, I thought I was still on hold."

She cleared her throat. "The man you're interested in has been arrested once for marijuana possession, back in 1987. He spent a month in jail and paid a fine."

Bingo. "Would it be possible to get a copy of his fingerprints?"

"Those would be at the State Identification Bureau. Hold on, I'll transfer you."

It took three more phone transfers for Cash to reach a person who could help him. "Yes, we have that record," the man said. "I can email it to you."

Cash gave him his work email address, thanked him, and ended the call. "Okay, Roy," he said to himself, "we'll find out if you're blowing smoke up my ass."

***

While Cash was fighting his way through the California Department of Justice's phone maze, Roy Baxter was halfway through his third beer of the morning. Damn that kid Cash. If Baxter had known he was a deputy, he would have steered clear of him at the dance hall that night.

He dug his phone out of a pocket and made a call.

A man answered. "What is it?" He sounded irritated.

"Guess who came to see me last night."

"Stop fucking around. Just tell me."

"Adam Cash." When there was no response, Baxter added, "He's a Noble County deputy."

"I know who he is. Everybody around here knows who he is."

"We need to talk."

"So, talk."

"Not on the phone. In person."

"Forget it."

The man said nothing more, but Baxter decided to wait him out. This wasn't up for negotiation.

"All right. I can be there by five."

"Bring the money."

"No problem."

Chapter Thirty-Two

Silas Dudek sucked the last few drops of beer from the bottle and set it on the bar. He wanted another, but that asshole Reggie, owner of the Tall Tale Tavern on County Road 245, was charging five bucks a pop now. Couple that with the ten-dollar hamburger on Silas's plate, and he was already looking at a real splurge.

Silas stared at the neon Bud Light sign behind the bar and wondered what he would do if he won the lottery. First off, he'd buy a big house on at least a hundred acres. That amount of land should hold enough deer for him to take all he wanted each fall. Hell, he could run a deer lease on the property to bring in extra cash. That would be like free money.

Next, he'd get himself the biggest fishing boat he could find. He'd keep it on the Twin Buttes reservoir near San Angelo. He'd invite all his friends to join him every weekend for a day of beer and sunshine. No women, though. Too much drama.

Finally, he'd buy his girlfriend a new Lexus GX 550 Premium with all the features. That ought to keep the whiny bitch off his back. Maybe she'd take it on road trips with her friends. With her out of town, he and Savannah Parker could bang each other whenever they wanted. No more sneaking out of the house at three a.m. for a quickie in her beat-up Mazda.

Silas looked around the saloon at its plastic chairs, rickety tables, and dilapidated pool table and sighed. He'd never win the lottery. To win he'd have to buy a lottery ticket, and if he didn't have five dollars for a beer, he certainly had no business throwing money at a pipe dream. Still, his lot was about to improve, enough that he could buy a second beer. At least, if his friend was telling the truth.

Reggie hefted his enormous frame off a stool behind the bar and waddled over to Silas. "Get you another?"

"I wish."

"I'll buy him a beer," a man's voice said behind Silas. "Bring me one, too."

Silas spun around on his stool and smiled. "Hey, bro. Good to see you. Where have you been keeping yourself?"

"Oh, here and there," the man said. He held a fat manila envelope, which he set on the bar as he took the stool next to Silas.

Reggie plopped two beers on the bar. Silas raised one in salute and said, "Thanks."

"Any time, Hooch. What have you been up to?"

Silas winced. He hated that nickname. "Don't call me that. I hear it enough from my bitch of a girlfriend."

The man threw up his hands. "Sorry. No offense intended."

"Forget it," said Silas. "Anyway, I've mostly been sitting on my ass. I got laid off six months ago."

"I'm sorry to hear that. Things must be tight for you."

"Tight?" Silas rolled his eyes. "Hell, I can't afford to flush the crapper more than once a day."

The man laughed. "I could help you with that."

"Flushing my crapper?"

"Don't be an idiot." The man's smile was gone. He stood up. "Bring your beer."

Silas followed him to a table on the far side of the room. Only one other table in the place was occupied, and they sat well away from that.

"All right," said Silas, "What's the big secret?"

"I've got a job that needs doing."

"Speak up. I can hardly hear you."

"Then lean in closer, dumbass. Nobody else can know about this."

"I don't like the sound of that."

"How do you like the sound of twenty-five thousand dollars?"

Silas answered by taking a long pull from his bottle. "I like it fine. I also think you're full of shit. We never came close to that kind of money."

"That's because we were setting our sights too low. This one brings us into the big time," the man said. He slid the envelope across the table. "Have a look in there."

Silas picked it up. What the hell was going on? He peeked inside the envelope. "Holy shit. How much is that?"

"Ten thousand."

"Ten thousand! For real?"

"Keep it down, would you? Yes, it's for real. Like I told you, we're moving up to the majors."

Silas eyed the money. It was more than he had ever seen in his life. It wouldn't make him rich, but it would certainly lift him from the dirt of the poor. But then his eyes narrowed. The offer was too good to be true. "What would I have to do for it?"

"Nothing all that different from what we've done before."

"I ain't robbing no more liquor stores."

"I'm not asking you to. But what's the big deal? We were never caught."

"Getting shot at ain't my idea of a good time."

The man grabbed Silas's arm. "Look, dude, we go back a long way. You've always come through for me. You're good at this shit."

Silas straightened, puffed up by the compliment. "What's the job?"

"It's simple. I've got a problem. I need you to make it go away."

"What problem?"

"His name is Adam Cash. He lives in Noble County."

"You want me to get rid of a guy? You mean, like make him leave town?"

"No. Something more permanent."

Silas gulped.

"Is that a problem?" The man tapped the envelope. "Once he's gone, there's a lot more money to be had. This isn't even half of what you'd get."

Silas took a deep breath. Sure, he'd roughed people up before. He'd even put a guy in the hospital once. But he'd never intentionally killed a man. Of course, he'd never been offered so much money, either. "Fifty thousand," he said. "And I want half of it up front."

"You drive a hard bargain, Hoo—I mean, Silas. Fifty thousand it is."

This was too easy. "Where's this money coming from?"

"You know how we always talked about finding that one big score? The one that would put us on easy street?"

"Yeah."

"Well, this is it." He took a long pull from his beer. "If you play your cards right, that is."

Silas resisted the urge to perform a fist pump. "Okay, you've convinced me. How do I find this guy?"

The man smiled. "That won't be hard. He works for the Noble County sheriff's department."

"He's a cop? He's a fucking cop?"

"No, he's a deputy."

"What's the difference? No way, man."

The man pressed his lips into a thin line. "I can't believe I'm saying this, but I'll give you a hundred thousand dollars."

A hundred thousand bucks? That would bring him a helluva nice boat with enough money left over to buy his girlfriend a new car. Maybe not the Lexus, but something that would get him back into the house. "What's his name again?"

***

"So you've got squat."

Cash held up a slice of tomato and Canadian bacon pizza. He didn't need Steve to remind him that his investigation was stuck. "Your pizza isn't good enough for me to listen to your insults."

Steve shrugged and leaned on the bar. The lunch rush was over and the Packsaddle wasn't busy, so he had time to shoot the breeze with his friend. "Then I guess you're here for the beer."

"Don't kid yourself," Cash said with a snort. "I haven't forgotten that avocado-flavored crap."

Steve filled a sample glass from one of the taps and gave it to Cash. "Okay, so that one didn't fly. How about Jalapeño Jeaven? Heaven is spelled with a J but pronounced like an H."

"I know how Spanish pronunciation works. And you need to hire a marketer to name your beers." He tasted the sample. "I'll admit, that's not bad."

"Sort of tickles the tongue, doesn't it?"

Cash's phone rang and he glanced at the screen. "I've got to take this."

Steve took the hint and wandered off. Cash said, "Hey, Reid."

"When are you going to quit harassing our drummer?" His brother sounded pissed.

"I'm not harassing anybody."

"Really? First, you sneak into our practice session to steal his fingerprints. Then you accuse him of robbery and murder. Then, even when you find proof that he didn't do it, you badger him with more questions. Enough is enough!"

Cash forced himself to take a deep breath. Hard experience had taught him that reacting to his little brother's snits in kind was counterproductive. "First, I didn't sneak into your practice. You invited me. Second, nothing I've done has been unreasonable. Hell, Reid, we're trying to find a killer. Even now that I know Eddie wasn't at the scene of the robbery, I can't rule out his involvement in the planning."

"What, you think he was in on it?"

"It's possible."

"Bullshit."

"We'll have to agree to disagree."

"The only thing I'll agree with is that you're being a dick. Just leave him alone."

Now it was Cash's turn to be angry. "I'm just doing my job."

"Yeah? Well, you suck at it."

The line went dead. Cash fought back an urge to strangle a certain someone who luckily wasn't present. Right about now he could use a couple of pints of Jalapeño Jeaven.

Cash's phone rang again. "I hope you have good news for me," he said.

"Sorry, no," Frida said. "The print on that bullet doesn't match Rick Smith."

He sighed. "Okay, thanks." Now he really wanted that beer.

Chapter Thirty-Three

Baxter pulled his eyes away from the TV to glance at his watch. Five-twenty. That son of a bitch Hooch better show up.

He was watching one of his favorite movies, *The Usual Suspects*, for the umpteenth time. Despite knowing all the twists, he still found the plot compelling. A group of con men outplayed by the master con man of them all. A ruthless bastard, too. The first time he saw the film years ago, the finale blew his mind.

Baxter heard a car pull into the driveway and got up to look out the window. An aqua blue Prius. That was a surprise. He would have expected a pickup truck from that redneck.

The man he knew only as Hooch got out on the passenger side and shut the door. In his hand was a large duffel bag that Baxter recognized as the one at the robbery. The Prius backed out of the driveway and drove away. Must have been an Uber ride. Weird.

After letting his visitor inside, Baxter got right to the point. "You guys really fucked me over. Nobody was supposed to get hurt. Now I've got a deputy sheriff breathing down my neck, asking all kinds of questions."

"If nobody was supposed to get hurt, then why did we bring guns?"

"You guys brought guns. Not me. You weren't supposed to start a shoot-out."

"How do you know we started anything? Your ass was back on the road safe and sound in your fucking Civic."

"It's an Accord."

"Who gives a shit?"

Fighting the urge to shout, Baxter said, "Sit down."

They sat, Baxter in his favorite recliner, Hooch on the couch.

Baxter noticed something odd. "Why are you wearing gloves?"

"To keep my fingerprints off of this." He nudged the bag with his foot.

"Is the money in there?"

"What do you think?"

"Have you counted it?"

"Of course."

Baxter waited but the guy didn't elaborate. "Goddamn it, Hooch. How much is in there?" he said.

"About a million and a half," said Hooch. He pulled a fistful of wrapped candies from his pocket and held one up. "Want one?"

"No, thanks."

"Suit yourself."

"Getting back to the subject at hand, that's more than I thought there'd be. And that was only half?"

Hooch laughed. "Are you fucking kidding me? No way I'm leaving that much money behind."

"You took it all? You weren't supposed to do that."

"Why the hell not?"

"Because it's not fair to Dieter. I just wanted my share."

"What the fuck do I care about Dieter? And speaking of shares, I'm keeping Cobb's."

"Shouldn't the girlfriend get that?"

"She's dead."

Baxter stiffened. "What do you mean, she's dead? What the hell happened?"

"Somebody broke into her house and killed her. It was in the paper."

"Was it you?"

"Maybe you shouldn't ask me that."

Shit, it was him. Two deaths now. Baxter felt sick. This was not a guy to argue with. "All right, you can have her share. That makes a hundred grand for you."

"And one point four million for you."

"If you say so."

Baxter ran his fingers through his hair. "How *did* the shooting start?"

Hooch looked away. Baxter interpreted the move to mean a lie was coming. "Cobb was an idiot. He made all kinds of noise. Some old guy came out and saw us. It was the same guy that yelled at us the first time. This time he didn't say anything, he just started blazing away. Cobb shot back and hit him, but not before taking a slug. He made it across the creek, but that was as far as he got. I would have brought him with me, but he was dead."

"Two deaths," Baxter said, shaking his head. "They were just kids."

"Yeah, well, shit happens."

Baxter leaned over and pulled the duffel bag over. "Before we divvy this up, tell me why you put that gun in Eddie's car."

"Do I have to spell it out for you? I wanted to confuse anyone investigating the robbery. Like that deputy."

"Eddie is my grandson."

"Like I don't know that."

"You could have landed him in prison. The only thing that saved him was the tape at the gas station he stopped at on the way back to Austin."

Hooch shrugged. "No harm, no foul then, right?"

The nerve of this guy. "All right, let's have a look at this money."

As Baxter unzipped the bag, Hooch slipped a crescent wrench out of his back pocket. He stood up and watched Baxter lean over the bag.

"What the hell is this?" Baxter said. "There's no money in here."

The blow caught Baxter behind the right ear. He emitted a soft moan and slumped to the carpet. Hooch swung the wrench twice more, just to be sure. He flipped the limp body over and watched for signs of life. Seeing none, he zipped up the duffel bag and took it out onto the porch. Had he touched anything? It didn't matter, he was wearing gloves. After checking again for a security camera on the porch and again seeing nothing, he used his phone to summon an Uber. His foresight in keeping his car off any cameras in the neighborhood gave him a feeling of smug satisfaction. The Uber would take him to his car at Hula Hut on Lake Austin. He'd drop Willa's phone in the lake, grab a bite to eat, and head back to Pinyon a wealthy man.

Chapter Thirty-Four

Cash lay awake for most of the night after arguing with Reid. He gave up on sleep at four-thirty, wandered into the den, and fooled around on his guitar until almost six. Time to put the instrument away, get his butt off the couch, and go to work. He was kidding himself if he thought he'd ever be good enough to sit in with Reid's band. Then he remembered that, even if he was, Reid probably wouldn't let him do it. He hadn't forgotten the venom in his brother's voice during their last phone conversation.

The buzzing of his phone in the bedroom interrupted his thoughts. He hurried to answer it. It was Reid. "Eddie's grandfather is dead," his brother said.

In his sleepy state, Cash didn't immediately process the statement. "Did you hear me?" Reid said, urgency in his voice. "Somebody killed Eddie's grandfather."

"Whoa, whoa," said Cash. "What are you talking about?"

"Eddie just called. He said he couldn't make our practice session later today because his grandfather was murdered."

Cash's head cleared. Roy Baxter was dead? "Where did this happen?"

"In his house."

"Eddie's?

"No, his grandfather's, dumbass. Eddie went over there last night to shoot the shit. He found him on the floor. Somebody bashed his head in."

Cash ignored the "dumbass" jab. His brother was shocked and upset. "What else do you know?"

"Just that Eddie needs a few days to figure things out. He said after the police arrived last night, two detectives questioned him."

"Did he tell you their names?"

"No."

"Okay, relax. I'll call APD and find out who they are." APD was the Austin Police Department.

"What then?"

"I'll do my job. You know, the one I suck at."

Reid took his time answering. "I'm sorry I said that last night. You don't suck at anything."

"Except for the guitar."

After ending the call, Cash thought over his next step. Recalling the second vehicle they heard but didn't see on Emil Bergheim's game camera footage, he wondered if the driver had been Baxter. The murder would make sense if Slater Cobb's killer was trying to cover his tracks. Or maybe the killer had gotten greedy and decided partners were superfluous. Maybe that's why Cobb was dead. And Cash still suspected Willa Dearborn's involvement. Is that what had gotten her killed?

Cash called Santos. A sleepy woman answered. "Hello."

"Hey, Katrina." It was Santos's wife. "Sorry to wake you. Is Gabe up yet?"

"He's in the shower. Can I have him call you?"

"Yeah, thanks."

Cash went to the kitchen to make breakfast. Before he could decide on what he wanted, his phone rang.

"We've got another murder on our hands," Cash told his boss.

"Shit. Who's the victim?"

"Roy Baxter. Remember, he's the guy—"

"That used to be Rick Smith. I remember."

"Kincaid found the body at Baxter's house in Austin. APD is investigating."

Santos said, "We need to compare notes with them."

"I'll call and find out who's on the case."

"Let me talk to Hodge first. Maybe she knows somebody from her time with the department." She had spent two years with the APD before taking the job in Pinyon.

"Okay. I'll see you at the office."

***

Cash entered the conference room to find Conrad, Hodge, and Santos waiting for him. Four boxes of donuts were spread out on the table.

"Holy cow," said Cash. "Are we feeding the whole town?"

Hodge said, "Deke brought them."

Conrad swallowed the last of one donut and reached for another. "I'd rather have too many than too few."

"With you around, the day we have too many will never come."

"Keep it up and I won't give you any."

Hodge took a donut. "Try and stop me."

"Are we gonna talk about the case or argue about donuts?" Santos said. That got everyone's attention. He continued. "An APD detective Hodge knows was able to give us the name of the lead detective investigating Baxter's murder. His name is Henry Stallings. I haven't been able to reach him yet but did leave a voicemail."

"That's three deaths now," said Cash. "Cobb, who we know was involved in the robbery; Willa Dearborn, Cobb's girlfriend; and Roy Baxter, who was Dieter Bergheim's business partner. I see a pattern here."

Everyone murmured in agreement. Conrad said, "Don't forget about the gun in Eddie Kincaid's car."

"I haven't. But I don't see him killing his grandfather. And my brother insists that he's innocent."

"Is your brother a detective now?"

"No," said Cash. "But he knows Kincaid and we don't. And he's not an idiot."

"He's not a cop, either."

"I guess you're smarter than him?"

"Settle down, guys," said Santos. "Cash, I agree we should keep your brother's opinion in mind. But Deke has a point. He's biased."

Santos was right, but Cash didn't want to admit it. "How about if I go to Austin to question Kincaid again?"

"Don't. That would just piss Stallings off and we need him on our side."

Cash conceded the point. The boss was right again.

Santos said, "Does anyone have anything more on Dearborn or Cobb?"

"I spoke with the people at Speedy Chicken," Hodge said. "Nobody knew shit. And that manager is a lecher."

"Did he hit on you?" Conrad asked.

'Yeah. Gross."

Santos shifted his attention to Cash. "What about Aiden Camp?"

"He denies everything," said Cash.

"Do you believe him?"

"We can't cross him off the list, but I have to admit there's nothing to suggest his involvement other than the fact that he lived with Cobb."

Santos waited, but nobody had anything to add. "All right. I'll let you know when I hear from Detective Stallings."

Chapter Thirty-Five

Santos had told Cash not to go to Austin to question Eddie Kincaid, but he hadn't said anything about speaking to him on the phone. Cash therefore felt only a little guilty when he pulled up the number and hit the call button. After four rings it went to voicemail. Cash ended the call and tried again with the same result.

He looked up the number for Avonwick, hoping to catch Kincaid at work. A receptionist put him on hold for what felt like an eternity before telling him Kincaid wouldn't be in that day. "There's been a death in his family."

Temporarily stymied, Cash drove to the Firewheel. Edie was working the breakfast shift today. Maybe it would be slow and she could steal away for a quick chat. He wanted to continue their discussion from the other evening.

No luck, the place was packed. Cash saw Edie rush out of the kitchen carrying a tray loaded with burger plates. He tried to catch her eye but her focus was on her customers. Sighing, he walked over to the cooler and grabbed a carton of chocolate milk. He paid for it, giving the clerk an extra dollar for the newspaper he took from the stack.

He spread the paper out on a table and opened the milk carton. "Murder Comes to Noble County," read the page one headline. An article about the robbery at Bergheim's was coupled with the deaths of Slater Cobb and Willa Dearborn. Cash rolled his eyes when he saw himself referred to as "the well-known Deputy Adam Cash."

His phone rang. He pressed it to his ear. "This is Cash."

"This is Santos. I spoke with Stallings. He said they don't have much to go on."

"Nothing at all?"

"Nothing he feels is important. He and his partner are going door to door to see what the neighbors know."

"Is he going to call you back after that?"

"He said he would."

"Well, crap," said Cash. "I guess all we can do is wait."

"It shouldn't be too long. I'm meeting with the commissioners in ten minutes to discuss funding for another deputy. I gave Stallings your number."

Cash wished Santos luck in the meeting and returned to his newspaper. While reading about the Pinyon Javelinas' victory over Ozona in the state high school baseball playoffs, he received another call. It was Detective Stallings.

"What have you got so far?" Cash asked after introducing himself.

"Slow down," Stallings said. "First tell me why you were interested in this guy."

Cash explained about the robbery and Baxter's connection to Dieter Bergheim. "He hated the guy. He thinks Bergheim cheated him out of a lot of money."

"Your sheriff told me you'd send me everything you have on that case."

"I can do that. Now tell me what you know about Baxter's murder."

"That won't take long," Stallings said, "because we don't have much. Somebody caved his skull in with a blunt object. We didn't find the murder weapon in the house or any fingerprints that can't be explained."

"That's it?"

"He didn't die right away."

"How do you know that?" Cash said.

"We found him in a pool of blood. He dipped his finger in it and wrote the word 'Hooch' on the floor. Any idea what that means?"

Cash knew exactly what that meant. "It's a name. Slater Cobb's roommate said some guy named Hooch had come around a couple of times. He didn't know a last name."

"Looks like we need to find this guy. Hey, there's one other thing. I don't know if it's related, but we found a bunch of candy wrappers on the coffee table."

"Were they Jolly Ranchers?"

"How did you know that?"

Cash told him about the wrappers he found at the robbery scene, ending with, "Did you look in the kitchen for the bag?"

"Yes. Didn't find one."

"Our sheriff said you were questioning the neighbors."

"That's right. All they could tell us is that the guy arrived in an Uber."

"How do they know that?" Cash asked.

"Maybe not an Uber, but a rideshare. He got out of a Prius from the back seat and then it drove away."

"Did they see the guy leave later?"

"No."

Cash said, "How about a description?"

"He's tall."

"That's it?"

"What can I say? People are lousy observers. Anyway, I'll put in a request to Uber for information about that ride. If we're lucky, they'll be able to tell us the origin point and identity of the person booking it."

Cash said, "What about the other ride-share companies in Austin?"

"I'll check those, too."

"How about if I lighten your load and do it for you?"

Stallings stopped to consider that. "I'm tempted. We've been slammed the past couple of days and two of our guys are out with Covid."

"So let me help you."

"You'll call me as soon as you learn anything?"

"That's a promise."

"I'll hold you to that."

The conversation with Stallings gave Cash fresh hope. Surely, one of the ride-share companies would have a record. That could lead them directly to the killer. On the other hand, what if somebody paid for the ride on behalf of the perpetrator? Or used a fake profile on the app?

Cash drove back to the station and fired up the conference room laptop. An internet search brought up several rideshare options in Austin. Uber and Lyft dominated the market, but several smaller companies also serviced the area.

Since Uber held the lion's share of the Austin market, Cash started there. The company's U.S. base was in San Francisco. Its website described a twenty-four-hour "dedicated team that responds to requests for information from law enforcement and public health officials." Requests could be made through an online portal intended solely for law enforcement agencies.

Cash navigated through the portal, first by attesting that he met the definition of a law enforcement officer, and next by filling out a form detailing the information he was after. After checking the box that said "Emergency request," he hit "Send." A box popped up promising a response "as soon as possible." He hoped that Uber's "as soon as possible" was sooner than that of most government agencies.

***

Over the next hour, Cash filed information requests with Lyft and the smaller companies. With no other solid lead to pursue, he returned to Willa Dearborn's neighborhood to knock on doors. He found more people at home this time, but none offered anything helpful.

He got similar results in Slater Cobb's neighborhood. One person remembered Cobb but didn't know anything about his associates. The two others he found at home claimed not to know him. He tried Will Anson again, but his knock at the door went unanswered. Nor was Aiden Camp at home.

Cash returned to the station to think. Armed intruders stole over a million dollars in cash from Dieter Bergheim. One of the robbers shot and killed his partner. The dead man's girlfriend was killed later. A third person who might have been Dieter's one-time business partner had been at the scene but wasn't picked up by the game camera. Last night Baxter became the latest murder victim.

Cash's gut told him the same person had committed all three murders. No other explanation made sense. And the killer was smart, given the lack of definitive clues left at the murder scenes. Figuring that into the equation damaged Cash's confidence that the rideshare angle would pan out. Surely the killer knew there would be a record of the ride. He wouldn't have been stupid enough to book it using his own phone. Still, maybe they'd get lucky. Criminals did stupid things all the time.

He recalled the Jolly Rancher wrappers at the robbery scene and in Baxter's den. It was a common candy. The killer hadn't necessarily left them, but what if he had? Maybe he wasn't as smart as Cash was giving him credit for. The thought gave him hope.

Cash tried Kincaid again. This time the drummer answered. "Hel-lo." He sounded like he might have been crying.

"This is Adam Cash, Eddie. I—"

"What the fuck, man? Are you ever going to leave me alone? My grandfather's dead"—his voice cracked—"and I don't have time for this shit."

"I'm sorry, Eddie. I liked your grandfather." No point in mentioning his suspicion that Baxter was involved in the robbery. "I'm going to do everything I can to find his killer."

Kincaid didn't respond.

"Did your grandfather like Jolly Rancher candy?"

"What the hell kind of question is that?"

"I can't tell you the reason, but it's relevant to his murder."

That seemed to change Kincaid's attitude. "No. He liked chocolate. He always said if it didn't have chocolate in it, you might as well give it to the dog."

Chapter Thirty-Six

Chez Abby was full tonight. When Cash called to make the reservation, he was told he got the last available table. When the woman asked him if he would be celebrating a special occasion, he told her no. But it felt special to him. Any night out with Edie felt special.

Looking fabulous in a sleeveless green A-line dress, Edie handed her menu to the server, a young woman named Candy, and said, "I'll have the crab cakes."

Cash winced. Only the ribeye steak was more expensive. He looked over the menu again. He had been planning on ordering the pork chop, but there were cheaper options. "Bring me the chicken fried steak. No gravy."

"What about the potatoes?" Candy asked.

"Yeah, gravy on the potatoes, none on the meat."

After Candy left, Edie smiled. "There are other things to eat in the world besides chicken fried steak."

"I like chicken fried steak."

"I know. With ketchup."

"Ketchup is just red gravy."

She laughed, a ringing crystal sound that shot straight to his heart.

"You look beautiful tonight," he said.

She took his hand. "Does that mean I don't look beautiful on other nights?"

"What I meant to say," he said, stroking her thumb, "was you look more beautiful tonight than usual. And your usual is stunning."

"Good recovery." She wrapped his hands in hers. "Guess what? I got into UT."

Before Cash could react, Candy returned with the wine. "Here you go. Sauvignon blanc from the finest vineyard in Noble County."

Cash started to make a joke about Noble County vineyards but noticed she had said it without irony. He watched her pour a sample and took the glass from her hand, which he then handed to Edie. "You try it. I'm more of a beer and chocolate milk guy."

She sipped. "Nice."

Candy poured two glasses and left. Edie said, "So, UT."

Cash forced a smile. "Congratulations."

"Now I have to decide between there and Tech."

"Surely you wouldn't pick Lubbock over Austin."

"I was joking. UT it is."

Cash felt chilled, and not from the wine. "When will you move, do you think?"

"The semester starts in three weeks. I'd like to be settled a few days ahead of time."

"What about your lease here?"

"I gave my notice two weeks ago."

He raised an eyebrow. It was just like Edie to have confidence enough to cancel her lease before being accepted into a nursing school. "That was gutsy."

She said nothing, just waited to see what else he had to say.

"Have you looked for a place in Austin yet?" he asked.

"No. I'll go this weekend."

Cash sipped his wine to buy himself time to think. He didn't want to say anything stupid. Or provocative. The last thing he wanted was to spoil an expensive meal with a fight.

Edie said, "You look like your cat just died."

"I don't have a cat."

"I know. It's just an expression. What's eating you?"

What's eating him? Wasn't it obvious? She was leaving town. "I'm just trying to adjust to the idea of you not being around."

"It's not like I'm moving to China. I can visit on weekends."

"Won't you need a job? How will you support yourself?"

She studied her wineglass. "Yes, I'll need to work some. Maybe I can pick up weekend shifts at the Firewheel."

"What about Luke?"

"I could ask Julie to watch him." She locked eyes with him. "Or you could."

"Me?" he said, surprised. "I don't know anything about watching a kid."

"What's to know? You play with him, take him swimming, feed him if he's hungry ... it's not rocket science. And besides, you do have a daughter."

The idea didn't appeal to him at all. "I'll think about it."

She frowned. "Don't you want me to spend weekends in Pinyon?"

"Of course I do. I just thought I'd be seeing *you* when you did, not babysitting a five-year-old."

Edie stared past him. Butterflies fluttered in his gut. He had definitely said something stupid. Perhaps even provocative.

Edie said, "You know we come as a package, Luke and I."

Cash gulped but said nothing.

She continued. "I need the man in my life to be comfortable with my son."

Before Cash could respond, Candy arrived with their food. Cash thanked her and asked for ketchup. Smiling, she plopped a bottle on the table and said, "I had a feeling."

When Candy was gone, Cash said, "Am I that predictable?"

Edie picked up her fork. "In more ways than one."

Cash could tell by her sour expression that he had indeed spoiled the meal. "What does that mean?" he said. He was unable to hide his irritation.

"It means"—she took a bite of crab cake—"I should have known this was coming."

Chapter Thirty-Seven

After a date that could only be called tense, Cash dropped Edie at her house. She hugged him so briefly he didn't have time to hug her back. She finished it off with an air kiss. There was no flirtatious small talk, no invitation to come in for a drink. He watched her disappear through the doorway with a heavy heart.

On the drive home, he replayed the evening in his mind. He cringed at some of the things he had said. They could only be classified as childish. He knew Edie wouldn't put up with that for long. He had to spiff up his act or he'd lose her.

At home, Cash ate a late snack of peach ice cream before showering and going to bed. Sleep proved elusive. His mind raced with thoughts of the murders he was investigating. For all he knew, the killer had other victims in mind. Maybe Emil Bergheim or his brother Dieter. Maybe Eddie Kincaid. Maybe somebody he didn't know about yet. Cash had to get to the bastard first.

At two a.m. Cash got out of bed and went into the den. The hall light provided enough illumination for him to see his guitar. He picked it up and sat on the couch.

After running through all the chords he could remember, Cash tried again with "Folsom Prison Blues." This time he thought he sounded better, both with the instrument and his voice. With a little more time he just might be able to join Reid on stage.

Cash returned the guitar to its stand, leaned back on the couch, and closed his eyes. Just as he was drifting off to sleep, a noise jerked him awake. Was it a dream? No, there it was again. A scratching at the back door.

Cash retrieved his Ruger from the bedroom. He tiptoed toward the door, but before he could reach it, the door swung open a foot. A man stepped into the house, holding a gun.

"Stop right there, buddy," Cash said. "I've got a gun, too."

In a lightning move the man turned and fired. The bullet whizzed past Cash and smashed apart a floor lamp across the room. Cash fired back, but the man had disappeared. Cash raced outside and another bullet thudded into the door frame. He fired at a retreating shadow and gave chase.

The man was slow. He ran down the driveway toward a pickup parked behind Cash's Ram. Cash would be on him in seconds. The man ducked behind the Ram and fired again. Cash started to shoot back but didn't want to hit his truck. He shot into the air, causing the man to duck. This gave Cash enough time to sprint wide and flank the intruder.

Another shot from the man smashed open Cash's living room window. "Shit," Cash muttered and took aim. The man peered around the other side of the truck. "You're in my sights," Cash said. "Put the gun down."

The man spun around to shoot, but Cash hit him in the chest with two well-placed shots. The intruder fell backward and thudded into the ground. Cash ran to him and kicked his gun away. He knelt. For the first time he got a good look at the guy's face. It was a man in his forties. Cash recognized the desperation in his eyes; he had seen that same look on wounded soldiers in Afghanistan. "Who are you?" Cash said.

The man sputtered and coughed. "Call an ambulance."

"I will as soon as you tell me your name."

The man coughed again, bringing up dark froth that dribbled down his cheek. "Hooch."

Cash froze. Had he caught the killer? He recovered and said, "Hooch what?"

"Dudek."

"Is there anybody with you?"

"No. Now please get some help."

Cash gathered Dudek's gun and jogged inside to get his phone. When he returned, Dudek issued another forceful cough and lay still. Cash knelt and felt for a carotid pulse. He detected faint pulsations and called nine-one-one.

"Nine-one-one. What is your emergency?"

"This is Deputy Adam Cash with the Noble County sheriff's department. I just shot an intruder at my house."

"Shall I send an ambulance?"

Cash watched Dudek's chest for movement and saw none. He felt again for a pulse. "Don't bother."

***

"How many times since you came back to Pinyon has somebody tried to kill you?"

Santos stood next to Cash as emergency personnel loaded Hooch Dudek's corpse into an ambulance. Floodlights bathed the driveway in harsh light, casting hard shadows across the crushed gravel.

"What am I going to tell Edie?" Cash said.

"Tell her the truth. There's no fooling that woman."

"Don't I know it?" He looked at Dudek's truck parked behind his Ram. It didn't completely block the Ram from leaving, but Cash would have to drive over several yaupon holly bushes he had recently planted. Even then it would be a tight squeeze to avoid hitting his water tank. "Can we get that thing towed by morning?"

"I'll call Chuck when we're done here." Santos stuck his thumbs in his belt. "Tell me what happened."

Cash took him through the entire sequence, from not being able to sleep, to fooling around with his guitar, hearing a noise, and Dudek breaking into the house.

"And you had to shoot him, right? He gave you no choice."

"I gave him every chance, Gabe. The guy wouldn't quit."

Santos nodded. "Who is he?"

Cash held out an evidence bag containing a wallet. "I found this. Don't worry, I was wearing gloves."

Santos took the bag. "And?"

"His name is Silas Dudek, but he called himself Hooch."

Santos raised an eyebrow. "Is this our guy?"

"I'm not so sure. The killer has been described as tall, and this guy doesn't fit that description. He's from Sonora. Lives with a woman named Addie Stockdale."

"How do you know that?"

"I looked him up on the internet. I didn't learn much else. Just that he has an arrest record that includes a couple of bar fights and domestic disputes. But nothing that would suggest armed robbery."

"So, this guy who's not our killer drives all the way from Sutton County to break into your house," said Santos, scratching his chin. "Why?"

"Exactly. If he was after money, he could have picked richer targets. I think he was here to kill me."

"Why you?"

"Maybe we were closing in on the guy who hired him."

The ambulance driver climbed into his vehicle and started the engine. Santos said, "Let's go inside."

Cash led him into his den. "Want some coffee?"

"No, thanks. I'm hoping to salvage some sleep when I get home."

They sat. Santos said, "Would you like some time off?"

Cash scoffed. "What, mental health leave? Sessions with the department psychiatrist? No, thanks."

"You know we don't have resources like that. I meant, just take a couple of days to wrap your mind around the fact that you killed a man tonight."

"As you know, it's not my first time." He thought of Maurice Trahan, the Louisiana con man who had tried to kill him earlier in the year. Cash's well-aimed shot had knocked Trahan into a stock pond that was home to his pet alligator. The end was grisly. "I don't lose any sleep about defending myself. As I recall, neither do you."

"True." Before Trahan, Santos had killed fellow deputy Judd Noteboom, who had been neck-deep in a ruthless human-trafficking scheme with Deputy Sheriff Clovis Vaughn. While not technically self-defense, his intervention prevented Noteboom from shooting Cash. "And then there's Afghanistan."

Neither one of them would ever forget their time in that godforsaken land.

Cash said, "I'll check out Dudek's house tomorrow. See what I can learn from the girlfriend."

"Are you sure? I know how much you love delivering bad news. Hodge could do it."

"I want to go. The guy broke into my house and tried to kill me."

"Want to take Deke with you?"

"Deke's a good man," Cash said, "but he's best in a brawl, not an interview."

"I know what you mean," said Santos, conceding the point. "When I first started, we were called to break up a fight at the Dizzy Dillo. I had no sooner stepped into the bar when one of those yahoos decked me. Deke had him on his back and in handcuffs in nothing flat."

"What about the other guy?"

"One look from Deke and he lay down on the floor and put his hands behind his back. I'd take Deke beside me in a foxhole any day. But, yeah, he's not a thinker."

"All right. Hodge it is."

Chapter Thirty-Eight

Cash asked Hodge to drive to Sonora. He wanted time to think without being distracted by eighteen-wheelers and idiots in sports cars. How many times had he seen a BMW or Corvette race up behind him and slam on the brakes as the driver spotted the squad car? Once an inattentive driver even zoomed past him as he was pulling over another car. "I had the lights going, siren too. This guy flew by at ninety plus," he told Santos later. "He said he was getting a piece of gum and didn't see me."

"Did you give him a ticket?"

"You bet your ass I did."

Cash stole a glance at Hodge. She held her hands relaxed on the wheel while her face betrayed no sign of emotion. She drove like an automaton, which was how she seemed to engage in any activity. Whether facing down a suspect or thrashing Cash in a one-on-one game of basketball, her mien was always the same, that of a kid being forced to watch a documentary about sixteenth-century Poland. Today only her eyes showed life as they darted back and forth, monitoring the situation.

"You'd make a good soldier," Cash said.

She kept her eyes on the road. "How so?"

"Nothing flusters you."

"Why would I be flustered riding in a car with you?"

She had a point. Theirs was a relationship of equals. In the army, his seniority over her would have given him the upper hand, but the Noble County sheriff's department wasn't the army. Still, he was her mentor. Shouldn't she at least be a little nervous?

Hodge said, "I think I should ask the questions when we get there."

"Why is that?" Cash had assumed he'd take the lead. Seniority.

"Are you kidding?" she said with a scoff. "You killed the woman's husband."

Once again, she had a point. When Cash had called Addie Stockdale earlier in the morning, he hadn't told the new widow why they wanted to speak with her. He had only wanted to make sure she'd be home. The news they would deliver would not be pleasant. She would undoubtedly first ask about the cause of her husband's death. It was hard to imagine cheerful cooperation after they informed her Cash had shot him, self-defense or not.

"Fair enough," he said.

"You don't have to sound so cheerful about it."

They rode in silence through a landscape of cedar-pocked caliche. Only a few feathery streaks marred the otherwise solid blue sky. A dozen turkey buzzards clustered around a dead white-tailed deer beside the highway. The sight sent a surge of sadness through him. More death.

"There's the exit," he said, pointing.

Wordlessly, Hodge flipped on the blinker and eased the car onto the off-ramp. She followed Sonora's Crockett Street past a barbecue shack and the obligatory small-town Dairy Queen.

"Left on Poplar," said Cash.

"I remember."

As they passed the Sutton County courthouse, Cash said, "That was designed by the same guy that did the one in Pinyon. Oscar Ruffini."

Hodge grunted.

"He also designed the Old Main building at UT."

"I don't remember that one."

"It was torn down to make way for the Tower." When she didn't say anything, he added, "Do you know what the official name of the Tower was when they built it?"

"No."

"The New Main Building."

"How original."

Hodge turned left on Kieselburg and stopped in front of a rundown single-wide trailer resting on cinder blocks. Trash and nondescript rusted metal junk cluttered the weedy yard. A gutter above the door hung precariously from a strand of baling wire. To the side sat a red Chevy Cavalier with a dented passenger door.

They got out of the car. Before they reached the door a woman stepped outside. "Are you the deputies that called?"

Hodge said, "Yes, ma'am. I'm Deputy Hodge and this is Deputy Cash. We're with the Noble County Sheriff's Department."

"I'm Addie. Come on in." She disappeared back into the house, the screen door banging shut behind her.

They entered a room straight out of *Hoarders*, the reality TV show about people with an unhealthy inability to part with even the most useless of belongings. Addie sat in the only seating option not piled high with laundry or old magazines. "Sorry about the mess," she said. "I wasn't expecting company today."

Cash doubted that a week's notice would have made a difference. He caught Hodge's eye and nodded for her to begin.

Hodge said, "Ma'am, it's about your husband, Silas."

"We ain't married."

Hodge paused. "We're very sorry to inform you that he was killed last night."

Her eyes misted as she absorbed the information. "Shit, Hooch," she said softly. "What did you do?" She reached for a nearby can of snuff.

"You said he wasn't your husband."

"Naw, we talked about it but never got around to actually doing it. We weren't exactly a happy couple." She popped open the can and stuffed her cheek with tobacco. "He's really dead?"

"Yes, ma'am."

"What happened?"

Hodge told her about the break-in and ensuing gun battle, omitting any mention of Cash's role.

"I knew that son of a bitch would come to no good."

"What do you mean?"

"I mean," she said, picking up an empty Coke can and spitting into it, "he was always looking for easy money. Didn't want to work for it. He'd rather steal it. Whose house was he trying to rob?"

"That's the thing," said Hodge. "We don't think he was there to rob the house. We think he was there to kill the owner."

"And who's that?"

Hodge jerked a thumb. "Him."

Addie's eyes narrowed. "You killed him?"

Cash cleared his throat. "It was self-defense."

She pressed her lips into a thin line. Without warning, she shoved a lamp from an end table. It bounced hard off the musty carpet before rolling to a stop. "What the hell do you want from me?" she said with a sneer. "Are you here to arrest me? I didn't do nothing. And I don't know a damn thing about him breaking into your house. What that man does is his own business."

"We're not saying you did anything," Hodge said. "And I can't imagine how difficult this is for you. But we're trying to figure out why he did what he did. I was hoping you might be able to shed some light on that."

"I don't know shit. I told you I threw him out a month ago. I haven't seen much of him since."

"Where did he go after you told him to leave?"

"Hell if I know. Probably to a bar. I bet he slept in his truck."

"Who were his friends?"

Addie stared at the floor. Her demeanor softened. "He didn't really have no friends. I always felt sorry for him. When he wasn't working, he was drinking. And he wasn't working much." She looked up and caught Hodge's eye. "That's why I threw him out. I told him not to come back until he got a steady job."

"Did he?"

"Come back? I wouldn't let him."

"I mean, did he get a job?"

"Hell, no," she said with a snort. "There ain't no jobs around here."

Hodge said, "When was the last time you talked to him?"

"Last night around suppertime. He called to tell me he'd come into some real money. Ten thousand dollars. Said there'd be more coming. I thought it was bullshit. Figured he was just trying to weasel his way back into the house."

Hodge shot Cash a look. "Ma'am, we think Hooch was involved in a recent robbery in which a lot more than ten thousand dollars was stolen."

Addie fell back in her chair. "How much?"

"Over a million dollars."

"Shit." She stretched the word out into two syllables.

"That's not all," said Hodge. "He may have been responsible for several murders."

Addie opened her mouth to say something, but no words came out. When Hodge let enough time go by, Cash jumped in. "Where did he like to drink?"

Addie emitted a mirthless laugh. "Everywhere, I guess. But mostly at the Tall Tale. It's a real shithole."

Cash knew the place. When he and Steve were in high school, they had gone there to shoot pool a couple of times. The drive was worth it because the owner wasn't strict about checking IDs. Cash wondered if ownership had changed in the ten years since. "Did Hooch ever mention anyone named Dieter Bergheim?"

"No."

"What about Roy Baxter?"

She locked eyes with him. Her steely look was back. "I think y'all should go. It's one thing to waltz in here and tell me my boyfriend is dead. It's quite another to be put under the third degree about it by his murderer."

"Ma'am, I—"

Hodge cut Cash off. "Thank you, Addie. We'll let you grieve in peace."

***

When they left Addie Stockdale's trailer, Hodge headed toward the driver's side of the squad car, but Cash beat her to it. She froze momentarily before circling the vehicle to climb into the passenger seat.

"I've been to the Tall Tale Tavern," said Cash. "And she's right. It's a real shithole."

Hodge grunted.

"My friend Steve and I used to go there in high school because the owner didn't check IDs."

She grunted again.

"Is something wrong?"

A pregnant silence followed. Cash could see she was upset. He just didn't know why.

Hodge said, "I thought you were going to let me do the talking."

"What do you mean? I did."

"You did at first. You took over at the end."

He opened his mouth to speak but shut it again. Had he taken over? He was just asking logical questions. Questions that she hadn't asked. "I was just trying to figure out his possible involvement in the robbery."

"As was I."

"But you hadn't asked those questions."

"I hadn't asked those questions *yet*. You didn't give me a chance."

"You could have done so when I finished."

"I don't know if you noticed, but she shut things down in no uncertain terms. For precisely the reason I warned you about."

Cash took a deep breath to keep from snapping at her. She had never spoken this aggressively to him. But her toughness and willingness to stand her ground was a big reason he had supported her hiring, so it shouldn't surprise him.

He gave her a contrite smile. "Sorry. I could have handled that differently."

"Apology accepted."

Hodge changed the subject. "What do you think about Addie? Was she in on it?"

"I don't think so," said Cash. "Did you see the shock on her face when you told her about the money? That looked real. Plus, if she was involved, she wouldn't have mentioned him bragging about ten thousand dollars."

"Speaking of which, why so little?"

Cash thought it over. "Maybe Hooch isn't who we're after. Maybe the killer hired him to come after me."

"Why would he do that?"

"Because we're close."

Chapter Thirty-Nine

Cash stepped into the Tall Tale Tavern and let his eyes adjust to the dim light. The place looked and smelled just as he remembered. Stale air. Neon beer signs. Duct tape over the ripped Naugahyde covering the bar seats. The ancient wrinkled felt covering the rickety pool table. Cash wondered if Steve's barf stain was still visible behind it.

Hodge said, "Nice place. I can see why you and your friend came here."

"What can I say? We were desperate."

A beer gut on legs waddled out from a back room. Reggie. He froze at the sight of Hodge and Cash. The disapproving look on his face when he registered a Black deputy did not escape Cash. "Who are you?" he asked.

After introducing Hodge and himself, Cash said, "Are you Reggie?"

"Yeah."

"I remember you. I used to come here when I was in high school." He smiled. "We didn't need IDs."

Reggie put his hands up. "Hey, I don't do that anymore. Anybody shows up without an ID is drinking lemonade in my bar."

"Relax," Cash said. He put out a hand and they shook. "We're not here about that."

"What do you want?"

Cash glanced at Hodge to see if she wanted to start things off. She shook her head.

"Do you know a guy named Silas Dudek?" Cash asked.

"You mean Hooch?"

"Yeah."

"The guy likes his booze," said Reggie. "He practically lives here."

"He was killed last night." Cash explained about the home invasion, concluding with his suspicion that Dudek had gone there to kill him.

"That wouldn't surprise me," said Reggie. "He was a real lowlife."

"The question we're struggling with is whether this was his idea or someone else's."

"You mean like somebody paid him to do it?"

"That's right."

Reggie stroked his greasy salt-and-pepper beard. Was he searching his memory or trying to concoct a story? "There was this fella that came in a couple of days ago. Tall guy." He looked at Hodge. "About her age. I'd seen him before, but he wasn't a regular. He bought Hooch a beer." He pointed at a table. "They sat right over there."

"Do you know what they talked about?"

"That's the thing. At first they were at the bar so I could hear them. Then the big fella grabbed both beers and said, 'Let's go to that table.' I don't know what they said after that."

"What was this guy's name?"

"I don't know. I've seen him around, but he wasn't a regular."

"What did he look like?"

"Like I said, he was tall. Long face. No beard or mustache. Kind of in between dog butt ugly and movie star handsome.

"How long did he stay?"

"Fifteen, twenty minutes. He didn't finish his beer. The bottle was half full when I cleared the table."

"What did Dudek do after the guy left?"

"He stuck around a little longer. Shot a game of pool, finished his beer, then took off."

An idea hit Cash. "When the tall guy paid for the beers, did he use a credit card?"

"No."

Of course not. That would have been too easy.

"He used a hundred-dollar bill," said Reggie.

Cash recalled that the stolen money had all been hundreds. "Do you still have it?"

"Sorry, no. I took it to the bank yesterday."

Cash turned to Hodge. "Anything else?"

Before she could answer, Reggie said, "Yeah. The tall guy was a real jerk. I keep peanuts and candy at the bar. On his way out, he dumped the whole bowl of candy into his pocket. Looked at me like he'd kill me if I said anything. Asshole."

"Was it Jolly Ranchers?"

Reggie cocked his head in surprise. "Damn, you're good."

***

Cash didn't want to start anything with Hodge, but he had to know. "I thought you wanted to ask the questions."

"It's all about knowing who you're talking to," Hodge said, fiddling with her seat belt. "The widow of the guy you shot was unlikely to cooperate with you. A fat-ass redneck bar owner in Bumfuck, Texas would just as soon open a gay nail salon as talk to a Black deputy."

"Fair point." He should have thought of that. "What's your assessment of what the guy told us?"

"Hooch Dudek didn't think this up by himself. Somebody paid him."

"Our tall friend."

"Right. And this guy is local," Hodge said, "but probably not Sutton County, since Fat-ass has seen him, but not very often."

"Agreed. Anything else?"

"He paid with a hundred-dollar bill. It could have been one from Dieter Bergheim's stash."

"Could have been," Cash said, "but there's no way to prove it. I'm betting not too many hundreds get flashed in that dump. Anything else?"

She frowned. "That's all I got."

"What about the Jolly Ranchers?"

"Enlighten me."

"Jolly Rancher wrappers keep turning up. I found a couple in and around Emil Bergheim's tool shed. The Austin detective found one in Roy Baxter's den. Now the guy who we think hired Dudek pockets a bowlful at the bar."

"We haven't caught our killer yet."

"Bingo."

***

When they arrived back at the station, Santos sent Hodge to investigate two missing baby goats. "Chuck McDermott called it in," he said.

"He's certain it was his neighbor's kids that took them. I'd look in that culvert about halfway up his drive. I've told him a million times to put a grate over that thing but he never does."

"Got it," said Hodge.

"And don't stick your head in to look. Stand back and use your flashlight. Deke scared a skunk in there once and it did not end well for him."

After Hodge left, Cash took the opportunity to catch Santos up on what they had learned in Sutton County. He ended with his theory that Hooch Dudek was not the killer.

"Makes sense. We'll keep looking."

"Hey, what happened when you met with the commissioners?" Cash said. "Did they approve another deputy?"

"They did as long as we understand that raises wouldn't be in the budget next year."

"Have you posted the job?"

"It's on my to-do list for today."

"I'll let you get to it."

Cash grabbed a cup of coffee from the lobby and settled into a chair in the conference room. He logged onto the laptop and opened his email account. The first message was from Uber.

Thank you for using the Uber law enforcement portal. Here is the information you requested:

Date: August 21, 2024

Time: 5:52 p.m.

Pickup location: 3825 Lake Austin Boulevard

Destination: 4719 Galindo Street

Driver: Jesús Arroyo

Rider: Willa Dearborn

Date: August 21, 2024

Time: 6:31 p.m.

Pickup location: 4719 Galindo Street

Destination: 3825 Lake Austin Boulevard

Driver: Neil King

Rider: Willa Dearborn

The information was accompanied by a map of each ride as well as a stock photo of the vehicle model.

Cash cursed. Roy Baxter's killer had used Willa Dearborn's phone to book the rides. Which meant he was also her killer. That was good information, but he had been hoping for a name.

Cash searched the Lake Austin Boulevard address and found it belonged to a marina near Tom Miller Dam. He knew the place. It was located just upstream of the dam next to a row of restaurants and coffee houses. His parents took him there one evening for dessert at Mozart's.

Cash checked the time on the laptop screen. Four-fifteen. He knew Mozart's stayed open until midnight. He looked at a map for the name of one of the restaurants. Hula Hut. It didn't close until 9:30.

Cash raced out of the conference room to Santos's office. The Sheriff looked up from his computer. "What's up?"

Cash slipped his hat on. "I'm going to Austin."

Chapter Forty

Cash started with the restaurants. They would close earlier than the coffee shop, and he wanted to make sure he didn't waste his three-hour drive to Austin. First up was Hula Hut.

The manager, a reserved man with a face beaded in sweat, bustled up to him. "What's going on?"

Cash introduced himself and explained the purpose of his visit. Could he look at the restaurant's surveillance video for the times in question?

"We're pretty busy," the manager said. "Could we do this later?"

Cash shook his head. "I'm afraid not. I'm investigating a series of murders. Time is of the essence."

The manager turned. "Follow me."

Despite Cash's size advantage, he had trouble keeping up with the manager on the way to the back office. The room was barely big enough for the two of them. Cash squeezed behind the man and peered over his shoulder.

"What times are you interested in?" the manager asked.

Cash told him.

The manager fiddled with the equipment. "Here's the first one."

A grid of six views appeared on the screen. Four were interior views; the other two covered the parking lot and a portion of the walkway by the water. Cash focused on the parking lot. He saw nothing. No Prius and no tall man. "Let's try the next one."

Nothing happened at the departure time either. Cash thanked the manager. The harried man pushed past him and said, "Can you find your own way out?"

Cash next tried Quince, the sushi restaurant next to Hula Hut. The young woman manager exhibited more enthusiasm than the Hula Hut guy, but the results were equally disappointing. "Thanks for your time," Cash said.

The woman flashed a coy smile. "Want to stick around? Handsome deputies eat free."

"Maybe another time."

Next was Mozart's, the coffee shop and dessert bar. Cash's mouth watered as he inhaled the intoxicating aroma of baked goods and fresh-brewed coffee. He told himself he'd grab a pastry on his way out.

Despite the place being packed, the manager appeared in no rush as he took Cash to his office. He pulled up the relevant video and stepped away from the equipment. "You can use that mouse to control what you see."

Cash watched as at precisely 5:52 p.m. a black Prius eased to a stop in front of the shop and waited. A man who had been out of camera range darted into view. He wore a floppy, wide-brimmed hat and kept his head down. His clothes were nondescript: jeans and a plain T-shirt. Cash couldn't see his face.

The man climbed into the back of the Prius, which then pulled out of the lot and disappeared. "Back that up a few minutes," Cash said.

The manager complied. Shortly before the arrival of the Prius, the man in the floppy hat strode onto the lot from Lake Austin Boulevard. Again, his head was down. He also kept a hand over his eyes as if shielding them from the rain.

"That son of a bitch," Cash muttered. "Go on to the next one."

This time the man exited from a silver Highlander. The hat shielded his face from view. Instead of heading toward Lake Austin Boulevard, he hurried around the shop. Cash shifted his focus to the waterfront and saw him walk purposefully to the railing. He leaned over, pulled something out of his pocket, and dropped it into the water. He left in a hurry, taking care to keep his face from view.

"Where would this guy have parked a car?" Cash asked.

"He had a car? Why is he using an Uber?"

"Because he's smart."

"If he didn't park out front, he would have used the lot across the street."

"Are there cameras over there?"

"Not that I know of."

Cash turned to go.

"Anything else I can do for you?" the manager asked.

"Yeah," said Cash. "Get me a coffee and two chocolate chip cookies to go."

***

After calling Santos to let him know he'd be spending the night in Austin, Cash called Detective Stallings.

"It's late," said Stallings. "You must have found something."

"I did." He told Stallings about the information from Uber, as well as the man in the surveillance footage.

Stallings said, "You were supposed to call me as soon as you heard from Uber."

"My bad. In my rush to check out those restaurants, I forgot."

Stallings was willing to accept that. "What did he drop in the lake?"

"Either the phone or the murder weapon. Probably both."

"I can get a dive team there first thing in the morning," said Stallings. "Eight o'clock."

"I'll see you there."

***

Cash spent the night with his brother. When Reid expressed surprise he hadn't gone to their parents' house, Cash said, "I wanted to run through some songs with you."

"Great, I'll get the guitars."

Reid returned to the den with two acoustic guitars. As he handed one over, Cash smiled and said, "I don't get the Martin?"

"In your dreams."

They played for an hour, Cash strumming and Reid providing occasional solos between verses. Cash sang three songs, "Paradise," by John Prine, and the Tim McGraw tunes "Ghost Town Train" and "I Like It, I Love It." After finishing the latter, Cash put down the guitar and said, "I've tortured this poor instrument long enough."

"Don't sell yourself short," said Reid. "You're pretty good. Next time we come to Winkler's, I'm dragging your ass up on stage one way or another."

"You better wait until I'm drunk."

"Point taken. You might sing better drunk."

Reid went into the kitchen and returned with two beers. He handed one to Cash.

"Thanks." Cash sipped. The beer went down nicely after his long day. "How's your drummer doing?"

Reid's face darkened. "He's having a rough time. First, you hounded him about being a murderer. Then his grandfather was killed."

Cash chose his next words carefully. "Reid, I have to tell you, Eddie's not completely in the clear yet. I know he wasn't at the robbery, but now that we know his grandfather was involved, we have to assume he might have been as well."

"Do you have any proof?"

"No, and I'm hoping we don't find any."

"Great." Reid took a long pull from his beer. "He's a real mess, you know. He and his grandfather were tight."

"All the more reason to think he might have been involved."

Reid stood up. He chugged the rest of his beer and hurled the empty can across the room. "I'm going to bed."

***

"Odds are, they don't find anything," said Detective Stallings.

He and Cash stood on Mozart's deck, overlooking Lady Bird Lake. A uniformed officer sipped from a to-go coffee cup while two Austin police divers prepared to enter the water via a portable ladder hanging from the deck railing.

Cash said, "We know right where the guy was standing. Also, he didn't throw it out into the lake, he dropped it straight down."

"Yeah, but look at that water. Visibility sucks. And once they start moving around down there, they'll kick up so much mud it will be even worse."

"You're a ray of sunshine, Detective."

"I'm a realist."

The divers sank below the surface. Stallings said, "I'm gonna grab a cup of coffee. You want anything?"

"Chocolate milk."

"For real?"

Cash handed him a ten. "And a blueberry muffin."

***

Cash was beginning to wonder how much air the divers had when they both surfaced. One of them held up a hand. Something laden with gunk was in it. Cash couldn't tell what it was.

The divers climbed onto the deck and yanked off their masks. One of them said, "We found this." He held up a cell phone. "I don't think there's anything else down there."

"Are you sure?" Cash asked. "No heavy objects? An iron pipe? Tools? Nothing like that?"

"I'd stake my reputation on it. We went over a twenty-by-twenty grid with a fine-tooth comb."

Stallings held out an evidence bag, and the diver dropped the phone into it. "Thanks, Ward," Stallings said. "Good work." He turned to Cash. "We've got some savvy IT guys. I'll bet they can salvage the data."

"What if he removed the SIM card?"

"We should still be able to see the contacts and photos. They'll be in the phone's internal memory."

"You'll call me when you have the data?"

"Of course. In the meantime, you could track down those two Uber drivers and see what they know. Maybe one of them had a camera in his car."

"I'm on it."

***

Alone again, Cash bought another blueberry muffin and found a seat on the deck. He performed an internet search for the first driver, Jesús Arroyo. There were two men with that name in Austin. The first one he called wasn't an Uber driver. The second told Cash it had been him driving the Prius.

"Do you remember picking up a ride at Oyster's Landing recently?"

"Yeah. Tall guy. Didn't talk much."

"Is there anything that stands out about him?"

"When I say he didn't talk much, I mean he didn't say a word the whole trip. I tried making small talk but eventually gave up. I mean, it takes two to have a conversation, right?"

Cash said, "Did he have anything with him?"

"Yeah, a duffel bag. Black, I think."

"You wouldn't happen to have a camera in your car, would you?"

"No. I've been meaning to get one but haven't gotten around to it."

Cash thanked Arroyo and ended the call. He called the first of six Neil Kings in Austin."

"This is Neil."

"Mr. King, I'm Adam Cash with the Noble County Sheriff's Department. Are you an Uber driver?"

"Yes."

"What kind of vehicle do you use?"

"A Toyota Highlander."

Bingo. This was the right guy. "I'm investigating a series of murders," Cash said. "One of your recent passengers is a person of interest." He gave King the specifics of the ride.

"I remember that guy. He ran to the car like his hair was on fire. Couldn't wait to get in."

"Can you describe him?"

"Big guy. Skinny. Wore a hat. He had a black duffel bag with him."

"Is there a camera in your car?"

There was a pause. "I should probably get one of those."

Cash swore.

"Hey, man," King said, "they're expensive."

Not that expensive, Cash thought. "Don't worry about it. Thanks for your time."

Cash pocketed his phone and ran through his options. Beyond hoping that Stallings hit paydirt with the phone, he couldn't think of any. Time to go back to Pinyon.

His phone buzzed. He told himself it was too soon for Stallings to have produced results but held out hope anyway. The voice that answered his hello wasn't male. It was Bernadette.

Chapter Forty-One

Her voice sounded like her house was on fire. "I saw him, Cash."

"Who, Morgan?"

"Yes."

That son of a bitch. "Where?"

"He was sitting in his car across the street. Just staring at the house. It's happened twice now."

"When?"

"Yesterday morning and again just now."

"Did he see you?"

"I don't think so."

"Did he get out of his car?"

"He drives a truck. No, he just sat there for a few minutes, then took off. It freaked me out."

Cash thought it over. Morgan was stalking her. Bernadette was in danger. And if she was in danger, so was Emma.

"Bernadette, I'm in Austin. I can be there by noon. Will you be okay?"

"I think so. I'm about to leave for work. But Emma will be here with Momma."

"Tell her to keep that shotgun handy. I'll be there as soon as I can."

"Okay. Please hurry."

***

On his way back to Pinyon, Cash did his best to keep his speed at no more than ten miles per hour over the limit. Anything more and he knew that Santos would receive complaints about the speeding Noble County squad car. He was tempted to use the siren but didn't feel he could justify it if questioned about it.

He arrived at Bernadette's house at 11:45. Wanda Fenster answered the door. "Thank God you're here," she said. "I didn't want to have to use the shotgun."

Cash strode into the house. "Is Emma okay?"

"She's fine. I am too. Thanks for asking."

"I need to see Morgan."

"If you set and wait awhile, I'm sure the bastard will show up."

"Do you know where he works?" he asked.

"Over at the tire shop. Are you going to arrest him?"

"I haven't decided yet. Is your shotgun loaded?

"Wouldn't do much good if it wasn't."

"Don't put it away just yet."

***

Cash switched off the engine at Murchison's Tire Shop and forced himself to take a deep breath. What was his plan? His goal was to convince Morgan to leave Bernadette alone. Unless Bernadette changed her mind about filing an official complaint, though, he had no leverage.

He got out of the car and strode toward the open two-bay garage housing the work area. He saw two men struggling to pull an enormous truck tire from its rim. They each wore a grimy work shirt with a stylized M on the back. Cash recognized the shorter man as Russ Murchison, owner of the shop. The other was Morgan.

The men looked up at Cash's approach. "Hey, Cash," Murchison said.

Cash ignored the greeting and marched up to Morgan. "I thought I made myself clear when I told you to stay away from Bernadette."

Morgan glanced at his boss. "I haven't touched that woman since I saw you."

"You've been stalking her. Last night and this morning. She saw you in your truck."

"Is it against the law for a man to be in his truck on a public street?"

Murchison butted in. "Cash, is there a problem?"

"Nothing that concerns you, Russ." Cash returned his attention to Morgan. "Stay away from her house, stay off of her street, stay away from her workplace. I don't want you within a hundred yards of her. Got it?"

Morgan said, "Last time I checked it was still a free country. If I want to patch things up with my girlfriend, you have no right to stop me."

"Be smart, Morgan. Find yourself another girlfriend. As I recall, you already have."

"Yeah, but she doesn't have a cute baby like Bernadette does."

Cash grabbed the collar of Morgan's work shirt and pulled him in close. "Listen, you son of a bitch. Leave my daughter out of this." He released his hold.

Morgan flashed a wicked grin and said, "You should be more polite. I could be her daddy someday."

Unable to contain his simmering anger any longer, Cash threw a roundhouse punch that connected with Morgan's jaw and sent him reeling backward. Morgan charged but, before he reached Cash, Murchison jumped between them. "Stop it," he said. "Take it somewhere else."

Cash stepped back willingly. He had screwed up. Morgan had pushed a button and he hadn't been able to stop himself. But that was no excuse. Not when he was wearing the uniform.

Morgan said, "You saw that, Russ. That's assault."

"What I saw," said Murchison, "was a law officer telling you to quit harassing a woman and you telling him to take a hike. Now get the hell out of here."

Fuming, Morgan stomped toward the open bay door. "Fine. I don't need this fucking job."

"That's a good thing because you don't have it anymore."

Murchison and Cash watched Morgan climb into his Ford Ranger and speed off. Murchison said, "What's the matter with you, Cash? You can't just hit people."

Cash removed his hat and wiped his brow. "No shit. I'm probably facing a lawsuit."

"Forget it. All I saw was a man mouth off to a cop. As far as I'm concerned, he got what he deserved. But you've got to control that anger."

Cash donned his hat. "Right again."

***

As he drove away from Murchison's, Cash decided he needed to get ahead of the trouble he had just caused for himself. He parked in the department lot and entered the lobby. Vicky looked up and smiled.

"Hey, Cash."

"Hey, Vicky. Is the sheriff around?"

"He's at lunch. I think he went to Frank's."

"Thanks."

Before he could leave, Vicky said, "I haven't eaten yet. Want to go to Dairy Queen with me?"

"Thanks, no."

"Come on," she said in a pleading tone. "It's not a date. Just two work colleagues having lunch together."

Cash needed to put a stop to Vicky's constant flirting, and there was no better time than now. "Vicky," he said with authority. "I need to tell you something."

She cocked her head. Such a young kid, Cash thought, and too sweet for the world Cash knew.

"What?" she asked, all smiles.

"I'm not the guy you want. And I've got a girlfriend." At least he thought he did. "Okay?"

Her smile stiffened but didn't disappear.

"Please stop asking me to lunch."

Now it was gone. She wiped away a tear. "Okay."

Great. He had made her cry. "Are you all right?"

Instead of answering, she jumped up and bolted into the hall.

Cash sighed and headed for the exit. "Guess not."

***

Cash found his boss elbow-deep in a plate of pork ribs at Grumpy Frank's Barbecue. The owner, Frank Schwarz, was actually one of the most cheerful men in town. No matter how packed and hectic his restaurant was, Frank always wore a smile. He greeted most customers by name. If a stranger came in, he made sure to learn their name by the time they left.

Food was served cafeteria-style. Bread and beans were on the house. Patrons dined at one of eight picnic tables covered with brightly colored patterned oilcloth. There was always a bowl of fresh water set out for canine customers.

Cash paid for a brisket sandwich—he was starving after his drive from Austin—and found a seat opposite Santos. "I think I may have screwed up."

Santos looked up from his ribs. "Oh?"

Cash explained about his encounter with Clint Morgan. "I couldn't stop myself, Gabe. He mentioned Emma and my brain exploded."

"Were there any witnesses?"

"Just Russ. After Morgan left, he said he had it coming."

Santos waved a hand. "Then there's nothing to worry about, right?"

"I suppose not." Cash bit into his sandwich. "Sometimes I wonder if I have PTSD."

"Hell, we all have PTSD," Santos said. "Nobody came out of that place intact."

"What about you? You always seem so in control."

"Don't kid yourself. Ask Katrina," he said, referring to his wife.

"What would she tell me?"

"The usual. Nightmares. Short temper. It's pretty classic."

"What are you doing about it?"

"I see a therapist over in Junction. She's helped me a lot. You should give it a try."

"I don't know."

Santos locked eyes with him. "If you're wondering whether there's a problem, there's a problem."

Cash didn't know what to say. The notion of therapy terrified him. Sharing his deepest secrets with a stranger held not the slightest bit of appeal.

Santos said, "What happened in Austin?"

Cash filled him in, from the surveillance video at Mozart's to the divers' recovery of a cell phone.

"What about the Uber drivers?"

"Nada. All they could tell me is that the guy is tall and quiet. And no, they didn't have cameras in their cars."

"Of course not."

"I'm telling you, this guy is smart. He obviously planned Baxter's murder. Why else would he have used the Ubers? And he kept his face hidden the whole time. I couldn't see anything on the video."

"Where do we go from here?"

Cash shrugged. "I'm stumped. Stallings will let me know what they find on the phone, but we already know it belonged to Willa Dearborn."

Santos finished his last rib and tossed the bone on his plate. He licked his fingers. "Let me know when you hear anything." He stood up. "Oh, by the way, Emil Bergheim is coming home today. Maybe he's remembered something since you last saw him."

"Do you want me to go see him?"

Santos grinned. "I always knew you were smart."

Chapter Forty-Two

The old man's impassive gaze followed Cash's truck as it crunched along the gravel drive. His eyes were the only part of his body that didn't hurt to move. Any small motion tugged at his incision site to fire white-hot needles in every direction. He had to keep the porch rocker still so as not to aggravate the pain.

The truck braked to a stop and Cash got out. Emil Bergheim tracked his approach. Cash was a good man. He had been a reliable assistant back when he helped build fences. Always on time, never complained, never slacked off. Why he had quit an outdoor job that kept a man fit to write speeding tickets and tell folks to keep their dogs quiet was a mystery.

Bergheim sat motionless as Cash clomped up the wooden steps to join him on the porch. He gestured at the other rocker. "Have a seat."

Cash sat. "It's good to see you back home."

"Good to be home. What brings you out to see an old man?"

"Does there have to be a reason? I'm just making sure you don't need anything."

Bergheim scoffed. "Anything I need, I can get myself."

Cash pointed at the shotgun in Bergheim's lap. "Are you expecting trouble?"

"Squirrels. They get all my pecans."

"It's a bit early for pecans, isn't it?"

"They don't wait until they're ripe."

"Yep," said Cash. "They're a pain in the ass. How's the wound? Does it hurt?"

"Nope." He hoped Cash couldn't detect the lie. "Don't bother me at all."

Cash laughed. "You're a tough old buzzard, Mr. Bergheim."

Bergheim grunted. Why was the kid here? Sheriff's deputies surely had better things to do than waste their day with an old man.

Cash said, "We haven't caught the robbers yet."

There it was. He grunted in acknowledgment.

Cash continued. "We have some clues. The detective in Austin—"

Bergheim stiffened. Damn, that hurt. "Austin? What's Austin got to do with anything?"

"A man was killed there. We think it's related to your robbery."

"Who got killed?"

"His name is Roy Baxter."

Roy Baxter? Shit. "Don't know him."

"He used to work with your brother."

Another grunt.

"That's three people dead now. Baxter, Slater Cobb, and Cobb's girlfriend Willa Dearborn."

Bergheim shook his head. Three dead. Terrible.

"We're going to catch the guy that did it."

"It's just one guy?"

"As far as we can tell."

Three people dead was a tragedy. Yet there was a practical matter of great importance to Bergheim. "Any sign of the money?"

Cash shook his head. "No."

"I can't afford that fancy place Dieter's living at. And if he can't stay there, I don't know where he can go." He cleared his throat. "God knows I can't take care of him here."

"Is he that bad?"

Bergheim scoffed. "He can hardly take a piss by himself. And I'm no damn nurse."

"There's Medicaid."

"I talked to a social worker about that. It takes months to get approved. And the places that take Medicaid are real shitholes."

"It might be your only option."

Bergheim knew that. It sickened him.

"Mr. Bergheim," said Cash, "I was wondering if you remembered anything new about the robbery since we talked last."

Bergheim shot him a suspicious glance. "Why would I?"

"I don't know. I just thought I'd ask. Any little thing. You never know what might break a case."

Bergheim wished Cash would go away. It was hard to think straight with the pain meds on board. But his brother needed that money. He let his mind drift back to that night. "Like I already told you, I heard a noise and went outside. I saw two men, one short and one tall. I hollered at them and the big one shot me. Then he shot the other guy."

"Why would he shoot his partner?"

"How the hell am I supposed to know?" the old man snapped. "Ain't it your job to figure that out? All I know is he shot the guy in cold blood and lit out."

"Was the big guy carrying anything? A duffel bag, say?"

"I wouldn't know. It was dark."

"But the money is gone. He must have been carrying it."

"I reckon."

"How much money was there?"

What was with all these damn questions? "I don't know for certain. A lot."

"A million?"

"At least."

They sat in awkward silence until Cash stood up. "I guess I'll leave you with the squirrels. Is there anything I can do for you before I go?"

The old man thought about it. "Just catch the bastard."

Chapter Forty-Three

After leaving Bergheim on his porch, Cash drove to Shelly's Donuts. He bought two cherry kolaches to go. They were out of chocolate milk, so he settled for orange juice.

He strolled across the street to the courthouse lawn and sat on a park bench. He needed time to think. Bergheim had seemed reluctant to answer his questions. Why? And something bothered him about what the old man had said, but he couldn't put his finger on it.

His phone buzzed and he fished it from his pocket. "This is Cash."

"Hey, boy!"

It was his father. "Hey, Dad. What's up?"

"Your mother and I will be in Pinyon this evening, and we thought we could have supper with you and Edie."

He was sounding too hearty. "Why are you coming to Pinyon?"

"Do we need a reason to see our son?"

"I guess not," Cash said.

"I'm installing a new HVAC system in San Angelo tomorrow."

"San Angelo? That's a long way from Austin."

"Yeah," his father said. "It's for one of my fishing buddies."

Cash glanced at his phone screen. "It's almost five. Will you be here in time for supper?"

"We're already in Junction. We'll see you guys at the Firewheel around six-thirty."

Not the Firewheel. At least not until he set things right with Edie. "Can we make it the Packsaddle?" He thought up a white lie. "I ate at the Firewheel for lunch."

"Okay, the Packsaddle it is. See you—hang on, your mother wants to talk to you."

The phone was handed over, and his mother said, "Adam?"

"Hi, Mom."

"Reid told us you spent the night with him last night. Why didn't you call us?"

Thanks a lot, Reid. "I was working on a case. There wasn't time."

"There wasn't time to come see the woman that gave birth to you?"

"Come on, Mom, you know I—"

"Relax, I'm just busting your balls."

"Mom!"

"What? Did I not use it right? I heard that on *The Sopranos*."

"No, you used it right. You just surprised me. It's more of a north-eastern thing. People don't say it much around here."

"Well, I'm going to ask Edie about that. See you soon."

The line went dead. Good grief. Edie. What was he going to tell his parents about her?

***

"Where's Edie?"

Cash eyed his mother and muttered the lie he had come up with. "She had a PTA meeting." He had seen the meeting announcement when he drove past the elementary school on his way to the Packsaddle.

Janet's face contorted into a look of disbelief. "She chose a PTA meeting over dinner with her boyfriend's parents?"

"What can I say?" Cash said with a shrug.

"You can tell us the truth," his father said. "No way Edie skipped seeing us for a PTA meeting."

"Dad, I—"

"Did you guys break up?"

Cash hoped not. "No, it's not that."

"What is it, then?"

Cash took a long pull from his beer. He had hoped to avoid a discussion about his private life. "We had a fight."

"So? Your mother and I fight all the time," Del said. "That doesn't mean we don't eat together. Right, Janet?"

"That's right."

"What was this fight about?"

"She's going back to school."

"Good for her."

"In Austin."

"Oh."

Janet said, "She's leaving Pinyon?"

"That's right."

"Where will she live?"

What did he care? It wouldn't be in Pinyon. "I don't know."

"What will she study?"

"Nursing."

Janet's eyes lit up in understanding. "And you're afraid she'll find a rich doctor to marry. You know, if you were to become a lawyer—"

Why was it always a "rich" doctor? "No, Mom, that's not it."

"Let it go, Janet," Del said. "He's not going to law school."

Janet sighed. "I know. It's just ..."

"Just what?" Cash asked.

"Nothing."

Del said, "How are things with your job?"

"Not so good." Cash told them about the robbery, the murders, and the tension between him and Reid about Eddie Kincaid.

"Emil Bergheim kept a million dollars in cash in his tool shed?" Del asked.

"Maybe more. It was his brother's."

"That guy always was a nut."

"Del, that's not nice," Janet said.

Without warning, Steve's voice boomed out, "Hey, guys! What are y'all doing here?"

His parents stood up. After a round of hugs and polite chitchat, Janet said, "Won't you join us?" She glanced at Cash. "His girlfriend couldn't make it."

Please say yes, Cash thought.

Steve slid into a chair. "I'm a poor substitute for Edie, but sure."

Janet said, "They had a fight."

Steve caught Cash's eye. Cash shook his head to keep him from probing.

Catching the hint, Steve grabbed a menu right quick. "Have you seen the specials tonight?"

***

The next morning, Cash made migas for his parents. They had slept in the guest bedroom. Cash had offered the use of his room, which had once been theirs, but his father said, "It's your house now, son. We'll be fine."

After bidding them farewell, Cash was putting on his uniform when his phone dinged. It was a text from Stallings.

Check your email.

Cash fired up his laptop and opened his email account. There was a message from the detective.

We were able to retrieve the information from the phone. It did indeed belong to Willa Dearborn. We see the Uber rides but no calls since her death. I've attached her contact list and the photos we recovered. Let me know if anything jumps out at you.

Cash opened the attachment. Among the hundreds of names, he searched for Eddie Kincaid and found nothing. Nor was there a hit for the name Bergheim or Silas Dudek. Slater Cobb came up—no surprise there. Rather than peruse the entire list—he was already late for work—Cash shut down his laptop, intending to dive deeper at the station.

***

Cash entered the station with his head down. He had neither the time nor the desire to speak with Vicky this morning. Later, when he wasn't rushed, he'd apologize for making her cry yesterday.

Vicky didn't look at him. Thank God. Maybe she'd finally given up. Or was she intentionally snubbing him? Either way, he was in the clear. He reached the conference room as the morning meeting was breaking up.

"Glad you could join us, Detective," Santos said.

"Sorry I'm late." He took a seat and motioned. "I have news."

Everyone settled back into a chair. Cash relayed the news from Austin, which he realized consisted mostly of things he hadn't learned.

"I still say we ought to bust that guy Kincaid," Conrad said. "A few days in the slammer should loosen his tongue."

Hodge rolled her eyes. Santos said, "If we had more solid evidence of his involvement, we'd do that." He turned to Cash. "What did Emil Bergheim have to say?"

"Not much. He just wants us to find the money."

Conrad smirked. "Is there a reward?"

"Yeah," said Hodge. "You get to keep your job."

Cash went further with his report. "APD recovered Willa Dearborn's phone." He told them about the contact list.

"Who's on it?" Hodge asked.

"I haven't looked at it in detail yet. I was hoping you could help me with that."

"Sure."

Santos said, "Anything else?"

"No."

"All right. Let me know what you find."

***

Hodge and Cash stayed behind in the conference room when the meeting broke up. Cash texted her Willa Dearborn's contact list before booting up the laptop. Hodge used her phone to peruse the names.

After five minutes, she said, "I don't recognize anyone on here."

"I'm not surprised," Cash said. "You haven't lived here that long."

"What about you?"

"I know two so far. They're both the same age as her, so she probably knew them from school."

He kept scrolling. A name jumped off the screen at him. "Holy shit. Here's Hooch."

"She knew Dudek?"

"Apparently."

He took his phone out and made a call. A man answered. "This is Stallings."

"This is Adam Cash. Do you have Willa Dearborn's phone log handy?"

"I told you, there were no calls after her death."

"What about the day or two before she died? Is there anything then?"

"Hang on."

Cash waited. Hodge started to ask him a question, but he raised a finger to stop her. Stallings came back on the line. "There are three calls."

"Are there any with Eddie Kincaid?"

"No."

"What about Roy Baxter?"

"Would you hold on a second so I can tell you? They're all with that Hooch guy you told me about."

Cash's heart rate jumped a notch. "Did you get the number?"

"Yeah. It's no longer active. Must have been a burner."

"Okay, thanks." Cash ended the call. Hodge was fidgeting like a toddler in need of a bathroom. "What was that all about?" she said.

"Let's look at the pictures."

Cash opened the photo file from Willa's phone. There were maybe twenty pictures in all, most of them of her cat. The last two, though, were selfies of her topless.

"Why do women do that?" Hodge said.

"Only one reason. To send them to her man. In this case, Slater Cobb."

Hodge pointed. "What's that?"

Cash looked closer. Willa was standing in front of a wall-mounted TV. The reflection on the screen showed the back of a man a few feet away. Cash couldn't make out much detail, but the large M of Murchison's Tires on the man's shirt leaped out at him. "Holy shit."

"What?" said Hodge.

"Clint Morgan just jumped to the head of the line."

Chapter Forty-Four

Cash ended his call to Bernadette and looked at Hodge. "She says he only goes by Clint, not Hooch."

"I don't get it," said Hodge. "How would Willa Dearborn have known Silas Dudek?"

"I don't think she did. Hooch's number in her contacts isn't the same as Dudek's. I think the man she called Hooch is Clint Morgan."

"We need to tell Santos."

They raced each other to Santos's office. He flinched when they burst into the room. "Dang, guys. Where's the fire?"

"It's Clint Morgan," said Cash. "He stole the money and killed all those people."

Santos raised his hands. "Whoa, whoa." Who is Clint Morgan?"

"Bernadette's ex-boyfriend. The guy I hit yesterday at the tire shop."

Hodge gave Cash a puzzled look. "You hit the guy?"

"I'll tell you another time," he said. "But he had it coming."

Santos said, "Don't leave me hanging, Cash. Let's get back to Morgan."

Cash explained about Hooch being in Willa Dearborn's contacts before showing Santos the selfie with the man in the TV reflection.

"That's the logo at Murchison's Tire Shop. Look how tall that guy is. That's Morgan. Morgan is Hooch. He's our killer."

"I thought Hooch was dead."

"Hooch Dudek is dead. Hooch Morgan is very much alive."

"How sure are you?"

"Look at his height. That's not Murchison. And neither of the other two guys working in the shop are that big."

"Keisha, what do you think?"

Hodge pursed her lips. "I think we need to take a close look at Clint Morgan."

Santos looked at Cash. "What's your plan?"

"I want to search Morgan's house."

"Looking for what?"

"Any number of things. The murder weapon. Boots that match the imprints we found at Bergheim's. A million dollars in cash."

"We'd need a warrant. And you know what Judge Mixon will say."

Cash's heart sank. Santos was right. "She'd say we don't have enough evidence."

"Precisely."

"So, we're back to square one."

They sat in glum silence. A grackle cackled outside Santos's window. To Cash, it sounded like the bird was laughing at them. A sudden inspiration jolted him upright. "What if I could get in there without a warrant?"

"We're not breaking into anyone's house," Santos said. "Not unless we think we'll look good in orange jumpsuits."

"I wouldn't break in. He'd ask me to come inside."

"How in the hell would you get him to do that?"

Cash sat back. "I have an idea."

***

This time Cash drove home first to change out of his uniform. He stuck his Ruger in his belt and got into his truck. Second thoughts about the gun prompted him to stow it in the glove compartment.

Cash fired the engine and drove to Stripes, where he bought a six-pack of Packsaddle beer. When he arrived at Morgan's, he found the Ford Ranger parked in the driveway. He grabbed the six-pack and got out of the truck. The Ruger he left in the glove compartment.

Cash had to knock three times before Morgan opened the door. Before the tall man could speak, he said, "I'm here to bury the hatchet." He held out the six-pack. Morgan glanced at it and said, "Do you think you can buy me off with a few beers?"

"I just want to talk," Cash said. "The beer is a peace offering."

Morgan took the six-pack. Cash said, "Can I come in?"

Morgan grunted and backed into the house. Cash noticed Morgan hadn't done any housecleaning since his earlier visit.

Cash settled into a wingback chair. Morgan dropped onto a cushioned sofa. He set the beer on a coffee table between them. "Have one if you want," Morgan said. "It's too early in the day for me."

That was a surprise. Cash had pegged Morgan as a beer-for-breakfast guy. Also, he had hoped Morgan would take the beer to his refrigerator. That would have given him a chance to scope out the den.

Cash said, "I'm here to apologize. I was way out of line yesterday. I'm sorry."

Morgan laughed. "I'll bet you are. I could sue your ass off. The department too. That stuff doesn't fly these days."

"I know. Like I said, I'm really sorry. I'd like to make it up to you."

Morgan looked at Cash like his face had just split open to reveal an alien. "How would you do that?"

"I could talk to Russ. Maybe get your job back."

"No, thanks. I'll find me something better. Heck, maybe I'll win the lottery." His eyes lit up. "Hey, I know. You could—oh, forget it."

"What?"

"I was gonna say maybe you could help me straighten things out with Bernadette. But I know how you feel about that. And anyway, I fucked up. There's other fish in the sea."

Cash nodded. "She wants to move on."

"I guess that's her right."

Cash looked at the beer. "That's going to get warm."

Morgan rose from the couch and grabbed the beer. "I'll stick it in the fridge." He disappeared into the kitchen.

Cash took the opportunity to make a quick survey of the room. He spotted a small basket on an end table next to the sofa and stood up to see its contents. There was a stuffed keychain with a Ford Ranger key fob inside. Beside it was a solitary key fob. Cash flipped it over to see a Buick logo.

"What are you doing?"

The sound of Morgan's voice made Cash flinch. He displayed the fob. "I don't recognize the logo on this. Do you know what it is?"

"Nope."

Cash dropped it back into the basket. Morgan pulled something from his pocket. A piece of candy. He unwrapped it and tossed the wrapper on the end table. "Want one?" he asked.

"Sure."

Morgan extracted another piece and tossed it. Cash caught it and read the label: Jolly Rancher.

"Don't you like that flavor?" Morgan said. "I've got more."

"No, this is fine." Cash pulled off the wrapper and popped the candy into his mouth. "It's a shame about Willa Dearborn, isn't it?"

"Who's Willa Dearborn?"

"Slater Cobb's girlfriend. Bernadette said you knew her."

"Never heard of her."

"What about Slater? Did you know him?"

Morgan bit his lip. "I think we've buried the hatchet deep enough. Maybe it's time for you to go."

Cash hesitated, then stood up. "Okay." He walked to the door. "Thanks for the candy."

Morgan grunted but didn't say anything. Back in his truck, Cash looked at the Jolly Rancher wrapper in his hand and said, "Gotcha, you bastard."

Chapter Forty-Five

Cash groaned inside as Santos closed his eyes and massaged his brow. He knew that meant his friend was trying to think of a diplomatic way to express his disagreement with Cash's proposal. Sure enough, Santos said, "It's all circumstantial, Cash. We'd never get a warrant from Mixon, much less a conviction from Lars."

"Come on, Gabe. How many people do you know that walk around with Jolly Ranchers in their pocket?"

"That's not the point. And I'm not saying he's not our guy. I'm just saying that a good defense attorney would blow holes in our—" he made air quotes— "evidence."

Cash threw himself back in his chair, looked up at the ceiling, and let out a long sigh. "What about the key fob?"

"What about it? Unless you can prove it belongs to Willa Dearborn's car, it doesn't mean anything. And the only way to do that would be to get it through a warrant."

Cash sat up. "There you go. We have a specific question that needs answering."

Santos squinted his eyes in thought. "Maybe you're right. All Mixon can do is say no. I'll ask her for one first thing in the morning."

"I can do it."

"Let me." He massaged his brow again. "Your track record with her isn't so good."

***

Cash left the station in a foul mood. Not only had Santos thrown shade on the results of his investigation, but he had also cast doubt on his ability to handle Judge Mixon. What did that say about his boss's confidence in him as a deputy?

Cash had to admit that his confidence in himself was waning. It seemed that every promising lead in this investigation had flamed out. He must be missing something. Someone with more experience—no, more skill—would have made an arrest by now. Or at least have gathered enough evidence to justify a warrant to search Clint Morgan's house.

Morgan. When Cash first met him, he never would have guessed what he was capable of. If his hunch was right, Morgan had killed three people so far. And he shot Emil Bergheim. Too bad Bergheim didn't see enough at the encounter to identify the bastard.

Wait a minute, Morgan didn't know that. As far as he knew, Bergheim knew who shot him and, now that he was recovered enough to return home from the hospital, would finger him as the shooter. Which meant that Bergheim was in danger.

Cash turned his truck around and raced to Bergheim's place. Five miles later, he turned onto Bergheim's drive and breathed a sigh of relief when he saw the old man sitting on his porch in the fading light. He tensed when he saw the shotgun in Bergheim's lap. That wasn't for squirrels. Not this time.

Cash got out of his truck and hustled to the porch. Bergheim sat motionless, tracking his approach with disapproval. "What are you doing here?" he said with a growl.

"Mr. Bergheim, I'm glad to see you're okay," Cash said.

"Why wouldn't I be?"

"I want you to spend the night at my place."

Bergheim scoffed. "Unless you've got Scarlett Johansson over there, I'm not going anywhere."

"Your life is in danger."

"Bullshit."

Cash pointed at the shotgun. "That's not for squirrels. You're worried too."

Bergheim grunted but didn't say anything.

"Okay, Mr. Bergheim. Here's the deal," said Cash. He explained his theory about Clint Morgan. "Since the night of the robbery, he's killed two people that knew he did it. Not to mention Slater Cobb. You're the last loose end."

Bergheim started to rock his chair but caught himself. "Ah, brother, that hurts." He fixed Cash with a glare. "You ain't leaving here without me, are you?"

"No, sir."

"All right, then. I'll get my toothbrush." He climbed slowly to his feet and turned toward the house.

"Mr. Bergheim?" Cash said.

"What?"

"Bring the shotgun, too."

***

The sun dipped below the horizon just as Cash turned onto his property, meaning the unbearable summer heat would soon drop into the merely miserable range. He gulped when he spotted a familiar vehicle parked in front. Edie's Prius. Leaning against it was Edie.

Bergheim said, "I'll be damned. You do have Scarlett Johansson over here."

"Close," said Cash. "That's my girlfriend, Edie James."

"I know who she is. She works at the Firewheel."

Cash parked and got out of his truck. Edie opened her mouth to speak but shut it when she noticed his companion. Recovering from her surprise, she said, "Hello, Mr. Bergheim. What brings you here?"

Bergheim fetched the shotgun from behind the seat. "Your boyfriend wants to babysit me tonight."

Edie turned expectant eyes on Cash. "I'll explain later," he said.

Cash approached Edie for a hug. A painfully brief, impassive one. He led them into the house. "Keep the shotgun by your bed, Mr. Bergheim. Your room is this way."

Bergheim followed Cash into the guest room, while Edie waited in the den. The old man leaned the gun in a corner and dropped into a padded armchair. "You gonna lock me in here?"

"Mr. Bergheim, I know you don't see much sense in this, but I strongly believe your life is in danger. Once I clear a few things up, you'll be able to go back to your house."

"Yep," Bergheim said. He surveyed the room. "You got any magazines?"

After rustling up an old *Field and Stream*, Cash returned to Edie, nestled into the sofa. "I didn't expect to find you waiting for me," he said.

"We need to talk."

Cash winced. Those were the four most dreaded words in a relationship. "Okay." He sat in the lounge chair. "Let's talk."

His throat constricted as several seconds of awkward silence dragged by. Edie said, "I guess I'll start. You said some disappointing things the last time we were together."

"I said some really stupid things."

"Like what, if you don't mind."

His mind as clear as a sandstorm, Cash said, "I can't remember all of it, but I didn't mean it the way it came out."

"You wouldn't have said those things if there weren't some feelings behind them."

Cash's brain scrambled to come up with what to say. "I'll grant you that. Let me just say a few things, though, and then we can dissect what I said the other night, if you want to. Okay?"

She nodded.

"I totally support your decision to become a nurse. You're one of the smartest people I know. You could do anything you put your mind to. And this is something you've wanted for a long time. Not only will it make your life easier by bringing you a better salary, you'll be doing something you love." He paused. "Like me."

She didn't say anything, so he continued. "Obviously, to pursue this goal, you need to leave Pinyon for a while. I'd be an idiot to get in the way of that."

"On that we can agree."

Ouch. "So if you need to move to Austin for a couple of years, then by God, you do it. I'll help you do it. I'll miss you, but I'll get over it."

"It will be temporary," she said.

"Hang on, I'm not finished." He felt himself gathering momentum. "What I want for us is to be together long-term. I'm not proposing marriage—yet—but that's in the five-year plan for sure. When we broke up after high school, I spent the next ten years telling myself I should move on, but I couldn't. Every girl I dated only made me want you back. I know now that's because you're the woman for me. You're smart, you're kind, you're a hard worker. Not to mention gorgeous."

She sniffed. "Looks fade."

"They haven't yet. When they do, it won't matter. You've got all that other stuff going for you, and those things won't fade. The point is—I'll say it again—you're the perfect woman for me. I love you. I always have. What I don't know is if you still love me."

He stopped. He had just spilled more about himself in the past five minutes than in the previous ten years.

Edie said, "This must be hard for you."

He emitted a nervous laugh. "A little."

She stood up, crossed the room, and settled into his lap. "I do love you. And I don't expect perfection, but you're close." She smiled and gave him a playful arm punch. "Just stop saying stupid stuff."

"I can't promise that," he said with a grin. "But I can try."

She draped her arms around his neck and gave him a lingering kiss. "That's all I can ask."

Cash ran his fingers through her hair. "How about spending the night with me?"

"Do I need my own shotgun?"

"I've got an extra."

"What about your guest?"

"Sorry, I'm not into threesomes."

"That's okay." She kissed him again. "Neither am I."

Chapter Forty-Six

Cash awoke feeling as relaxed as he had in weeks. The pleasant scent of Edie's hair reminded him why. She lay on her side, still asleep, her soft breaths as rhythmic and soothing as a ticking clock.

Hard footsteps in the hall spoiled the atmosphere. Bergheim. Cash heard him clomp into the hall bath, flip the commode lid up, and let loose a steady stream. No prostate problems there.

Edie stirred. "Good morning," Cash said.

She smiled. "Good morning." She rubbed her eyes. "What time is it?"

"Time for a quickie."

The commode flushed and the lid slammed down, eliciting a grimace from Edie. "I don't think so."

Cash's phone rang from its place on the nightstand. "So much for a peaceful morning," he said, reaching for it. "This is Cash."

"I got it."

Who was that? Santos? "Got what?"

"The warrant, dumbass. Mixon came through."

"You woke her at"—Cash glanced at the phone screen—"seven-thirty?"

"I called her last night. She wanted to think on it. I just got off the phone with her. When can you be at Morgan's house?"

He sat up. "Twenty minutes."

***

Cash kissed Edie goodbye. "I'll swing by the café for lunch. Can you get Mr. Bergheim some breakfast?"

"I can get my own breakfast," Bergheim said.

Edie said, "I could make pancakes."

He grunted. "I wouldn't turn them down."

Cash said, "You'll be here when I get home, right?"

"I sure as hell ain't walking anywhere."

"If this goes like I think it will, I'll have you home this evening."

"We'll see."

***

Cash turned onto the street and saw Santos waiting in a squad car two houses down from Morgan's. He parked behind it and got out. Santos, Hodge, and Conrad emerged from the vehicle.

"I brought reinforcements," said Santos.

Santos led the way to the house. He rapped on the door and stepped back. Morgan answered wearing gym shorts and a T-shirt. He was barefoot.

Thrusting the warrant at Morgan, Santos said, "We're here to search your house."

Morgan took the document and read it. "What's this about?"

"Please step aside."

Scowling, Morgan handed the warrant back and complied.

When they were all in the den, Morgan shut the door. "Do you mind if I go finish my breakfast?"

"As a matter of fact, I do," Santos said. "Please have a seat."

With an exaggerated eye roll, Morgan flopped into the wingback chair. Santos sent Hodge and Conrad down the hall and turned to Cash. "I'll start in the kitchen. You start here."

Cash donned gloves. His eyes locked immediately on the end table. The basket was still there. It held Morgan's Ford Ranger key fob but nothing else. "Where's that other key?" he said.

Morgan remained deadpan. "What other key?"

"The one with the logo I didn't recognize. I asked you about it."

"I don't know what you're talking about."

Cash silently cursed himself. He had tipped Morgan off during his visit. Now they'd never know the significance of the mystery key. That had been the main justification for the warrant.

He searched the rest of the den, knowing he wouldn't find anything. If Morgan was smart enough to get rid of the key, he was smart enough to ditch anything else that might tie him to the murders. And the money? Surely, he'd have that stashed somewhere else.

Santos returned from the kitchen. "Anything?"

Cash shook his head.

Morgan said, "If you'd tell me what you're looking for, maybe I could help."

"Where's the attic entrance?" said Cash.

"In the hall."

Santos stayed with Morgan while Cash went to look. He pulled the stairs down and climbed the steps. The attic was small. And empty, except for a single cardboard box within arm's length. Cash slipped a hand behind it and tried to pull it toward him, but it was too heavy. Could this be the missing money?

He stepped higher on the ladder and manhandled the box closer. He held his breath as he lifted the lid off. No money. Only dozens of tightly packed vintage LPs. He pulled one up so he could see the cover. It was Elton John's "Yellow Brick Road." He removed a handful of albums and reached into the gap. Nothing. As he returned the albums he noticed the names Johnny Cash, Merle Haggard, and Loretta Lynn. "Dad would love this," he muttered.

He found Santos and the two deputies back in the den. Santos said, "Deke, go see if there's a crawl space under the house. Cash, let's look in the garage." He nodded at Hodge. "You stay here with him."

The one-car garage was large enough for a workbench beside the space for a vehicle. Tools hung from a pegboard nailed to the open studs above the bench. Next to the bench was a single shelf, empty except for three quarts of motor oil. There were no vehicles or lawn care tools.

Santos said, "Doesn't look too promising."

Cash examined the tools. Screwdrivers, a rip saw, chisels, a mallet, and a claw hammer: standard stuff. He peered closely at the hammer and mallet, looking for signs of blood, but saw nothing suspicious.

Four identical crescent wrenches hung from a row of hooks above the saw. Or were they the same? "Gabe, look at this."

Santos strolled over.

"Notice anything about these wrenches?" said Cash.

"Can't say that I do."

He pointed. "Look at that one."

"What about it?"

"It's different." Three of the wrenches were smeared with oil and grime. The fourth looked like it had just come from the store. "Why is that the only clean one?" he asked.

"Good question," said Santos. "Bring it with you."

Cash found an evidence bag in his pocket. He stowed the tool, sealed the bag, and said, "Let's go."

Conrad and Hodge waited for them in the den. Conrad reported, "It's a concrete foundation. There is no crawl space."

Morgan said, "I could have told you that. I haven't done anything."

The smug bastard. If only there was a way to wipe that smile from his face. Then Cash had an idea. "We'll be back. We have a witness ready to spill his guts about who shot him. He's seeing his doctor over in Junction today, but in the morning, bam. You should start looking for a good lawyer."

Morgan hesitated long enough for Cash to know he had struck a nerve. Finally, Morgan said, "Do you want your shitty beer back?"

***

Out in the street, Hodge said, "What was that all about, Cash? Who's this witness?"

"Emil Bergheim."

"He already told you he doesn't know anything."

"Morgan doesn't know that."

"So?"

"So he's a loose end."

Santos said, "We can't use an old man as bait."

"We won't."

Chapter Forty-Seven

Emil Bergheim pried the lid from the foil to-go dish and inhaled the steam rising from the plate. Chicken enchiladas, rice, and refried beans. "How did you know what I'd want?" he asked Cash.

Cash pulled three other plates of Tex-Mex from the plastic bag and set them on his dining room table. "It's what you always wanted when I worked for you."

Bergheim snorted. "Didn't know I was that predictable."

Cash slid a plate to each of his parents. "Taco salad for you, Mom." He pushed the other to his dad. "Beef fajitas for you."

"Thanks, son," Del said as he ripped the lid from the plate and dug in.

They ate in silence. Cash exchanged an awkward glance with his mother. His father was already face-deep in his food. Cash cleared his throat. "Thank you, guys, for coming to pick Mr. Bergheim up on short notice."

"Hell, we didn't have anything better to do," said Del.

His mother said, "I was going to clean out the hall closet."

"Eat your salad, Janet."

Bergheim said, "I still don't understand why I can't just stay here at your house."

"This could take a few days," said Cash. "You just got out of the hospital. You shouldn't be alone."

"If this mess wasn't happening, I'd be by myself at my house."

"But it is happening. I can't leave you there. You know that."

"Because the bogeyman might get me," Bergheim said with a snort.

"He's killed three people," said Cash. "And he sent that guy Dudek to get me."

"I thought you said you didn't know that for sure," Del said.

"It's the only explanation that makes sense."

Janet cleared her throat. "We're pleased to have you stay with us, Mr. Bergheim. There's a Chuy's near our house. You can have all the chicken enchiladas you want."

Bergheim grunted and shoveled a forkful of refried beans into his mouth. He swallowed. "If you catch him, will I get the money back?"

Cash sipped his iced tea. "One step at a time."

***

Morgan turned onto the farm-to-market road that led to Emil Bergheim's property and squeezed the steering wheel. He smiled at the strength of his grip. The old man's larynx would crumple in his hands. Morgan would watch the life drain from his face and know he had tied up the final loose end. After that he'd wait a couple of months, toss the money in his truck, and start a new life in another state. Maybe another country. He'd heard Costa Rica was nice. He'd have to learn Spanish, but how hard could it be? And the señoritas would flock to a rich American.

Of course, there was still Adam Cash. Not exactly a loose end, but an itch that Morgan yearned to scratch. The deputy couldn't touch him—hell, he'd already searched his house and come up empty—but Morgan would love to pound that smug expression from the asshole's face. Maybe he'd pay him a nighttime visit after taking care of the old man. After that, perhaps a final roll in the sack with Bernadette, willing or not. As for the old lady? He'd shove that shotgun up her ass and pull the trigger.

Morgan reached the familiar turnoff and steered his truck onto the unpaved road. He switched off the headlights and relied on the running lights to illuminate the night. A half-mile later he eased to a stop fifty yards from where he had parked Willa's car the night of the robbery. He slipped on a ski mask, got out of the truck, and used a flashlight to look for security cameras. Seeing none, he patted the disposable lighter in his pocket, fetched the gasoline-filled Coke bottle from the truck bed, and headed into the woods.

***

Cash pulled his Ruger, opened the door, and entered Emil Bergheim's house. Stepping softly, he searched the premises and found no one there. He was alone.

He made his way to the den. There he found a five-year-old copy of *Field and Stream*. He stretched out on the couch and tried to read, but it was too dark. He didn't want to turn the light on and make himself visible, so he gave up and tossed it aside. He pulled out his phone, opened a *New York Times* crossword puzzle, and told himself to be patient.

Pondering the first clue, Cash wrinkled his nose. What was that smell? Rotting fruit? A dead mouse? He got up and followed his nose into the kitchen.

The trash can. Of course. It hadn't been emptied since the night of the robbery. Cash opened the lid and gagged. Rotting chicken bones, banana peels, and an unidentifiable glob of goo had combined to create a stench powerful enough to floor a mountain lion. But he found something else as well. Cash peered closer. Beneath the goo lay an empty plastic bag that changed everything.

Chapter Forty-Eight

Ten minutes after finding the bag in Bergheim's trash can, Cash was mulling over the crossword clue "Peer Gynt's mother" when he caught a flicker of light through the window. He pocketed his phone and crossed the room. Parting the curtains a crack, he saw flames licking the sides of the workshop. What the hell?

It had to be Morgan. He had set a fire to lure Bergheim outside where he could kill him. If that was the case, exiting the house through the back door would be suicide. Cash would be a sitting duck.

Cash retrieved his phone and made a call. "Do you see that?" he said.

"See what?" said Hodge.

"The workshop is on fire."

"I'll check it out."

"Hang on. I'm coming out front. Meet me there."

As quietly as he could, Cash opened the front door and stepped outside. Hodge had pulled her gun and was holding it at her side. He put a finger to his lips. Using hand motions, he told her to circle one side of the house while he went the other way.

Cash unholstered his own gun. He hurried into position and peeked around the corner. Flames stretched into the sky high enough that he worried about nearby trees catching fire. He crouched and approached the shed. He glanced to his right and saw Hodge emerge from behind the house.

A shot split the night. A bullet thudded into the house not far away. He dropped to the ground and fired twice into the trees where he thought the shots had come from. Hodge fired as well. Cash caught her eye and pointed to her right. She nodded and, using an enormous live oak as cover, worked her way toward the workshop.

Cash stood up and, gun raised, made a wide circle in the opposite direction. As he moved past the workshop he tensed, ready to shoot, but no one was there. He jogged closer, stopping when the fire's heat became too intense.

Hodge stepped into view. "Did you see him?" she asked in a loud whisper.

"No," said Cash. "Did you?"

"I didn't see shit."

Cash looked past the creek into the woods. "He must have come from back there by the road. That's where he parked last time. We should have thought of that."

"Let's go get him."

Cash thought it over. Had Morgan left? By now he knew that Bergheim wasn't in the house. But could he take the chance that they hadn't seen him? If not, he'd have to kill them both and worry about Bergheim later.

"You check the woods," Cash said. "I'll search the house. If you get to the road without seeing him, come running."

Hodge nodded and took off across the creek. Cash stepped back around the shed and studied the house. Nothing had changed. A light still blazed through the kitchen window but otherwise, everything was dark. Fearing a bullet at any moment, he sprinted to the back door and listened for movement in the house. He heard nothing.

Cash eased the door open and stepped inside. He strained to hear something other than the thumping of his heart, but nothing else broke the silence. He crept into the kitchen, saw no one, and returned to the den.

He inched into the hall. Three dark doorways loomed up ahead. Cash swung his gun into the first. The bathroom. It was empty.

Moving stealthily, Cash approached the first bedroom. He paused to listen. Silence. Leading with the gun, he stepped into the room. No one was there.

By now Cash's breaths were coming in short bursts. His heart banged in his chest so hard he was sure that anyone else in the house must hear it. He felt transported back to Afghanistan, where terror dogged him on every mission.

One bedroom remained. If it, too, was empty, Morgan must have fled through the woods back to his vehicle. Cash took a deep breath and bolted into the hall.

A noise reached his ears. Not too loud, just a soft rubbing sound as if someone had brushed up against a wall. It was too late for Cash to stop his momentum. He flung himself to the ground as two shots rang out, the bullets zipping past him and shattering a lamp in the den. Cash rolled and fired. Something heavy crashed against a wall and thudded against the carpeted floor. A body. It lay still. Cash kept his gun trained on it and waited. He heard gasping breaths.

"Can you hear me, Morgan? Or should I call you Hooch?"

There was no answer, only a weak cough.

Without taking his eyes from the wounded man, Cash stood up and flipped the light switch. Morgan sat against the wall, a bloody streak painted above him. His arms hung limp at his side. He had pulled the ski mask off. A pistol lay a foot beyond his grasp.

Cash stepped to the gun and kicked it aside. He knelt. "Can you hear me?"

Dull eyes. A vacant expression on Morgan's face. He nodded.

"Is there anyone with you?" said Cash.

A shake of the head.

The back door crashed open. Cash tensed and, gun raised, whirled around to face the new threat. Hodge charged into view. Seeing him, she lowered her gun and said, "Is that him?"

Cash relaxed. "Yep."

"Is he alive?"

"Yep."

Hodge stepped closer to Morgan and peered down at him. Her face twisted into a mask of contempt. "Too bad."

***

As Cash watched the paramedics load Clint Morgan into the ambulance, he wished they would accidentally drop him. As much pain as Morgan's chest wound undoubtedly brought him, the bastard deserved that and more. Three people were dead by his hand. Silas Dudek was dead because of him. He had asked Morgan about Dudek while waiting for the ambulance. Morgan didn't respond, but his guilty look gave Cash the answer.

A pair of headlights appeared at the road turnoff and sped toward the house. A white minivan stopped next to the ambulance. Santos spotted Cash and strode toward him.

"Are you all right?" Santos asked.

"I'm fine."

"What about Hodge?"

"Same."

Santos swiveled his head. "Where is she?"

"At the workshop with the firetruck." Cash pointed at the writing on Santos's T-shirt. "World's Greatest Dad?"

Santos grinned. "Katrina gave this to me. She's pregnant."

"Congratulations," said Cash, extending his hand. "But you mean *you're* pregnant, don't you? It's a team effort."

"Speaking of team efforts," said Santos, "great job tonight. I wasn't sold on the idea of Morgan showing up, but I gotta hand it to you. Your hunch paid off."

"Now all that's left is to find the money."

"We'll find it. We'll tear Morgan's house apart if we have to. And I'll have Deke check every storage facility within a hundred-mile radius of here. Then we can finally put this case to rest."

"Not quite," said Cash.

"What do you mean?"

"I need to talk to Bergheim."

"What about?"

Cash started toward Bergheim's truck. "I'll tell you after I see him."

Chapter Forty-Nine

Back at his house, Cash stripped and fell into bed. He lay on his back and stared at the ceiling, trying to slow the thoughts racing through his head. At last, he was able to quell them enough to fall asleep.

Mouth dry. Hands clutching his M4 while he trudged through an Afghan village. Cold terror. The inescapable thought that each step could be his last, giving his feet the feel of hundred-pound weights. Mud huts, choking dust, a relentless sun. Heat waves rising in the distance. Fatigues heavy with sweat. Enough perspiration pouring down his neck to drown him.

Pop pop pop. Automatic weapons fire from the house ahead. Men dropping all around. Running as fast as his leaden feet will allow him to peer through an open doorway. The certainty that a bullet awaits him. Seeing no one. Stepping inside. Ready to die.

A young boy. Twelve, maybe thirteen. Pointing a rifle at him. Cash squeezing the trigger of his M4. The boy dropping.

A noise from behind. Spinning around. Three Taliban fighters wielding long knives. Polished steel glinting in the light. Promising death. Cash firing but this time only water spurting from his gun barrel. The men with knives laughing and advancing. Swinging their terrible blades in a slow arc toward his face. Throwing his hands up and waiting for the metal to pierce his body.

Cash awoke gasping for breath. Another nightmare. Different this time, but with the same outcome as all the others, certain death for him and his buddies. And the boy. He had seen that face before in his dreams. It matched that of the boy he had shot one unforgettable day. At the time, all Cash had seen was the rifle. Only after he fired did he see the face of the man pointing it at him. But it wasn't a man, it was a child no older than Reid.

Cash sat up and told himself what he always did after these nightmares. Someday he'd meet the boy in the afterlife and beg forgiveness. Then he'd ask him why the hell he'd been holding that rifle.

Cash got dressed and wolfed down a breakfast of scrambled eggs and toast. He texted Santos that he was going to Austin to fetch Emil Bergheim. Santos replied with a thumbs-up emoji.

When Cash arrived at his parents' house, his father had already left for work. He found his mother in the hall, sorting junk pulled from the closet. "Where's Mr. Bergheim?" he asked.

"He's in the backyard."

"What's he doing back there?"

"Fixing the fence."

"Mom," Cash said with an exaggerated gasp. "He's recovering from surgery."

"You try and stop him."

Cash stepped onto the back porch and shook his head. A tree branch had fallen on the six-foot cedar fence, smashed three pickets, and cracked the runner supporting them in two. Bergheim had used the chainsaw at his feet to cut up the branch. When Cash reached him, he was using a rip saw to cut a new runner to size.

Bergheim paused only long enough to register Cash's presence before returning to work on the two-by-four. Cash said, "Should you be doing this so soon after surgery?"

"What else am I going to do?" said Bergheim. "Clean closets with your mother?"

"You should be resting."

"I'll rest when I die. But if you're so worried, you could give me a hand."

Cash sighed. "Give me that saw."

Bergheim measured him, then handed it over. He held the runner steady while Cash finished the cut. Moving quickly so the old man couldn't stop him, Cash snatched the cut board and nailed it in place. Fastening the three new pickets was then a simple matter.

"Like old times, right?" Cash said with a smile.

"Old times, new times, they're all the same to me."

Motioning for Bergheim to follow, Cash started for the house. "Do you want to know what happened last night?" He couldn't believe Bergheim hadn't pressed him for the information the moment he showed up.

"You can tell me in the car."

"Would you like to go see your brother on the way out of town?"

"Just take me home."

***

They were in Dripping Springs before Bergheim spoke. "Okay, what happened?"

Cash told him. The intruder shot. The workshop a total loss from the fire. "But nothing else burned. The firefighters did a great job."

"If they'd done a great job, I'd still have a workshop, wouldn't I?"

There was no pleasing this guy.

"Hooch is dead?" Bergheim asked.

"No. They took him to Junction for surgery. The ambulance guys said he'd survive. And by the way, his real name is Clint Morgan."

"Did he tell you where the money is?"

"No, but we're looking for it."

"Did he say anything else?"

"Like what?"

Bergheim turned his head and stared out the window. "Never mind."

Chapter Fifty

Although Cash had taken out the kitchen trash before Morgan's appearance last night, a lingering foul odor greeted them as they entered Bergheim's house. If Bergheim noticed it, though, Cash couldn't tell, as his bland expression betrayed no sign of emotion.

The shattered lamp still lay on the floor in the den. Bergheim paused when he saw it, then continued his slow pace to the couch. Cash picked up the broken base and set it on the end table.

"You don't have to babysit me anymore," Bergheim said. "I can take it from here."

Cash took a seat in the lounge chair. "There's an important question I need to ask you."

Bergheim turned his expressionless eyes toward Cash but said nothing.

"Why did you do it?" said Cash.

"Do what?" Bergheim said.

Cash thought he saw a flash of fear in the old man's face. He reached into his pocket. "I've got some Jolly Ranchers. Would you like one?"

"What the hell are Jolly Ranchers."

"Hard candy. They come in different flavors."

"No," Bergheim said. "I don't eat that crap."

"That's what I thought," said Cash. "So I'll ask again, why did you do it?"

Bergheim shot Cash an impatient look. "You might as well be speaking Chinese. What the hell are you getting at?"

Cash pulled his hand out of his pocket. He held not a piece of candy but an empty Jolly Ranchers cellophane bag. "I found this in your trash can."

Cash waited, but Bergheim said nothing.

"You say you don't eat them. Who does?"

Silence.

"Mr. Bergheim," Cash said. "Do you know who likes these things? Clint Morgan. There were several pieces in his pocket when we searched him last night. And once he's out of surgery, he'll start talking." He leaned forward. "You were in on it, weren't you?"

Bergheim drew a long breath and dropped his head. "It was never supposed to go like this. Nobody was supposed to get hurt."

"But they did, didn't they?"

Bergheim nodded.

"Four people are dead," Cash said.

Bergheim covered his face with his hands. When at length he removed them and lifted his face to look at Cash, his eyes glistened with moisture. "I have to live with that now."

"Tell me the story."

"God Almighty, such a mess." He leaned back and stared at the ceiling. "Dieter can be a real bastard sometimes. He's my brother but, Lord, the way he treats people . . ."

"Who did he mistreat?"

"Rick."

"Rick Smith?" Cash asked, recalling that as Roy Baxter's real name.

"Yeah, Rick Smith. Dieter screwed him out of a lot of money. Without Rick's help that company would have died on the vine. Thanks to him, it was taking off. But Dieter pissed and moaned so much about the finances that Rick wanted out. Hell, even I thought it was tanking. What Dieter didn't tell him was that the money had been flowing for months. He let Rick go on thinking they were about to go under. So when Rick told Dieter he wanted out, the greedy SOB was happy to oblige. He gave him back his original investment and sent him packing.

"I felt bad for Rick at the time. I should have spoken up, but I didn't yet know the full story. I only found that out later one night after Dieter was halfway through a bottle of Jim Beam.

"By then Rick and I had gotten to be good friends. Not best friends, but we hung out some when I'd come to town. Basketball games, pizza and beer, that kind of thing. I lost track of him after he went back to California. But then one day I got a call from him. He's moving back to Austin, he says. He's supposed to keep an eye on his sister's kid."

"Eddie?"

"Yeah, the one that plays in your brother's band. Anyway, he came to see me. Not here at the ranch, because Dieter was living with me by then and Rick didn't want to see him. When I told him how much money Dieter made when he sold his company—Rick's company, really—he was none too happy. Later on, I got to thinking about it and realized there might be a way to put things right. I thought I could kill two birds with one stone. Fix things right by Rick and get Dieter's cash to a bank, where it should have been all along. I never did like having all that money out in the shop. Dieter and his stupid ideas. Anyway, that's the story."

Bergheim folded his arms as if he had finished.

He'd left out the important part. "That tells me why," Cash said, "but not what. What was the plan and how did it go wrong."

"I'll tell you what went wrong." Bergheim spat the words. "Hooch, that's what. I never should have let Slater bring that guy in."

"Hang on a second," Cash said. He pulled out his phone and found a picture of Silas Dudek. "Is this him?"

"No."

Cash pulled up a picture of Clint Morgan. "What about him?"

"That's the guy."

"And the robbery was your idea?"

"Yes and no. Rick and I came up with it together. I told him about Dieter stashing a small fortune in cash in the workshop. He said half that money rightfully belonged to him. I said I agreed." He paused. "But that son of a bitch Hooch took it all."

"Start at the beginning, if you could," said Cash. "Take me through it step by step."

Bergheim glanced over his shoulder at the kitchen. "There's beer in the fridge. Get me one. Take one for yourself, if you're of a mind."

Cash got up to fetch the beer. Fearing that Bergheim might leave the room, he quickly snatched a can of Bud Lite and hurried back to the den. He handed it to the old man. "Here you go."

Bergheim popped the tab and sipped. "It started with Slater. I hired him to work fences with me."

"So I heard."

"He was lazy but seemed harmless enough. I figured him for a guy happy to make some extra cash without getting greedy. I told him where the money was. He was going to come in the night, take half, and give it to me. I'd pay him his share and give the rest to Rick."

"None for yourself?"

"Hell, I've got all the money I need. Dieter does too, even if you cut it by half. Anyway, the next day Hooch shows up at my door. Said he heard from his friend Slater about a job. He wanted in."

"Why did Slater tell him about it?"

"They'd been drinking. Hooch was half-plastered when he got here. He sat right in that chair"—Bergheim pointed at the lounge chair—"and sucked that damn candy. He wanted to hear the whole plan. I was afraid of what he'd do if I didn't tell him. When I was done, he thanked me and left. He tossed that bag on the floor. I told him to take it with him, but he just laughed and said I could afford to hire a maid."

Cash said, "They didn't take the money until the second time they came. Why?"

"That was Rick's idea. He said it would help make it look more like a real robbery. If they found it right away, the first time, it would look like an inside job. We thought it would hide the fact that they knew where the money was if they had to come more than once."

"Go on."

"I got to worrying about Hooch. Cobb was okay, but Hooch looked like a guy that would punch his mother for the last piece of bacon. I put them cameras up in case the robbery went south. Which of course it did."

"Did Cobb and Hooch know about the cameras?"

"No," said Bergheim. "Only Rick. Hooch must have found the one by the shop and taken it with him. He never knew about the other one."

"What happened when they came back the second time?"

"The plan was for me to come outside just as they were leaving with the money. I was gonna holler at them, and one of them would shoot at me and miss. But they were arguing with each other when they came out of the shop. Slater said they had to put some money back, and Hooch told him to go to hell. I asked what they were talking about, and Hooch shot me. After they ran off, I heard another shot. I guess that's when Hooch shot Slater. I made it back to the house and called nine-one-one. You know everything after that."

Cash pondered the information. Despite knowing the chronology of events, he still had questions. "Why didn't you just let Rick come and take the money?"

Bergheim laughed. "Are you serious? I bring Dieter out here on weekends. The first thing he does when he gets here is go look at his money."

"Why didn't Baxter do the fake robbery? Why involve Cobb?"

"I didn't want him accidentally leaving fingerprints or anything else behind that might give him away. Not to mention the game cameras. Cobb was my idea." He blew a long breath. "Stupid."

Stupid indeed, thought Cash. "How were you going to explain away the burglars leaving half the money?"

"Like I told you before, Dieter needs that money to pay his rent. I would have said I caught them in the act and ran them off before they could get it all. Then I would tell Dieter I was putting that money in the bank, no matter what he said, because I was afraid they'd come back."

"But they took it all."

"Hooch took it all. Poor Slater died by the creek." He sniffed and wiped his eye. "You said four people died. Who else besides Rick and Slater?"

"Slater's girlfriend, Willa Dearborn. She must have known what happened and Morgan didn't want her to talk."

"She was two-timing Slater with Hooch."

Cash raised an eyebrow. "Really?"

"He told me that when he came to the house. The son of a bitch bragged about it."

"Interesting," Cash said.

"The other dead person?" Bergheim said.

"The real Hooch. His name was Silas Dudek. He's the guy in the first picture I showed you."

Bergheim wrinkled his brow. "I never met that guy."

"He broke into my house one night with a gun. I shot him in self-defense. There was ten thousand dollars in hundred-dollar bills in his truck. I believe Clint Morgan—the guy you're calling Hooch—hired him to kill me."

Cash's phone rang. With an apologetic glance at Bergheim, he retrieved it from his pocket and answered the call. "This is Cash."

"Cash, this is Gabe. I've got good news. Deke just called. The money was in a storage locker in Junction. He and Hodge are there now."

"That was fast. Is it all there?"

"There's no way to know, but he said it's a helluva lot of cash."

"Thanks. I'm with Bergheim now. I'll let him know."

Cash ended the call. Bergheim leaned forward. "They found it?"

"Yes," said Cash.

Bergheim shut his eyes and emitted a soft moan. "Thank God." Moments later, his lids snapped open. "Are you going to arrest me?"

Was he? The old man had concocted a plan to steal a small fortune from his brother. The fact that it was well-intentioned made it no less difficult to ignore. Added to that were the four deaths. And the mental anguish Eddie Kincaid suffered when Cash suspected his involvement.

On the other hand, Bergheim hadn't killed, or even tried to kill, anyone. And would society be better off with him in prison? Cash didn't think so. Any punishment meted out would be for foolishness, not malevolence. The true bad guy was recovering from surgery in a Junction hospital. After that he'd stand trial for robbery, murder, breaking and entering, assaulting a law officer, and murder-for-hire. Cash had no doubt of a conviction and lengthy prison sentence.

Cash studied the old man's face, which had assumed its previous neutral countenance. Bergheim sat stiffly, stoically, ready to accept Cash's decision without complaint. Just like he had always accepted the notion that life meant work and work meant life. In prison, he would have no work. Nothing Bergheim would perceive as real, anyway. He'd shrivel up and die. And to what end? Justice? Not in Cash's view.

Cash stood up. "Your refrigerator is a little bare," he said. "I'll head into town and pick up some groceries."

"That's it?" asked Bergheim.

"That's it," said Cash. He headed to the door and turned. "This stays between us. Right, Mr. Bergheim?"

The faintest smile creased Bergheim's face. "Right."

Chapter Fifty-One

Cash intended to brief Santos when he returned to headquarters. He wasn't prepared to encounter not only his boss, but also Conrad, Hodge, Frida Simmons, district attorney Lars Newsome, and county commissioner Fred Uecker. They were arrayed around the conference table, munching pizza. That was a troublesome combination. "What's all this?" he asked, taking a seat.

Santos reached for a gallon jug of milk and filled a paper cup. He slid it to Cash. "It's chocolate."

Cash sipped the sweet liquid and cast suspicious glances around the room. The smiles plastered on the faces made him nervous.

Santos said, "Everyone's here to congratulate you on yet another outstanding job."

"Hear, hear," said Hodge, raising her cup.

Uecker patted Cash on the back. "Have some pizza."

Santos continued. "Kudos also to Hodge, for assisting with the arrest, and to Deke, for tracking down the money. Excellent work, folks."

As Cash took a slice of sausage and mushroom pizza, he caught Newsome's eye. "How does the case against Morgan look?"

"Solid," the district attorney said. "He's going away for a long time."

Frida spoke up. "In addition to the money, Deke found a pair of muddy boots in that storage locker. The imprint of the left boot has a broken tread that matches a print from the creek. I also found blood on the thumb screw of the wrench you and Santos took from Morgan's house. It's human. I've sent it for DNA analysis, but I think we know whose blood it is."

"That sounds cut and dried."

"That's not all. Remember that fingerprint on the Encore's lift gate? It belongs to Morgan."

"You've been busy," said Cash. "I can't believe he left his prints on the car. Or kept the boots. He was smart about everything else."

"What can I say?" Frida said with a shrug. "Criminals are stupid. Even the smart ones."

"Maybe. But all this time I thought I was looking for a guy named Hooch. It turns out the real Hooch was the guy that tried to kill me at my house. Morgan was calling himself Hooch with Slater Cobb and Emil Bergheim. Probably with Baxter, too. That way they couldn't ever name him. The real Hooch would be the fall guy if they talked. Of course, later he decided not to give them that chance."

Santos said, "How do you know Morgan was using that name?"

"Cobb's roommate told me he hung around with someone named Hooch. On the way over here, I stopped by his house to show him Morgan's picture. He said that was Hooch. And Bergheim said the same thing when I showed it to him."

"One thing puzzles me," said Uecker. "Gabe said that Rick Smith heard about the money from his grandson, who works in Dieter Bergheim's retirement home. But the grandson also said he didn't know where it was hidden, only that Dieter was keeping it on the property somewhere. How did Morgan know where to find it?"

Everyone looked at Cash. He bit into his pizza and feigned deep thought as he chewed. "I guess we'll never know."

***

The celebration broke up with handshakes all around. Cash pulled Santos aside and said, "Can I talk to you in your office?"

"Sure."

Cash followed Santos down the hall and closed the office door behind him. They sat. "What's up?" Santos said.

"Once Morgan can talk, we're going to hear him say some crazy things."

"What kind of crazy things?"

"Oh, things like it was all Bergheim's idea."

Santos blinked. "That does sound crazy. Why would he say that?"

"Maybe because it was."

Santos leaned forward, waiting for Cash to elaborate.

Cash continued. "He loves his brother. He was also friends with Roy Baxter. Dieter screwed Baxter in a business deal. Bergheim didn't like it. He also didn't like having a million and a half in cash stashed in his workshop."

"Okay."

Cash told the whole story. Bergheim's foolish plan. Morgan forcing his involvement. Morgan straying from the plan and betraying his partners. Morgan murdering three people so he could keep the entire haul. He finished by saying, "Mr. Bergheim's intentions were good."

Santos said, "The road to hell ..."

"I know. And you're right. But I don't see a point in putting him away. Going to prison would kill him. And his brother needs him."

"Well," said Santos, furrowing his brow. "Like you said, Morgan's going to say some crazy shit."

"Right."

"Because he's crazy."

"Right again."

"So it will be a crazy man's word against the word of an old man who's never broken the law."

"Yep."

"I'd say the old man's got nothing to worry about."

***

Cash rapped on the door and pushed it open. "May I come in?"

"Who is it?" shouted Dieter Bergheim.

"It's Deputy Cash."

"Come on, then."

Dieter sat at the card table with a partially completed jigsaw puzzle depicting a summer beach scene. "Nice picture," Cash said, pulling up a seat.

"What do I care? I ain't going to the beach no more."

"I used to do these with my little brother," Cash said, picking up a piece and trying to place it. It didn't fit. "He'd always hide a piece in his pocket so he'd be sure to be the one to finish it."

"I remember doing that as a kid. Emil would get mad as hell."

"Speaking of Emil, he's coming to see you tomorrow." Cash had tried to get him to come today, but he had an appointment with his surgeon. "He said to tell you hi."

"How's he doing?" Dieter asked.

"Recovering nicely. He already fixed a fence in my parents' backyard."

Dieter snorted. "Sounds like Emil."

"He opened a bank account with your money. That's one of the reasons he wants to see you. You need to sign some papers to be co-owner."

Dieter's eyes spit fire. "Co-owner? That's my money."

"He'll have his name taken off it at the same time. The bank will set up online payments of your rent and your other regular bills." Cash tried another puzzle piece without success. "It's too bad about Rick."

"He tried to rob me. He got what he deserved."

"That's one way of looking at it. Do you know why he came back to Austin?"

"Sure. To steal my money."

"He came back because of his grandson. Rick was the only family the kid had left. You've met him. He's a maintenance man here."

"I remember that kid. He's the one who told Rick where the money was."

"His name is Eddie Kincaid. He had no idea of your history with his granddad. Your brother tells me Rick only wanted that money to help him."

"What does that matter? It's against the law to steal another man's money."

Cash said, "Like you stole from Rick?"

Dieter pounded a fist on the table, sending a cascade of puzzle pieces onto the floor. "I didn't steal from that son of a bitch. I bought him out fair and square."

Cash scooped up the pieces and returned them to the table. "That's not how Emil sees it. He said you tricked Rick into thinking the company was about to go under. Meanwhile, you were negotiating a sale of a company that had soared in value in large part because of his expertise."

Dieter's face twitched as he picked up a puzzle piece. Cash could tell he had hit home.

"Of course, the money legally belongs to you," Cash said. "I'm just saying it wouldn't hurt to throw Eddie a bone." He paused. "In honor of Rick's contributions to your success."

The old man seemed to consider Cash's words. He tossed the puzzle piece aside.

Cash said, "Your brother would see it as the right thing to do."

Dieter cut his eyes up to Cash but said nothing. His hard look dissolved into one of self-pity. Cash took the discarded puzzle piece, studied the picture, and fitted that one into place. He hadn't totally lost his touch. He stood up. "It was good talking to you, Mr. Bergheim."

Chapter Fifty-Two

Del dunked his sandwich into the beef broth and bit off a chunk. He groaned with pleasure. "Nothing like a good French dip."

"Western dip, Dad," said Cash.

"What?"

"It has peppers and onions. It's a Western dip, not a French dip."

"Whatever."

"Mommy, can I have my cookie now?" said Edie's son, Luke. He reached for the plate.

Edie pulled the plate away from him. "Take three more bites of your grilled cheese first. And make them real bites, not mouse nibbles."

"Aw, man."

They sat around a table in the Lavender Café in Blanco, a small town an hour north of San Antonio. They'd traveled there to hear the Whistling Armadillos play. Reid and the rest of the band were busy setting up their equipment in front.

Cash ran his finger along the slick oilcloth covering the table. "What time should I come by Sunday morning?" he asked Edie.

"Seven o'clock. I want to get an early start."

Cash winced. He had been hoping to sleep in. "You haven't told me where you'll be living yet."

"I've got a room in Northwest Hills."

Cash gave her a surprised look. That was an expensive Austin neighborhood. Since his parents purchased their home there ten years ago, rents and real estate prices had skyrocketed. His father said they bought just in time. "How are you affording that?"

"Easy," she said. "Free rent."

"Free rent?"

"Yes, but I'll pay my share of the utilities and food."

"But why is there no rent?"

"Because we don't need it," Del said. "That room is just sitting empty. It might as well be put to good use."

Cash noticed the impish grin on his father's face. It matched those of Edie and his mother. Even Luke was trying not to laugh. "Okay, guys, what's going on?"

Luke couldn't contain it any longer. "We're gonna live with Grandma and Grandpa!"

Grandma and Grandpa? Edie's parents were dead. And Luke's paternal grandparents lived in Chicago.

Janet said, "Isn't that cute? That's what he calls us."

Cash's mouth fell open. He shifted his gaze to Edie. "You're going to live with my parents?"

"Yep."

"That way," said Del, "you'll be more likely to visit your old mom and dad more than once in a blue moon."

Edie would be living with his parents? He wasn't sure what to think about that. On the one hand, it would be easy to visit her in Austin. On the other hand, privacy would be nonexistent. And the implied commitment gave him chills.

"Don't worry," Del added. "You'll stay in her room when you're there."

"Unless you'd rather sleep on the couch," Edie said.

Cash broke into a sheepish grin. "No, your room would be fine."

Janet said, "And little Luke here will use Reid's old room. We'll just need to take down the *Sports Illustrated* swimsuit pictures."

"Don't throw them out," said Reid, who had just snuck up behind Cash. "I still want them." He slapped Cash's shoulder. "Are you ready for your big night?"

Butterflies fluttered in Cash's gut. "Second set."

"You better not chicken out."

***

The Whistling Armadillos played a forty-five-minute set. Cash and Edie danced to several numbers, as did Del and Janet. When Reid announced they'd be taking a short break, Cash felt needles pricking his spine. In a few short minutes he'd be onstage.

He excused himself and wandered to the bar, where a young woman refilled his iced tea. He had switched beverages after his second beer.

Cash turned around and bumped into Eddie Kincaid. "Sorry," he said.

"No problem."

They stood eye to eye for several awkward moments. Cash said, "I've got something for you." He pulled a folded check from his shirt pocket and handed it over. "This is from Dieter Bergheim."

Puzzled, Kincaid unfolded the check and read. His eyes bulged. "Holy shit. What's this for?"

"He screwed your grandfather." Cash explained the circumstances of Rick Smith selling his share of the business. "This is his way of apologizing"

"Half of that sale should have gone to Grandpa?"

"In a moral sense, yes. Legally, though, Dieter can keep it all."

Kincaid stowed the check in his wallet. "This helps. A lot. I feel like I should go to a bank right away."

Cash smiled at the irony of that statement. "Oh, and I want to apologize for giving you such a hard time. That must have been stressful."

"It was."

"I was just doing my job."

"Water under the bridge, man."

"I'm truly sorry about your grandfather. I liked him."

Kincaid nodded.

Cash said, "Well, I'll let you get your drink."

"Hey," said Kincaid. "I hear you're joining us after the break."

Cash swallowed the bile in the back of his throat. "That's right."

Kincaid smiled. "You're not half bad. You'll be fine."

***

When Cash was in college, he and three friends had taken a spring break trip to Nashville, where they attended a Grand Ole Opry concert at the historic Ryman Auditorium. The emcee introduced a singer making her Opry debut. Halfway through her first song, the young woman's voice cracked. She recovered, but when it happened again, she stopped playing her guitar and tried to compose herself. Cash recalled cringing as he watched her terror mount. The crowd kept silent until a man's voice boomed out, "We love you, sweetheart." The singer emitted a nervous laugh, took a deep breath, and resumed her song. When she finished, the crowd gave her a standing ovation.

Cash wondered if the diners in the Lavender Café would be so forgiving if he screwed up. Not if, when. He saw Reid signaling to him from the stage. Time to put up or shut up. His heart banged against his ribs. Sweat moistened his palms. As he trudged up to the stage, he feared he might throw up. He strapped on his guitar and wished he could be anywhere else.

Reid stepped before the microphone. "Ladies and gentlemen, may I have your attention, please?" The dining room went silent. "We have a true hero here with us tonight. Just last week he solved a robbery and three murders, recovered the stolen money, and brought the bad guy to justice. He's the singing deputy of Noble County, Texas, my big brother Adam Cash!"

Cash's knees wobbled as Reid finished his over-the-top introduction. He exuded such confidence in front of a crowd. How did he do it? Were they really related?

The crowd's applause died away. Reid nodded for him to start. Cash gulped and scanned the faces in the room. He saw nothing but smiles. Maybe these folks wouldn't be too hard on him when he bombed. Either way, his parents would still love him. Edie would still love him. And it was unlikely he'd ever see any of these people again.

A child's voice broke the stillness: Luke. "You're the greatest, Cash!"

Everyone laughed, Cash included. He felt the fear drain from his body. Screw it, this was supposed to be fun. He smiled, struck the first chord, and opened his mouth to sing.

Thank you ...

... for reading *Murder Creek*. Want to keep up to date on my upcoming books and giveaways? Sign up for my newsletter by **clicking on this link** or by visiting my website **jeffreykerrauthor.com** and I'll send you a free copy of ***Cash: The Prequels***, a collection of three exciting short stories that introduce The Adam Cash series.

Got a moment?

The best way to help an independent author like me is to post an honest review on Amazon or any other reading platform you use. Reviews are critical to a book's success. And success is what allows any author to continue writing the books you want to read.

To leave an Amazon review, click here.

Or...

If you're reading the paperback or pdf version, please visit the book's Amazon page and scroll down to the customer reviews. Then click on "Write a customer review."

Word of mouth and posting on social media also help. I appreciate anything you can do to spread the word!

If you enjoyed Murder Creek ...

... you'll love ***Blunt Force Trauma***, in which Cash finds himself accused of murdering the man who just trounced him in the election for Noble County sheriff. On the run and fighting to clear his name, Cash's secret investigation reveals a darker truth threatening to destroy countless lives. Only Cash can catch the killer and save the innocents. *If* he can avoid being captured ... or killed.

The doorknob jiggled. Cash inched his way toward the window, stood, and pushed up on it. It was locked. He found the latch and released it. As he nudged the window open, two shots in quick succession drilled through the door and penetrated the wall beside him. He leaped to the commode and propelled himself through the window's small opening, slamming into the ground as another shot shattered the glass above his head. Scrambling to his feet, he started to run when a shouted command froze him. "Hold it!"

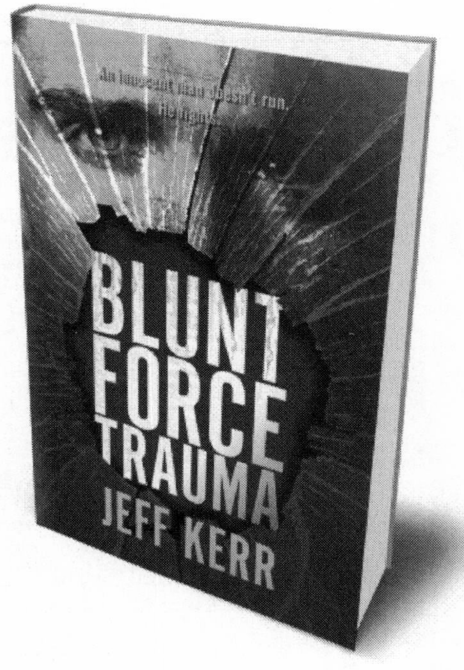

Buy *Blunt Force Trauma*

Here's the url for those of you reading the paperback or pdf version.

buy.bookfunnel.com/cnc3m2fvon

About Jeff Kerr

Jeff Kerr wasn't born in Texas but says "y'all" like a native. He wrote a poem in the third grade that earned him a school prize, a book about the American flag. You'd think that would have inspired him to become a writer but that came later.

Jeff wrote and published his first book twenty years ago. He hadn't planned on doing so until one night at supper his son interrupted a discourse about local history by saying, "Enough, Dad. Write a book!" So, he did. Eight books later, he calls himself an author.

When Jeff isn't writing you can find him floating a Texas river or battling cedar on his small slice of Hill Country land. When he *is* writing, he stays busy by creating pulse-pounding crime thrillers that, according to one reader, "move along like a runaway locomotive." Thank you, son.

Learn more about Jeff and his work at **jeffreykerrauthor.com**.

Drop him a line at **jeffkerr@jeffreykerrauthor.com**. He'll write back!

Twitter: twitter.com/jkerr50

Instagram: instagram.com/jkerr50

Facebook: facebook.com/JeffKerrAuthor

Bookbub: bookbub.com/authors/jeffrey-kerr

.

Also by Jeff Kerr

FICTION

Blunt Force Trauma

Second Death

Refuge

Lamar's Folly

The Republic of Jack

NONFICTION

Austin, Texas: Then and Now

The Republic of Austin

Seat of Empire: The Embattled Birth of Austin, Texas

Manufactured by Amazon.ca
Bolton, ON